Jerome Charyn was born in the Bronx in 1937. He lives in Paris and New York and is currently Visiting Distinguished Professor of English at the City College of New York. He is on the executive boards of P.E.N. and the Mystery Writers of America and is the American Secretary of the International Association of Crime Writers. He has received a John Simon Guggenheim Memorial Fellowship, the Rosenthal Foundation Award of the American Academy and Institute of Arts and Letters, and has twice been nominated for France's *Prix Medicis Etranger*. His graphic novel, THE MAGICIAN'S WIFE, received the *Prix Alfred* at the Angouleme in 1986.

His work includes WAR CRIES OVER AVENUE C, DARLIN' BILL, THE CATFISH MAN, PINOCCHIO'S NOSE and THE ISSAC QUARTET. His most recent book is MOVIELAND: HOLLYWOOD AND THE GREAT AMERICAN DREAM CULTURE.

Also by Jerome Charyn in Abacus:

WAR CRIES OVER AVENUE C
METROPOLIS

PARADISE MAN

JEROME CHARYN

ABACUS

SPHERE BOOKS LTD

Published by the Penguin Group
27 Wrights Lane, London w8 5tz, England
Viking Penguin Inc., 40 West 23rd Street, New York, New York 10010, USA
Penguin Books Australia Ltd, Ringwood, Victoria, Australia
Penguin Books Canada Ltd, 2801 John Street, Markham, Ontario, Canada l3r 1b4
Penguin Books (NZ) Ltd, 182–190 Wairau Road, Auckland 10, New Zealand

Penguin Books Ltd, Registered Offices: Harmondsworth, Middlesex, England

First published in Great Britain by Michael Joseph 1988
Published in Abacus by Sphere Books 1989
1 3 5 7 9 10 8 6 4 2

Printed and bound in Great Britain by
Richard Clay Ltd, Bungay, Suffolk

For Eliza Kazan, Norman Mailer, and Arthur Penn, who taught me about the wicked witch of drama during the writing of this book.

The Leopard Girl

THEY WERE THE BANDIDOS, lunatics and murderers Castro had let out of his jails and shoveled onto the boats at Mariel harbor. They practiced a jailhouse religion called Santería, where saints turn into ferocious African gods who can toss thunderbolts, wrap themselves in a thick vapor, become a man or a woman at will. The Bandidos were beholden to Santa Barbara, "sister" and spirit of Changó, the thunder god who wore women's clothes some of the time. It wasn't Fidel who had inspired the boatlift, the Bandidos believed. Changó had arranged the whole thing. Changó sat on every boat, looking like an ordinary *puta* in a red dress, wearing his *collares*, red and white beads.

The Bandidos had no families to welcome them in Florida, not one fat uncle from Flagler Street, like the other Marielitos had, the good Marielitos, who'd never sat in jail, who'd come here to be with sisters, brothers, mamas, papas, uncles, and aunts in Little Havana. The Bandidos were herded into tents under a highway. The federales saw the tattoos in the webbing of their thumbs, on their lips, inside their mouths, and called them desperate characters. Most of the Bandidos couldn't read anything but their tattoos, which were the signals of their trade: kidnapper, executioner, stickup artist . . . Some of the Bandidos found a sponsor—a concerned "uncle" or "aunt"—who bailed them out of the tents. Others were shipped off to detention camps, like Indian Town Gap, in Pennsylvania. The luckier ones landed in New York, where they could pull stickups and pretend to be innocent Puerto Rican boys, or become thugs for La Familia, those Batista babies who'd left Cuba twenty-five years ago and had their own crime family now. The chiefs of La Familia were

9

educated men. They'd been judges, lawyers, and jewelers during Batista's regime. They despised the Bandidos with their silly god in women's clothes and wouldn't really welcome them into La Familia. The Bandidos had no discipline. They were little better than dogs.

That much Holden knew. His rats had collected information on the Bandidos and the boatlift. He had diagrams of all the tattoos and he could tell which of those monkeys was a murderer or a stickup man. Holden had to be careful, because he couldn't afford to fool with the Bandidos. They might send Changó after him, and he'd get bumped by a god in a red dress.

The man and woman he was after weren't Bandidos, his rats had assured him. The man had come riding out of Mariel with all the lunatics, but he didn't worship Changó and he'd never been in jail. He was known as the Parrot and he was a Cuban confidence man. The Parrot had been stealing money from La Familia and doing a lot of damage.

Holden was on a prairie in the middle of Queens. With a parking lot and a pizza restaurant. He saw a huge metal pie in the window. The pie blinked. Holden wasn't in the mood for pizza. He'd come by subway. There was a hospital on the prairie, and Holden could have produced some phony doctor's plates, but he preferred the anonymous drift of a subway rider. No one would see him disappear in a borrowed Lincoln or Dodge.

He crossed the prairie with a quarter of a million in a vinyl bag. Holden was like a mule, lugging packets of hundred dollar bills. But it couldn't be helped. He had to destroy the Parrot and his mistress. The Marielito would pose as a dealer from Miami, with keys of cocaine to sell. The woman was brainier than the man. She used a knitting needle on her gentlemen callers, catching them between the eyes.

The Marielito shouldn't have prospered outside Florida. It was the woman's beauty that saved him. No one would have cared about this Parrot. But the woman possessed a talent for disturbing very shrewd men, according to the file card Holden had. The Marielito was fond of a Llama .22 long. He couldn't afford to rely on knitting needles. He didn't have the woman's calves or her cleavage.

The couple should have gone back to Miami, settled in a houseboat, and preyed on Florida businessmen, because there wasn't much of a future for buccaneers in Queens, unless they were Bandidos. But the Parrot and his mistress had already murdered fifteen men.

Holden didn't find one Latin nightclub, or a bar that advertised yellow rice and beans. He couldn't have entered some secret Cuban zone. The apartment house was ordinary. Dentists and accountants, Holden figured. And furriers like himself. He was with the Aladdin Fur Company. But he knew nothing about pelts and skins. He'd never seen a live sable. He collected for the company. And the company's strange books had brought him to Queens. He was the wandering sheriff of Aladdin Furs.

The Marielito was in apartment 7B, under the name of O'Connor. Holden wondered how many apartments this Parrot controlled. He never struck from the same place twice. It was either a hotel room, where the woman could lure a man into bed and dig with her needle, the back of some nightclub, or an apartment with the name O'Connor on the bell. Holden pressed the button.

A woman's voice drifted down from 7B. "Who is it?" The voice startled him. Holden couldn't find much of a Cuban accent. Maybe it was the wrong O'Connor.

"Parrot," he said. "I'm looking for the Parrot."

Holden heard a click. *Parrot* had gotten him into the building. The Marielito was waiting upstairs to kill him and swipe the vinyl bag. Holden wished he had a gambler's gun in his shirt sleeve, a derringer he could have pressed against the woman's heart. He had to arrive with nothing but his baby fat, or he'd never get close enough to the Marielito.

He was only the courier, a common mule. The Parrot and his mistress had burnt every mule before Holden. They'd frisk him at the door, pull him inside with the bag of money. The woman

wouldn't bother to seduce a messenger boy. And that was Holden's
one advantage. He wasn't important enough to worry about. Holden
couldn't tell how the buy had been made, or the number of men the
Parrot's mistress had seduced. How else had they gotten a messenger
boy with a quarter of a million to come to Queens?

Holden didn't take the elevator. He climbed six flights. What
if Holden himself was being set up? The more of a history a bumper
had, the larger the feathers he built around himself, and the nearer
he got to his own execution. Holden was like a grandpa, an ancient
man of thirty-seven. He'd never come to forty. His feathers were
already too long.

Holden arrived at 7B. He was about to knock when the door
opened. It nearly broke his heart. That bitch was a perfect height
for Holden. Around five foot four. She'd come to him without shoes.
She didn't smile. The bitch was blonde and all business. Her hair
was almost white. She wore a polo shirt. It wasn't the outline of her
breasts that defeated him. It was the curve of her arms. Now he
knew why the other fifteen had failed. What the hell was a kilo
compared to her skin? And then Holden looked beyond the polo
shirt and the blonde, blonde hair and remembered the knitting
needle.

She cooed at him. "Come in."

He entered with his quarter million and the man appeared,
almost as blond as the bitch (there must have been a consignment
of blondies at Mariel harbor). The Parrot locked the door. He had
a .22 long tucked into his pants. Holden could have slapped his head
with the money bag and shot the Parrot with his own gun. But he
couldn't attend to the woman and dance around with the man. He
was in a blind spot near the door, some hurricane alley.

The bitch was staring at him. "I like your tailor." He'd worn
his crappiest clothes, because he couldn't look like Douglas Fairbanks Jr. on a prairie in Queens. But it was still a London suit from
Hester Street. Holden's tailor was a thief. He could pirate any style.

"That's a thousand-dollar suit," the woman said.

It was just Holden's luck that the woman he had to kill was a couturier in a polo shirt.

"Bella," the man griped, "leave him alone. Can't you see? He's just a kid."

A grandpa, and they called him a kid.

"Sonny, give us the satchel . . . nice and slow."

Holden held out the vinyl bag. The Parrot took it and said, "Now hug the wall with your palms, sonny, and keep your ass high." The woman searched inside his collar. She fondled his neck while she searched, and Holden had an erection. She dug into his pockets, patted his thighs, held his penis for a moment, as if it were all part of some inscrutable frisk. Holden had to endure the metaphysics of her hands.

The Parrot sat on a table six feet from Holden and unzipped the bag. He started to play with the money, building a tower with the packets of hundred dollar bills, while he dangled one knee over the table, contemptuous of Holden, who was still standing in that hurricane alley.

The bitch rubbed him with her body, her breasts like gloves in his back. Holden didn't like it. He saw the needle rise up from her dungarees. He struck her once in the throat, with the needle almost at his ear, and she made a strangling noise as Holden grabbed the Parrot's leg, brought him down from the table, and socked him three times in the temple. The Parrot was dead.

The woman choked quietly in a corner. But he couldn't take a chance. He walloped her where her brows began. The needle fell out of her hand.

"Fuckers," he said, and then Holden saw a pair of eyes under the table, in all that dark and dust. Like a leopard that had come to haunt him with fevered animal eyes.

The leopard was a little girl. Darkhaired. A Marielita in a red dress.

Changó, he muttered. That little girl was the Bandidos' god. But Holden didn't believe in jailhouse cults. She was a Marielita, that's all. He had to make sure. He stooped to find out if the Parrot was wearing Changó's red and white beads. But the Parrot had nothing inside his shirt—no necklace, no tattoos, no prison scars. Silly, Holden said to himself.

He trembled now, because Holden didn't have a choice. The little girl wasn't little enough. He couldn't leave a witness like that. Some police artist could compose a portrait of him from the little girl's nods. "*Chiquita,*" the artist would say, "was the bad man's forehead high or low?"

He'd have to smother her with his hand, feel her hot mouth and the fiddle of her throat.

There wasn't supposed to be a little leopard girl. That bit of news would have been somewhere in the file cards Holden kept. It was a stupid trick. The Parrot was minding the little girl until her mother came home. What mother? Would they let some neighbor's little girl watch while the woman finished Holden with her knitting needle? He understood enough Creole talk to ask the Marielita her name. But he didn't want to know.

He stuffed the money back into the bag and listened to an odd chirp. He stooped. The Marielita wasn't crying. She looked up at him with her leopard's eyes. It had to be that other bitch. But she lay dead in her polo shirt. The noise had come from him.

Holden didn't care. He went about his business. But the chirping didn't stop.

"Jesus," he said, shoving the bag under his arm and grabbing the Marielita's fist while he wiped the doorknob with his handkerchief.

"*Querida,*" he said, "you be quiet."

The girl hadn't made a sound.

Holden knew the Marielita would mark him. It was like carrying a tag on his back. *Take a look. I'm the man who did the piece of work in 7B.* And what if he should meet the mother on the stairs? He'd have to waltz her out the window and run with the leopard girl.

But he got to the front door without the slightest complication. It was just a building in Queens with a coachman's circle to let accountants deposit their wives on the doorstep, like some fat Cinderella escaping from the rain. The Marielita didn't struggle. Her own fingers tightened around his hand.

They passed a bunch of nurses on the street and he was afraid she might bolt from him. The nurses paused in the middle of their conversation to admire the Marielita. He couldn't pluck his head somewhere like an ostrich. He had to acknowledge his right to the girl.

"Isn't she the prettiest thing? . . . Johanna, look at those eyes. A regular Rita Hayworth."

They pulled at her, these busybodies with their capes and their nurses' bonnets.

"A devil, but so sweet . . . honey, who's that holding your hand? Your uncle, or your dada?"

Holden tried to release her hand. He'd have to pardon himself, take long steps to the subway, and hide in a closet for six months, but the Marielita held tight.

"Dada," she said. And he wasn't sure if he should groan or smile or deliver up the Marielita to those tall women in their bonnets. He'd found himself a leopard girl in Queens.

2 HOLDEN WENT DIRECTLY to his tailor. He could have shopped the brat to some orphanage, but he hadn't dealt with children before, and he wasn't familiar with the rates. Goldie would know. Goldie was his tailor.

Samuel Goldhorn, Esq., had a storefront in the ruins of Hester

Street. He was a London Jew. He'd arrived here without his father before he was ten. He'd served in the army with Holden's dad. Spent most of World War II attached to one general or another, in the arts and archives division. That's where he'd become a forger and a thief. Holden's dad was a military cop with the same division. The two of them had dealt in stolen documents.

The store was full: six sewing machine operators. Chinese women who assembled Goldie's counterfeit suits. They pretended not to look at the little girl Holden had brought in. But she caught them with her leopard's eyes. They couldn't defend themselves against the Marielita. He laughed to himself. The little girl was like an X-ray gun.

He traveled around the bend of the store, with patterns everywhere, bolts of cloth, designer dummies, the collar and cuffs of some exquisite shirt Goldie hadn't gotten around to yet.

Holden knocked on the tailor's door. "Goldie, it's me."

And Goldie buzzed him into the back office, where the tailor ruminated and stitched, giving himself a week to finish a cashmere coat. He'd lost track of time and money. The madman sculpted clothes.

He stopped working the moment he saw the Marielita. He tossed the cashmere coat aside. "A little complication?"

"No. A casualty. She was under the table."

"A gift, then," Goldie said. "From the Cuban Santa Claus."

"Something like that. But you can't bring her back to Macy's. I'll have to board her somewhere. I was thinking of that old woman in South Jersey. Mama Bell."

Goldie whistled, and the noise seemed to wind through his skull. "She's a bit compromised at the moment. Surrounded by Marielitos, that Union City bunch. I wouldn't go to Mama Bell."

"Fine. No Mama Bell. But I'm short in that category. I never needed a nursemaid."

Goldie hadn't listened. He was watching the Marielita. "What's her name?"

Holden shrugged. "Will you use your charm on her, Goldie? She saw me in the act."

Goldie reached under his desk and fished out a lollipop. He unwrapped it for the Marielita like a perfect gentleman. Had he picked up his manners from the generals at arts and archives? Holden Sr. had been through the same generals, but he couldn't have unwrapped a lollipop like that. Holden Sr. had to flee the army and live like an outlaw in France, where Holden was born.

The little girl sucked the lollipop. Goldie placed her on his lap and chatted to her in the king's own Spanish. He wouldn't talk Newyorican with a leopard girl. Whole melodies passed between them, mountains of talk. Holden was very bitter. The Marielita had been silent on the subway into Manhattan.

"Goldie, who is this girl?"

"She won't say."

"You've been jabbering with her for five minutes. She had to tell you something."

"She did. She told me about her dolls and her favorite dish of ice cream."

"Thanks," Holden said. "You solved the riddle. What the hell was she doing in Queens?"

"She doesn't remember. She was sleeping under a table and you woke her up."

"Women," Holden muttered. "They're all alike. Walk around with mysteries in their brains. Will you ask her who her dad is?"

Goldie smiled. "You're her dad, she says."

"I give up. She's an elf. Her only past is dolls and ice cream."

"It's a blessing. You went out on a kill and inherited a daughter."

"Is that smart?" Holden asked. "Did you have to say kill?"

"Holden, she's not a dummy. She talks like an adult."

"Not to me," Holden said.

"You're a little rough with her. That's the problem."

Holden cracked his teeth. It was a habit he picked up from his dad. "Rough? I was a lamb."

"You didn't buy her a lollipop or ask about her dolls."

"Goldie, I had other things on my mind . . . like what happens when the cops discover she's missing. Whatever she told you, the little bitch has a family somewhere."

"Shame on you," Goldie said. "The girl decides you're her dad, and right away you call her a bitch . . . take off your clothes."

"What?"

"How can I dress you with your clothes on. Take them off."

"In front of the girl?"

"Holden, she must have seen men in their underpants. I guarantee you. She's quite mature."

Holden got undressed and stood around in his socks and shorts, like a doll in the window. Goldie gave him a silk shirt. The silk sent shivers along his spine. The tailor himself knotted Holden's tie. Then he took a blue Beretta out of a bag and attached the gun to Holden with its leather cup. And he dressed Holden in a dark wool suit that was made to wear with this gun. Holden saw himself in the mirror. The suit hugged his skeleton like some armor of skin out of the Middle Ages, and there wasn't the hint of a holster under Goldie's wool.

Goldie had draped him like Douglas Fairbanks Jr., the best-dressed man in the world. London elite, Goldie called it. Wine-colored shoes and a display handkerchief that cost twice as much as a hat. Holden couldn't walk in off the street and visit Doug Jr.'s tailors. He had to depend on Goldie to steal the tailors' styles. Goldie had a carton of patterns from all the best shops. The classiest tailors didn't have a public address. Would lords and earls wander into the marketplace with wild, anonymous men? The quality of a tailor was determined by who he wouldn't dress.

"Goldie, what about the kid?"

"Offer her to Mrs. Howard."

"I don't get it. She's not a nursemaid."

"That's the point. Nobody will know where to look."

Mrs. Howard was a widow who'd once worked in the shop. She'd been a tailor up in Harlem with some tough gang, but she fled

St. Nicholas Avenue years ago to stick pins in trouser cuffs for
Goldie. She'd dress Holden when Goldie was ill. She'd had as good
a hand as Goldie himself but she suffered from arthritis and could
no longer grab a needle or a pin. Holden hid his file cards with Mrs.
Howard, and the record books of the spies he carried. Holden had
to keep spies, or he couldn't have lasted. He'd almost been killed
twice on a poisoned contract. His rats had saved him. And she ran
them for Holden on her telephone line. She'd become Holden's
answering service. He hadn't bought her loyalty. He loved her. She'd
lived with his dad for a while. She was the only one of his father's
women he'd ever liked.

He walked out of Goldie's with the Marielita, her lollipop, and
his quarter million and took a cab to Mrs. Howard, who kept a flat
on Oliver Street across from the old mariner's church. She had her
own back yard, with pigeon coops and a tiny barn for neighborhood
cats. She wore a holster, like Holden, and the same blue Beretta,
because he didn't want anyone to surprise her in that yard, not a
thief, or one of Holden's enemies.

He rang three times and let himself in with his key. Mrs.
Howard was waiting for Holden. Goldie must have phoned ahead.
She had pudding for the Marielita. She was tall as Holden, a beautiful black bitch with arthritis. Holden wished she'd shed a generation
somewhere. He'd have married her then. His own marriage had left
him with a fist inside his heart.

"Holden, that's one hell of a suit."

"Cost three thousand for the pattern alone. Goldie uses expensive gyp artists . . . Loretta, will you mind the girl? She was part of
that trick in—"

"You don't have to explain. She's a lovely creature, Holden.
We'll do fine."

"There'll be an extra allowance . . . for the girl and everything."

Her eyes tightened, and he recalled how angry she could get at
his dad. She was Holden's dream girl when he was twelve. She'd
parade in her panties and high heels, and he'd want to disappear into
her flesh. He hated his father for having her. And hated him more

when his father ditched her after a drunken brawl. She'd wanted to
take Holden, and his father threw her down the stairs. That instant
of Loretta flying, her long legs kicking out at random, stayed with
Holden.

"Shut up about money," she said. And he was that unhappy
child again, mourning the loss of Loretta Howard.

"Any messages, Mrs. H.?"

"Nothing important," she said.

The Marielita spooned her pudding, oblivious of him. Don't
forget dada, he almost said. He kissed Mrs. H. on the mouth, felt
her gun against his heart, while the Marielita looked at dada once
with her leopard eyes and returned to the pudding with a pledge of
chocolate on her mouth.

3 IT WAS NEAR MIDNIGHT when Holden arrived at
the fur market. The streets were black around Seventh.
The storefront gates were locked on West Twenty-ninth.
Holden had to ring for the watchman. He took the elevator up to
Aladdin Furs, toyed with the alarm, and walked in. He could see
the factory lights. His partner, Nick Tiel, was preparing for the
Paris show. Nick hired fur cutters who went into the gloom with
him. The cutters were faithful to Nick. Holden saw to that. One
cutter, who'd waltzed off with a paper sleeve, was found with a
bullet in his head.

It was a business where everybody stole. Manufacturers, cutters, mannequins, office boys. Nick Tiel didn't care about the sables.

He could survive the loss of a few dozen skins. But he guarded every scribble. No one could enter the designer's room without a nod from Nick. He was the most inventive designer in New York. The company whirled around Nick Tiel. He controlled the cutters, design assistants, salesmen, some of the buyers themselves. He could always anticipate a shift in the market. He was months ahead of other manufacturers' lines. But Nick had been knocked senseless by a gang of Greeks when he'd first come into the business. And he never quite recovered from that beating. He'd fall down after one of his flurries, and Holden had to fit him together again. Holden was his gun and his glue. He guarded Nick when the madness appeared, kept him away from people, or Nick would have offered his designs to any beggar, and sold his company to the Greeks.

The Greeks had more than half the fur market to themselves, but they couldn't contend with Nick's genius to marshal a company for an important show. The Greeks were waiting for Nick to fall and not have Holden around. But Holden was always there.

It might have been a marriage. Nick Tiel was president, Holden was senior vice president and service man. And Holden's services went beyond sables in a drawer. He killed people for Aladdin Furs. That was the complication. Nick had another partner. He owned Aladdin with Bruno Schatz, a Swisser who lived in Paris and was eighty years old. Schatz scheduled Holden's calendar of hits. Holden and Nick barked and wore the best clothes, but they were the Swisser's slaves. It irked them, but they didn't have the capital or the connections without Schatz. They would have been adrift in a universe of Greeks.

Holden caught Nick Tiel eating a sandwich in the designer's room with a team of cutters around him. They'd completed half a coat. Nick would never allow the same cutters to see a whole design. He himself was the joiner, the ultimate pattern man. "Kids," he said. The cutters were as old as Nick Tiel. "There's no money in couture. You're much better off putting your money in shoelaces than sables."

The cutters agreed, but they'd have sold their sisters for Nick

Tiel's ability to design a coat. And they were all snobs. Nick abused them, but they were sable cutters, princes of the line.

"Go into laces," he said and dismissed the cutters, ordered them out of the designer's room.

When a coat was very important, Nick lured Goldie uptown, because a thief like Goldie would never steal from him. Goldie would pin the canvas model onto the designer dummy, and Nick Tiel could walk around the dummy and imagine it in sable.

He offered Holden half his sandwich. "How was it in Queens?"

"Satisfactory," Holden said, dumping the vinyl bag on Nick Tiel's table.

"That's no answer. Give me a nibble. Did the woman have a moustache? Did she make you?"

"She's dead."

" 'Course she's dead. That was the idea . . . any particular problems?"

"No."

Holden had a sliver of Nick's ham. "I'm tired. I'm going to bed."

"I'll give you something to dream about . . . your next case."

"I thought I'm going to Paris tomorrow with your prelims." Holden always brought Nick's patterns to the Swisser before the Paris fair.

"Something came up," Nick said. "You'll have to cancel the flight."

"What could be as important as prelims?"

"Abruzzi's daughter-in-law."

"What the hell is she to Nick Tiel?"

"I love you, Holden, but don't you ever watch the tube? She was kidnapped this morning."

"Who would be crazy enough to kidnap a district attorney's daughter-in-law?"

"The Pinzolo brothers," Nick Tiel said.

Paul Abruzzi was the grand old man of Queens. He was waiting for the right judgeship to come along. Meanwhile he hunted the

Mafia in his own county. He'd begun to make a stink about an undiscovered tribe of garbagemen, the Pinzolos, whom he liked to call the Sixth Mafia Family.

Holden yawned. "I'm going to bed."

"You ran with those imbeciles once upon a time."

"I did not. I went to high school with Mike Pinzolo. We were friends. And why are you so sure Red Mike grabbed the Abruzzi bitch?"

"I'm not sure. But it makes sense. He's a Pinzolo. His father is in jail. The family suffers from malnutrition and a million other diseases. They're out of their heads."

"Nick, I'm not buying this one. I took the Parrot. I'll have my rest. I don't do anything back to back. It's a bad policy."

"You've been sworn to it, Holden. By the Swisser."

"Fuck him. I'm going to bed." Holden walked out of the designer room, past the nailing boards of silver foxes and sables, that marvelous assembly of skins he'd never understand. A fur coat was a miracle to him. Skin upon skin, like the perfect bolting of a bat's wing. He went into an office with his name on the glass. S. HOLDEN, VICE PRESIDENT. The S. was for Sidney. But no one had ever called him that. He was Holden at home, Holden at school, Holden in this fur factory.

The office was a huge loft, with windows over Manhattan. Holden moved in here after his marriage broke up. He was still in love with his wife. He'd found her in the showroom at Aladdin Furs. She was a mannequin who belonged to Nick Tiel. He couldn't take his eyes off her. She called herself Andrushka. She was seventeen, and she was sleeping with half the buyers. Holden went crazy. He'd just turned twenty-seven. He was the boy wonder who'd been bumping people for nine years. He walked up and down the showroom with deep splits in his forehead. The buyers fled from Andrushka.

"Mister," she said, "who are you and what do you want?"

"I'm Holden, vice president."

"Well, Holden, vice president, you're scaring my best customers away."

She was a little taller than Holden liked, and built like a twig, but her hair was wild, and she wasn't like the other mannequins, who traveled the circuit of showrooms with a bored, lascivious look. This Andrushka had a rough innocence. She probably loved every man who bought her a meal. Holden didn't dare mention marriage. She'd start screaming.

"So talk?" she said, painting her eyes.

"I'm one of your bosses."

"I've got lots of bosses, Holden, vice president."

"I'd like to take you to lunch."

"Salami and cheese?" she asked.

"No. Caravelle, if we can get in. Or Lutèce."

"I've been there," she said. "All the men stare down my tits."

She had no tits. But Holden wouldn't call her a liar.

"Then what would you prefer?"

"The kosher deli on Twenty-ninth."

"They won't serve you salami and cheese."

"They will if I ask for separate sandwiches."

He took her to the kosher deli and she wondered why in the middle of the twelve o'clock rush, with furriers everywhere, Holden got a table.

"I remember now . . . you're the bumper."

"Who told you that?"

"I listen," she said.

They were married in three weeks. Holden had to doctor her birth certificate, because Andrushka had no legal guardian, and she was a lousy minor. Her real name was Ann Rosshoven. The Russian princess had been born in Green Bay.

They lasted two and a half years. Andrushka ran to Europe before she was twenty. She married the Swisser without divorcing Holden. He dreamt of murdering them both. But it was one hit that would never happen. He lay down and watched *The Deer Hunter* on his video machine. Then he started *Destry Rides Again*.

The phone rang at five in the morning. He recognized the wind and static of a European call.

"Holden, are you up?"

"Wait," he said. "I'll turn off the cassette."

The machine froze on Marlene Dietrich's face.

"What can I do for you, Swiss?"

"It's a pity you'll have to postpone Paris for a while. Somebody's daughter is missing. And you've been elected to locate her."

"I elect my own projects, Swiss. There's too much notoriety attached to this one. I might disappear after the package has been returned."

"Your safety's been assured," the Swisser said.

"Too bad."

"Holden . . ."

"What?"

"You're an original, and I tolerate your bad manners and all your moods. But I've promised you, Holden. And I can't go back on my word. You're invaluable to this project."

His head throbbed. Where the hell is Andie, he thought, his Andrushka, wearing silks with an eighty-year-old man?

"I'm freelance, Swiss. That was our bargain. I can say no."

"Not when it involves the lives of our friends."

Holden understood the Swisser's Morse code. The Mafia didn't like the idea of Italian mavericks stealing a district attorney's daughter-in-law. It killed their bargaining power with all the U.S. attorneys who were after their skin. The Pinzolos were making the Mafia look like pigs.

"Why can't our friends use their own material? They have the best merchandise in town."

"Don't play dumb with me, Holden. They can't afford the publicity right now."

Was Andrushka undressed? What time was it in Paris? One in the afternoon? She wouldn't rise before two.

"I'll think about it, Swiss. I had a hard afternoon."

"There'll be a bonus. That bundle you were carrying. Half of it is yours."

The Swisser was nuts. A hundred and twenty-five thousand for some bitch no one had heard about until today? The best Mafia piece man would have done it for free in honor of his padrone. And they had to reach for Holden. Because they couldn't get near the wild man, Red Mike, and his brothers.

"Swiss," Holden said through that wind in the wire. "We have a problem. I can't go in wearing a mask. The daughter will see my face and tell the district attorney."

"No harm in that, Holden. He won't disturb whatever angel brings her out."

"What about the other side? I'll have a family of crazies on my back once it's finished."

"That family doesn't have much of a future. The garbagemen will go to their graves. The daughter's the ticklish thing. We can't have her damaged. We need some custom work."

The wind cracked in Holden's ear and the line went dead.

He didn't think about daughters-in-law. Not even the Pinzolos he'd have to kill. He thought about the man with Andrushka, eighty years, and that Swisser would outlive Holden.

He tapped his video machine and Dietrich's face unfroze. She was round and lovely, not like that twig he'd married. Destry Rides Again.

4 HOLDEN GOT OUT OF BED at noon. He didn't need a file card on Red Mike Pinzolo. He'd had target practice with Mike and his brothers, Eddie and Rat, a month ago. They used the old police range at Rodman's Neck. An Italian detective was always smuggling them in. Mike was the family's main enforcer. He controlled half the garbage routes in Queens. He'd walk into some restaurant and kill a rival with thirty men and women eating around him. All the witnesses went dumb. Abruzzi couldn't indict him. But Mike's father, a kindly old man who fed Holden gnocchi he'd made with his own hands, was caught trying to strangle a bartender who happened to be an undercover dick. Red Mike considered that unfair. Two of his sisters had been fingerprinted and shoved inside a detention cell. Mike wanted Abruzzi to understand the insult of having your father and your sisters fondled by cops.

A neighbor had once stolen Mike's parking spot. He brooded for a month and then shot the man's home with a submachine gun. It was this romantic, Red Mike, who had the district attorney's daughter-in-law.

Holden began seeing her picture in the papers. Fay Abruzzi, who'd gone to Swarthmore College with Abruzzi's boy. She was a year younger than Holden, thirty-six. She'd been a sociologist until she had her second child. Red Mike had plucked her off the streets of Manhattan. The *Post* called her the Vanishing Ph.D.

She wasn't Holden's type. She wore eyeglasses and her figure was much too full. He almost sympathized with Red Mike. But it was a stupid act. Crooks should leave civilians alone.

Holden went to his spies. It took six days to uncover Red Mike. The idiot had brought Abruzzi's daughter-in-law to a house in Far Rockaway, a half-deserted stretch of summer bungalows. Holden didn't have to wonder why he'd found Red Mike. The cops and all the Mafia families were helping his spies. It should have been a honeymoon hit. But he was too damn fond of Mike.

He rode out to the Rockaways in a Lincoln that was registered to a dairy farm in Pennsylvania. Goldie had come along. He was Holden's package man. He provided guns as well as silk ties. Holden couldn't trust some kid with a suitcase of hot guns to sell. Goldie's guns came out of a freezer that couldn't be traced. They were assembled for Holden, custom-built. Goldie himself buffed and filed each grip. Because Holden's life would depend on how he pulled.

He had to go against three crazy brothers, and Goldie had given him a Llama .22 long, just like the Parrot wore in Queens. It was a good sheriff's gun, accurate and swift to the touch. Holden always took his target practice with a .22 long.

"It's not Eddie and it's not the Rat," Goldie muttered. "It's Mike. Mike will smell us from the beach." His mouth began to quiver.

"You promised me you wouldn't cry," Holden said.

"Who's crying? I'm worried about Red Mike. You won't get past the door."

"You promised me," Holden insisted. "If I took you along, you'd sit like a gentleman and wouldn't twitch."

"I am sitting like a gentleman."

"Then how come your whole face is moving?"

"It likes to move," Goldie said. "You need a back-up man."

"You get killed faster with a back-up man. They're always fucking up. You have to start thinking about them, and it hurts your timing. I'm better off alone."

"Not against wacked-out brothers who'd steal family from a D.A."

"They had cause," Holden said. "Abruzzi stole from them."

"Yes. A father who strangles people. Sisters who'll cut off your arm if you look at them the wrong way."

"They're still family," Holden said, and Goldie held his trembling lip as they traveled on Seagirt Avenue. Holden stopped the car along the beach. Goldie listened to the tear of the ocean. He thought of London and his childhood digs. He'd been a thief since he could remember, swiping nails and bolts from an ironmonger, hurling them into the damp sky. His bones were always cold.

"Goldie, are you in a trance?"

"It's not important. I was recollecting a few nails out of my rotten past."

He removed the .22 long from an old paper bag. Holden took the gun and stuffed it into his pants without inspecting the magazine. He knew Goldie had licked every bullet in its copper jacket. Nothing had ever gone wrong with a tailor's .22.

"Don't you consider following me inside, Goldie."

"I wouldn't dream of it. But kiss me," the old man said.

They hugged in front of the car like a couple of bears.

"I never failed you, Goldie."

"I know, but I'm getting superstitious. A kiss brings good luck."

Holden walked toward a line of shabby summer houses and Goldie got back into the car. He had a second .22, a Llama short, in the glove compartment. He didn't care what promises he'd made. If Holden didn't come out in a reasonable time, Goldie would have to give his regards to Red Mike.

"Careful, God damn you," he muttered as Holden halted outside a bungalow. A body appeared in the door, lean as a snake.

Holden nodded to Red Mike, whose hair wasn't noticeably red. He had lighter skin than his dad, and must have seemed like a ruddy man to the rest of the Pinzolos.

"Hello, Frog," he said from the door. "Have you come to kill me?"

"Yes."

"Good. Then come on in."

Holden climbed the steps of the bungalow with the Llama high against his waist, so there wouldn't be any confusion about the gun. Mike had a Walther PPK 7.65 in a cream-colored holster under his heart. He'd picked up that gun at the movies. It was a James Bond Special. Red Mike had modeled himself after Sean Connery ever since junior high. He hated Roger Moore. He felt as if the Secret Service had betrayed him when Roger Moore grew into 007. And he was the one man Holden would allow to call him Frog. Red Mike had given him that name because Holden spent the first three years of his life in France.

He entered the bungalow. Eddie and Rat stood in the living room with deer rifles trained on Holden's groin. They were older than Mike, had little mouths and little, searching eyes.

"Mikey," Rat said, "should we lend him to the sharks?"

Red Mike smiled under his dark brown mustache. He had three mistresses and two wives. It depressed Holden to think of all the widows he'd have to make.

"Relax, relax," Mike said to his brothers, pointing one of the rifles away from Holden's crotch. "It's a friendly chat. We haven't gotten to the bargaining stage."

"What's there to bargain about?" Eddie asked, his eyes searching hard.

Holden loved all three brothers. Eddie with the crazy eyes. Rat who always had tonsillitis. And Red Mike, who'd taught him to hold a gun.

"There's plenty to bargain," Mike said, patient with his brothers. "We don't even know who sent the man."

"It don't matter," Rat said, with a sudden surge of intelligence.

Mike pinched his mustache. "What's wrong with you? Didn't you eat stracciatelle with this man? Frog never fucked us. The D.A. did."

"Mikey, Mikey," Rat said. "He's the D.A.'s boy."

Mike turned to Holden, his mustache flaming in the sun that broke through the porch. "Frog, is that right? Did the D.A. deputize you?"

"I never worked for Abruzzi."

"It don't matter," Rat said. "It comes to the same thing."

"It's not the same thing . . . Frog, the D.A. is practicing genocide on my family. You know that."

"But if you hadn't touched his daughter-in-law, I wouldn't be here."

Mike's eyes went beady the way his brothers' did. "Frog, who's sitting in your car? Some ice man you brought? I pity the bastard."

"It's Goldie. He came along for the ride."

"You should have said so. Invite him inside. He'll have some spumoni with us," Mike said, fondling his holster. And Holden shivered under his shirt, shivered for Goldie. He shouldn't have brought his tailor on the job. And then Rat intervened.

"Mikey, should we show him the little darling?" Rat said. "She can have some of our ice cream." He left the living room, returned with Fay Abruzzi, and began to titter with Ed. The daughter-in-law wasn't wearing any clothes. Holden didn't go searching below her neck. But he couldn't avoid the woman's breasts. She had big shoulders. There weren't any bruises on her arms. She looked at Holden and lowered her eyes.

"She does the cooking," Rat said.

"Frog, we didn't touch her," Mike insisted. "I'm a married man."

"She does the cooking," Rat said. Holden pulled the .22 out of his pants and shot Red Mike. Mike's lips pursed as he fell. The hole in his forehead could have been a red dime. Ed and Rat were horrified. Holden shot them both before they remembered the deer rifles they had.

The woman never screamed. She watched the three dead men, her neck high as a swan.

"Come," Holden said. "Where's your clothes?"

He had to ask her twice.

"They ripped them," she said, "ripped them up and used them for rags . . . so I couldn't escape."

He'd never heard a woman talk with such a fine melody. Her voice was softer than Goldie's wool. But he didn't have time to chat with the bitch. And the open forks of her body made him uncomfortable. He couldn't relax around a naked woman he didn't know. Her ripeness bothered Holden, obliged him to consider Andrushka's chest.

He wasn't going to pull clothes off three dead men. He'd have to find other things for Fay to wear. He went into the closets and discovered a whole new wardrobe each brother had. He dressed Fay Abruzzi like some kind of man. She didn't object. Her bosoms disappeared under the drape of Red Mike's shirt. Holden felt relieved.

He had to send her out of the bungalow in a pair of Eddie's sandals. Goldie stood on the porch with a .22. Now she could identify his tailor.

"I was worried," Goldie said.

"Get back into the car."

"I heard three shots, and—"

"Get back into the car."

Goldie returned to the Lincoln.

A limo seemed to come out of the sand dunes with venetian blinds. Holden never looked. One of his stoolies, Harrington, owned a car service, and Harrington himself had arrived in the Rockaways.

Holden led Fay to Harrington's limousine. She tightened under the shirt. "Where are you taking me?"

"Home. But I'm not taking you. My associate is."

"Do you work for the police?"

"Not very often," Holden said.

She entered the limo and Harrington took off.

Holden didn't like it at all. He'd killed three men and she'd never cried. He'd expected her to shove around in a shaky dream. But she talked like a music teacher.

He got to the Lincoln. Goldie sat like a guilty child. "Give me that gun," Holden said. He took the tailor's .22 short, removed the cartridge, then banged the gun against the dashboard until the gun broke. "Some terrific back-up man. A .22 short? You could hit a guy in the head and the bullet would stand there, stuck in the flesh. Wouldn't even penetrate the skull. Goldie, who asked you to bring a gun?"

"There were three maniacs. I couldn't help myself."

"But Jesus, I have to depend on you. You're my package man. And you pick yourself a stupid gun."

"Not so stupid," Goldie said. "The bullets dance a lot. I always aim for the ear."

"Then I'll use a .22 short next time," Holden said. "But you keep your guns in the closet."

5 HOLDEN KNEW he was near the end. He sat in the kosher deli with all the Greeks who'd discovered pastrami for themselves and couldn't go back to a diet of olives and brittle white cheese. And a police captain from the old burglary squad had come in to congratulate Holden.

"That was a beautiful piece of work."

This captain had no influence at all. He couldn't have gotten close to Abruzzi, and yet he'd learned where Holden had been. Holden didn't even bother to deny it. If a disconnected captain had tied Holden to the Rockaways, then the story had to be out on the street.

The captain had mustard on his collar. His clothes were full of dandruff. He wore hand-me-downs from a bargain basement. Holden wanted him to disappear. But he couldn't pinch a captain in public. He had to wait until the captain grabbed a few of Holden's half-sour pickles.

"You need a favor, Holden, you come to me."

And the captain walked away in filthy trouser cuffs, collecting gifts from the Greeks, because he was supposed to discourage burglars. It was a scam, but why should Holden warn the Greeks, who would love to have him dead? If a captain could finger him that quick, Holden was lucky he'd last the week. Bumpers couldn't afford to be movie stars. Holden had to depend on the anonymous lair of a fur company. Clients might develop a sudden itch if Holden could be traced back to them.

"Mikey," he said. "Red Mike."

He left a five-dollar tip, but the waiter followed him out the door.

"Mr. Holden, please . . . I'll get into trouble."

Holden forgot. The kosher deli wouldn't take his tips. The owners liked to have him around. They hadn't been held up ever since the sheriff of Aladdin Furs started swallowing their pastrami.

Holden went up to Nick Tiel. There was a glaze in Nick's eye. Holden wondered if Nick was about to unravel. He'd have to take the designer along to Paris, or the Greeks would steal from Aladdin. And Holden couldn't shoot half the fur market to get back Nick's designs. But Nick lost that crazy luster. "You did it, Goddamn."

"Couldn't you be a little more quiet?" Holden said. Nick Tiel's assistants were nailing skins a few yards from Holden.

"Ah, so what?" Nick said. "If people like to listen, they'll have to suffer the consequences of their own ears."

The nailers picked up their boards and moved to the end of the factory.

"Holden, it was just on the radio. They called you the mystery man. You could run for mayor, start your own ticket."

"But that ticket might come home to you."

"Let it come," Nick said. "There's no danger to us. Holden, you're a hero."

"Good. I'm going to bed."

"Infante is here."

"What does he want?"

"Be a little human, Holden. The man admires you."

Robert Infante was their lawyer. He was also the lawyer of the biggest Greek furriers and a peacemaker for all the crime families. He'd settled the policy war that broke out between the Italians and the Cubans in 1980. The Italians couldn't keep La Familia under their wing. It was during the boatlift from Mariel. La Familia had hired the Bandidos to bomb Mafia betting parlors. Italian bumpers looked everywhere for the Bandidos. But the Bandidos dressed in women's clothes like their god Changó, and the bumpers could never find them. That's when Infante was brought in, an Italian lawyer who pleaded La Familia's case. The Italians sold half their betting parlors to the Cubans. And La Familia became one of Infante's clients. He sat around with the Cuban chiefs, lawyers like himself, drank bitter coffee and discussed politics.

Infante had his own office at Aladdin Furs. It belonged to the Swisser before the Swisser moved to France. Infante had started out as a prosecutor in the Queens district attorney's office. Now he controlled every piece of sable that moved into the fur market. He was the most feared lawyer in town. Once, only once, the cops had put handcuffs on Holden. Infante was there when Holden arrived at the central booking station. The cops removed the handcuffs, and half the sergeants in the house apologized to Holden.

Infante was forty-five. His wife Florinda ate at Mansions restaurant with a lot of kings. Infante would ask Holden to be her bodyguard from time to time. Holden had become a big hit. He was a bumper with better clothes than any billionaire.

Holden knocked on Infante's door and went in. The lawyer sat behind his desk, counting furriers' markers and notes. He tied them with a rubber band and stood up to paw Holden. He had an elegant stink of toilet water. Holden used nothing but slightly scented soap.

"Holden, Holden," the lawyer said. "I'm proud . . . you sneak Fay back into Manhattan in a man's shirt and pants. Who else would have thought of that?"

"I had to, Robert. Red Mike destroyed her clothes."

"Then Mike deserves a bit of credit, eh? Credit he'll never claim."

"He was my friend. I can't celebrate his not being here."

"I know," Infante said. "I was fond of the big bastard myself. But he went too far. He wants to machine-gun a house, okay. Bump a couple of competitors, fine. But steal Abruzzi's daughter-in-law?"

"He never really harmed the girl. He burnt her underwear, so she couldn't run away."

"That's sick," Infante said. "But why are we arguing? Abruzzi sends his regards. He's awful fond of Fay. You met her husband a

couple of times. Rex, a tall guy who likes to scribble. I got you tickets
for one of his plays, *The Purple Farm.*"

Holden remembered now. He'd gone to that play with Nick
Tiel. It was three hours of talk. There were no purple farms. The
play was about a sea captain and the voyages he took, the women
and children he acquired, all the different crusts a man can wear.
Holden had never been to sea. And he couldn't sympathize with this
sea captain. Nick Tiel had his fun in the dark, watching fur coats.
Nick could tell the quality of any mink draped over a chair. Holden
had nothing but the sea captain . . . and Rex, a giant who sat through
the performance holding his jaw.

"Robert, I didn't care so much for Rex's play."

"That's because you're a snob, like your London tailor. It bothers me, Holden. No matter how rich I am, I'll never dress as well
as you."

"Hire Goldie."

"It's not that simple," Infante said. "You're practically his kid.
He's devoted to you."

"Make him an offer."

"I already did. I offered him ten thousand a year not to dress
you, and he laughed in my face."

"Well, you're industrious, Robert. You have a lot of bumpers
in your back yard. You could convince one little tailor."

"Fat chance," Infante said, "when the tailor has you on his
side."

"I'm just your servant," Holden said.

The lawyer started to laugh. He was vain about his narrow,
birdlike body and wore the tightest clothes he could find. But his vest
rippled with short explosions of laughter and broke his trim, mata-
dor's line. Infante realized this and stopped laughing.

"I'd like to meet a servant that draws your kind of salary."

"I'm expensive, but so what? The Swisser owns me."

"Own? You're the lord of the fur market. Everybody begs
favors from you . . . including myself. You've been ignoring Florinda,
Holden. Every time you disappoint her, she takes it out on me.

Florinda thinks I can produce her Holden like a bunny out of a hat
. . . she's expecting you at Mansions for a late lunch."

"Sorry," Holden said. "I have other plans." He felt unwired
after the Rockaways and wanted to disappear into his office-home
and watch *The Third Man* or sink into his tub like a sea captain.

"Holden," Infante said, "will you meet my wife? . . . as a favor
to the firm."

He walked into Mansions wearing a dark velvet suit. His display
handkerchief was a piece of pure red silk Goldie got from a Pakistani
merchant who once supplied household goods to a colony of rajahs
and royal Brits. The handkerchief sat like an exquisite blood clot on
Holden's heart. His shoes were from Seville. Goldie had buffed the
leather to look like burnt clay. Holden's tie, also red, had come from
the closets of the late King George. His shirt, with broad blue stripes,
had another king's signature on one of its tails. Holden could have
been some apparition off the streets. Goldie had designed him to
move like a sculpted man.

No one stopped him near the door. He didn't need a reserva-
tion. The owner, Count Josephus, hobbled next to Holden and
shook his hand. The count had been wounded in some mysterious
war. He spoke half a dozen languages, his shirts carried the mono-
gram of kings, but Holden knew that Josephus had been a convict
before he was a count. He had the same tiny tattoo hidden in the
webbing of his thumb that the Bandidos sometimes wore. A heart
with the word *"madre"* in the middle. An executioner's sign. Holden
had wondered for half a year why the count liked to curl his left
thumb and keep it closed against his hand. And then, while the
count was in the middle of a story about his boyhood in Albania, he'd
gestured with the wrong hand and Holden saw that heart under the
thumb. The count could blab about Albania until he was blue in the
head, but he'd done some time between his royal birth and his
restaurant.

"Good to see you," said the count. "How are the sables doing?"

"You'll have to ask my partner Nick. He's the creative one. I wouldn't know how to design a coat."

The count brought him to Florinda Infante's table. She haunted Mansions' window like a huge, angular cat. Florinda was descended from a noble Tuscan line—had an emperor somewhere in her house, and a couple of whores, Holden could imagine. She was a tall beauty with a purple streak in her hair. Holden sat down and Florinda put a leg in his lap. She bit his ear in front of the count.

"What can I bring you?" the count asked.

"Go away," Florinda said.

The count laughed, then bowed to Florinda, and hobbled toward that cave beyond the bar where most of the aristocrats liked to eat lunch. Mansions was a cafeteria for countesses and kings.

"Why won't you sleep with me?" Florinda asked, swallowing half of Holden's ear.

"Because of Robert," he said.

It was a lie. He had slept with Florinda, but Holden was still in love with his wife. And he grew sad in bed with Florinda Infante, who hugged him like a cobra and had all the passion of her ancient house, and he'd think of Andrushka's face glowing under him and want to cry.

A king arrived at the table. Holden couldn't tell one king from another, or recollect the thrones they'd lost. This king was new. His name was Alfonse, but Florinda called him Fatso.

"Fatso, come and meet Holden . . . he kills people."

"Darling," Alfonse said, "who doesn't?"

She thrust two fingers out at Alfonse to form a gun. "It's not a joke. He's a bang-bang boy."

"Then I'd like to borrow Holden."

"Fatso, you couldn't afford him," Florinda said, her mouth shining near the window. The king walked away.

Holden took Florinda's leg off his lap.

"You're cross," she said. "I love it when you're cross. Your brow wrinkles, and you look like Galileo, or some deep mysterious Jew."

"Florinda, you shouldn't give out all my tricks. Fatso might take you seriously."

"Then sleep with me."

"Let's have lunch."

Other kings came over. Or counts. Holden couldn't say. They kept asking him about his tailor. They were jealous of his handkerchief, the ribs on his shirt, the green line of his socks, the bewildering orchestration of the colors he wore. Every part of Holden had been fitted by hand. The men at Mansions were always morose around him. They couldn't solve the mystery of his clothes. They didn't care what Holden did. He could have been a gravedigger. But they had to know who dressed him.

Florinda's face developed a dark blush. Holden was in trouble. She was crazy under that burning skin.

"Holden, how did you like her ass?"

"Whose ass?"

"Fay's," Florinda said.

Holden growled inside his chest. Did Infante have to tell his wife all of Holden's tricks? Every king in the cafeteria would soon be aware of his business.

"Do her tits sag?"

She'd bite his head off if he didn't give her some satisfaction. "I think so," he said, dreaming of Andrushka's tiny breasts.

"Her husband ought to thank you. I'll tell him that the next time he comes to my table. He's a big oaf with curly hair. Always signing autographs . . . he signed one for you."

How could he remember Rex Abruzzi's signature among all those counts and kings? He couldn't concentrate on the rich. He closed his eyes at Mansions.

"Holden, he's hardly ever here. Rex prefers the Odeon. With all the art glitz. The count doesn't seem to care about playwrights."

Holden ordered asparagus for lunch.

"It's depressing," Florinda said. "You can't just sit there with a plate of asparagus."

"Why not?"

"People will laugh. They'll say I have lunch with barbarians."

"I am a barbarian."

"You are not," Florinda said. "You're a misguided little boy."

She ordered a rack of lamb for Holden and herself.

He watched the bones under her mouth as she chewed. He finished his asparagus. She was like a sleek tub of electricity. He'd get a tiny shock whenever he touched Florinda.

Holden looked across the street. One of his rats was waiting.

"Florinda, I have to go."

"Stay," she said, clutching Holden's pants. "I never eat dessert alone."

"You have the goddamn restaurant. Everybody knows you. Sit with a couple of kings."

"If I wanted a king, I'd have come in with a king. I'm warning you. Don't leave."

Holden tried to stand up, but Florinda dug into his jacket and went for Holden's gun. Holden had to squeeze her fingers around his heart.

"It's sexy," she said. "Feeling you like that."

Her perfume clogged his head like some kind of monstrous vapor. While he struggled with her, his eyes caught the purple streak in Florinda's hair. She had no shame. Mansions could have been her private cafeteria. She ruled the chef, the count, all the little kings. He sat down again, let go of her hand, watched her dissect a glazed pear with a miniature knife and fork. She drank her coffee and let him drift.

"Holden, I'll come and visit you one night. You'll see."

"And what if Robert's in the next room?"

"He'll have to suffer," she said.

Holden passed a few countesses and kings, with tiaras and scarfs and centuries of royal blood. He tipped the headwaiter, some lesser prince who'd lost his country and his title.

"Goodbye, Monsieur."

Holden was always Monsieur in the cafeteria. He couldn't get out the door. Count Josephus tugged at his sleeve.

"Congratulations."

"I'm not getting married," Holden said. "Why congratulate me?"

"For solving that kidnappers' case."

"Count, you'd better keep quiet."

Holden crossed Lexington Avenue and approached Gottlieb, a seventeen-year-old boy with delicate features. Gottlieb had the hands and face of a girl. He was a runner at a high-priced whorehouse. He collected sandwiches, shined shoes, slipped from door to door like a ghost with big ears. He was the best agent Holden had ever had. But he was reckless. He'd bound himself to Holden's fortune, and he'd fall when Holden fell. He talked like Holden, dressed like Holden, had the same library of video cassettes. He couldn't live without *Destry Rides Again*.

"Holden, get off the street."

"Are Red Mike's sisters coming after me?"

"Forget Mike. That's ancient. Have you been messing with the Mariels?"

"I did them a favor. I took out the Parrot and his woman. They were giving the Bandidos a bad name. The Mariels should offer me a medal."

"They will. After they put you in a basket."

"Talk sense."

"Some of the *jibaros* are after you."

"Then find out what I did to them. How can I do penance when I don't know my sins?"

"I'm not a mind reader, Holden . . . sorry, I gotta blow."

The kid danced around the corner and Holden stood on Lexington Avenue in a priceless silk tie. He couldn't walk around all the time looking like Douglas Fairbanks Jr. Goldie had a saying: the finer the clothes, the more anonymous the man. One duke was like any other. But what if it was all a tailor's dream?

He took a cab down to the Manhattan Bridge and hunkered in the shadows, sniffing cold air. He couldn't win a war with the Mariels. They worshipped chicken blood and little dolls and would cook Holden into a soup and suck his bones if they were unhappy with him. They did voodoo with their rice and beans. Holden wouldn't interfere with a god in a red dress. The kid had to be wrong.

Holden snuck into a cellar on James Street and took the underground route to Mrs. Howard, landing in her back yard and knocking on her window before he let himself in. A guy could get shot in the pants if he didn't establish the right code.

He searched the apartment for Mrs. Howard and the Marielita. "Mrs. H.?"

He went from living room to bedroom to Mrs. Howard's telephone bank where she deciphered all the messages from Holden's rats. He loved listening to her on the telephone with a rat. Her dialogue could have been pieces out of Rex Abruzzi's play. She developed particular songs with particular spies. He'd hear her talk about rocks and oceans and cattle on Mars and then she'd get off the wire and the cattle became Coke bottles filled with gasoline or another kind of bomb. Mrs. Howard never put anything on paper. She wouldn't declare what she had until she saw Holden himself. None of his spies could get into trouble, no matter whose phone was tapped. All they ever talked about were rocks and heavenly cattle.

Holden looked up and saw Mrs. Howard with a gun in his face. She held onto the Marielita with her other hand.

"You shouldn't pounce on people, Holden. You frightened the girl."

"Did you learn her name yet?" Holden asked.

"She's not into names. Names aren't her thing."

"Then what is her thing?"

"You," Mrs. Howard said. "She's in love with you, Holden. I tried to talk her out of it. Loving you can get a little hairy."

"She talks English?"

"When she's in the mood."

The Marielita looked funny to Holden. Mrs. Howard had dressed her in satins and silks from her personal closet. Holden forgot. Mrs. Howard was a tailor too.

"Loretta, can you send her somewhere? We have business to discuss."

"Christ, Holden, she hears me on the phone. I don't keep secrets from her."

"Well, I do . . ."

Mrs. Howard whispered to the Marielita and the little girl disappeared in her silks. She could have been the queen of Persia, or an island princess. She wore lipstick, and her tiny nails were polished.

"Holden, you're the rudest man around."

"I still need my messages."

"Then that's what you'll get. Carmen Pinzolo wants to kill you, but she can't." Carmen was Red Mike's baby sister. She'd had a crush on Holden for years and years. He'd fed her ice cream on his lap. But he couldn't keep her there after she was nine or ten. She developed breasts and started to bleed like a woman. Red Mike had to take his sister out of school. Teachers were proposing to her in the hallways. Mike got her a tutor. The tutor proposed. Mike broke the tutor's mouth and started teaching her himself. But Carmen's musk drove him crazy. He created a convent for Carmen, sent her to live and learn with an old Italian witch. She stayed in exile until she was seventeen. And then Mike begged Holden to marry her, so at least his little sister would go to a friend and his heartburn wouldn't be so heavy, but all Holden could think about was Andrushka. Red Mike locked Carmen in the house. She'd escape, look for some man to be with, and Mike would destroy the unlucky bastard. Now, Holden thought, now Carmen can get married.

"Why can't she kill me?" Holden asked.

"Because the girl will never find a gun. The whole family is in the toilet. The Pinzolos can't touch you."

"I'm glad . . . Gottlieb says the Bandidos are after me."

"Bandidos? I'll check it out."

"Are you sure nothing came through the wire? Gottlieb isn't a romantic kid. He doesn't fantasize—"

"Holden, either fire me or trust what I say. No one's mentioned any Bandidos. I'll start calling. Now get out of here and play with the little girl."

Holden left Mrs. Howard to her telephone bank and looked for the Marielita. He found her under a table, like the first time, with those big leopard eyes.

"Dada," she said.

"I'm not your dada. I'm Holden. *Querida,* talk to me."

"Dada," she said.

"All right, I'll be your dada. But talk to me."

He got nowhere with the girl. She sat under the table, staring out at Holden in her silks. The little harbor lady, queen of Mariel. And Holden had a sudden shiver, like a bag of light in his skull. He was her dada in some way he couldn't define. Holden had conceived a leopard girl. He'd been born in Avignon, the city of popes, with a stitch under his heart; the stitch grew. He had no mom he could remember, though his dad talked of a woman who sprang out of dark medieval streets. He was supposed to look like that phantom lady. Now a daughter had popped out of his chest.

"Mademoiselle, what can I bring you from Paris? Perfume? A new doll? A lollipop that looks like a bridge? Or a sable coat from the Swisser's French collection?"

"Holden, are you propositioning that little girl?" Mrs. Howard asked, standing in the door. And for a moment, in that trick light of a room masked with metal blinds, Mrs. H. was his father's mistress again, the longlegged beauty of his boyhood, the woman he desired most.

"I was being friendly, that's all," Holden said. "Christ, will you give her a name? I have to know what to call her."

"She's yours. You name her if you want."

"I can't," Holden said. "It's not decent, picking names for a girl who's already formed."

"You can always form her again."

"That's playing with God."

"But you were born in God's home town."

He was sensitive about Avignon, where the popes had gone to live hundreds of years ago, seduced by some French king. It felt like a holy place to a boy who never had much religion. Holden Sr. despised God and His papal palace. He was like a prisoner in Avignon until Goldie rescued him.

"I called every contact we have," Mrs. Howard said. "There's nothing on the street about the Mariels. It's a whisper, Holden. Get Gottlieb to reveal his source, and we'll know."

"I can't compromise the kid. The Bandidos would roast him alive."

"Then you'll have to suffer the suspense. No one can help you, Holden."

"Dada," the Marielita said.

Loretta scowled. "That man doesn't deserve you, child. He talks about Parisian lollipops. But you wait. He won't deliver."

Holden stooped to nuzzle the leopard girl and tasted her lipstick.

"Go on," Mrs. Howard said. "Cozying up to a child like that. You ought to be ashamed."

"I am."

He hugged Mrs. Howard before she could escape. He recalled her aromas when she'd lived around him, a black woman in a white brassiere who smelled like sweet country grass. He'd loved her all through junior high. It was only Andrushka who'd relieved him of the spell. It was Holden's misfortune that he was a monogamous man. He couldn't exist with more than one sweetheart in his head.

Andrushka

6 HE HAD A *CROQUE MADAME* at a café near the Swisser's office. He loved grilled cheese crowned with an egg. The *croque madames* at American bistros were a tasteless pile of toast. He gorged himself whenever he got to Paris. The Swisser had found him an apartment on the rue du Dragon. But Holden preferred a hotel. There was no one to greet him at the apartment, nothing but neighbors who never smiled and a concierge who wondered why the mysterious American didn't need a mailbox. The apartment looked out onto a wall and the lower margins of a roof; it felt like a prison with tiled floors. Holden had gone from the airport to the apartment, stood on the tiles, stared at the pocked white wall, and registered at a hotel on the Place St. Sulpice, where no tourists ever went. The manager always seemed to have room for Monsieur. Holden's French was rotten. But he could gesture with his mouth, make the little explosive noises of a Frenchman. He'd lost a mom in Avignon, but he must have picked up something from the frogs.

He had his second *croque madame* and suddenly he could feel a pair of eyes, soft as a spider, sitting on his chest. Holden smiled. His shadow had come into the café. Billetdoux. Billetdoux always followed him when Holden came to France. He worked for a French furrier who was scared of Holden. Holden had kidnapped the furrier five years ago, a certain Mr. Bronshtein, who was feuding with Holden's senior partner, Bruno Schatz. Bronshtein had insulted Bruno's mannequins at the Paris fair, corrupted his messengers, and stole Nick Tiel's designs. It was a disaster for Bruno Schatz. His whole inventory had been compromised. That's when Holden kidnapped the furrier, brought him to one of Bruno's warehouses behind the Gare d'Austerlitz, sat him down in a huge, empty loft, so that Bronshtein had a world of ceilings to look at, and waited until the furrier began to weep.

"Don't kill me," Bronshtein had said, crawling to Holden on his knees. He had a lot of metal in his mouth, a face of golden teeth, and Holden felt sorry for him, because he hadn't been instructed to hurt the furrier, but to tease him and harrow his life a little.

"Will you make restitution to the Swisser?" Holden had to ask.

"Certainly," the furrier said.

"You'll repay him for ruining his winter line."

The furrier took a checkbook out of his pocket that was like a long flat boat and began to scribble numbers in the book.

"Mr. Bronshtein, this is a deal between gentlemen . . . we'll take cash."

"How much?"

"Swiss will leave that up to you. He knows you'll be generous about the damage you've done."

Holden escorted the furrier out of Bruno's warehouse and put him into a cab. Now Bronshtein had a fever the minute Holden was in town. And he hired Billetdoux, a bumper from Marseilles, to watch Holden. It was almost like a friendship, Billetdoux and him. The big bumper could have hid a gun factory inside his overcoat. His head looked like it had been assembled with a hammer. Billetdoux had seams under his ears. He reminded Holden of a bionic caveman, a brute with interchangeable parts. Holden asked the waiter to bring Billetdoux a glass of lemon water.

"My treat," Holden sang across the tables. "How's Bronshtein?"

"Bronshtein misses you," the bumper said.

"I'm glad. I'm going to the Swisser. Want to come?"

The bumper sipped his sour water and Holden left him in the cafe. He went up the rue du Four and landed on the Swisser's boulevard. Holden was like an infant in his partner's territories. But Holden didn't care. It pained him that Andrushka was in Paris. His own little bride who'd married Bruno Schatz without divorcing

Holden. Andrushka was a bigamist. Holden could have hired a lawyer to keep Andrushka out of the Swisser's bed. But he didn't have much contact with lawyers other than Robert Infante. And Infante worked with the Swisser cheek to cheek. Holden had rats and money and he knew a couple of kings, but there wasn't any way he could buy Andrushka back.

The Swisser was expecting him. That old man sat in his office overlooking the church and courtyard of St. Germain des Prés. He was dressed in silk, wore a pale suit that matched the color of his eyes. Holden was pissed off. Schatz seemed more energetic at eighty than Holden could ever hope to be.

The Swisser came out from behind his desk like a short fat engine with the pinkest shirt cuffs in St. Germain des Prés.

"Holden, it's embarrassing. I can never tell if you've come to kiss me or kill me."

"I work for you," Holden said.

"Work for me? You're my bloody partner. But no one's safe with you around . . . where's the sketches? Let's have a look."

Holden wore Nick Tiel's designs in a special pouch that was tied to his ribs, like a money belt. He didn't trust briefcases. Any band of pickpockets could have bumped into him at Charles De Gaulle and disappeared with Nick's designs. Holden unbuttoned his shirt, removed the pouch, and then unrolled the pattern paper. The Swisser's hands were trembling, but it had nothing to do with his age. He was excited. He read Nick Tiel's designs like a musical score, but those scribblings were an act of genius Holden would never understand. The Swisser could imagine a coat in his head from pieces of paper that Nick had numbered and cut. Holden was left out. He couldn't hum with the Swisser, who tacked Nick's designs to the inside door of his closet and stared at all that paper as if he'd discovered the clockwork of a doll.

"I'm in love," the Swisser said.

Holden felt a panic in his gut. "What's that, Swiss?"

"You heard me. I'm in love with Nick Tiel. I'd like to marry him."

You already married my wife, Holden wanted to say. But he'd go mad if they got on the subject of Andrushka. "Well, what's stopping you, Swiss? Marry the man."

The Swisser smiled. "I'd have a permanent guest in the house. You know Nick. He can't get along without you, Holden."

The Swisser removed the tacks from the closet door, rolled up Nick's designs, and locked them inside his safe. It startled Holden how swift Schatz was on his feet. His own arms and legs ached all the time.

"Do you think I look like Lord Weidenfeld?" the Swisser asked.

Holden shrugged. "Who's that?"

"Don't get slow on me now. Weidenfeld is one of the top dressers in the world. I'll bet he's on Goldie's list."

"Could be," Holden said. "But I'm not doing Weidenfeld this year."

"You ought to. He ducks into the closet with all the fancy ladies . . . Holden, you're as thick as your dad."

Holden Sr. had been Schatz's bodyguard until he died. He'd met Swiss during the war. Schatz was a consultant with arts and archives, a temporary colonel or something like that. He'd taught Holden Sr. how to steal. And Holden Sr. had remained with Schatz half his life, a bodyguard and a chauffeur. He'd never graduated beyond that. He was like a truculent child on the Swisser's payroll.

"You shouldn't knock a dead man, Swiss. My dad was devoted to you."

"And you're not," the Swisser said. "That's why you're my partner, and he never was."

"Don't blame him, Swiss. He wasn't into bumping people."

"That's because he didn't care enough. He wasn't ambitious. Would he have gone into the Pinzolos' den and faced up to Red Mike and his brothers?"

"I'm not proud of that, Swiss. Red Mike was my friend."

"But your dad, rest his soul, couldn't have saved the Abruzzi girl. That's why you're vice president, and he was a chauffeur."

"I wouldn't mind being a chauffeur, Swiss."

"Don't kid yourself. You're a celebrity now. You're on the map. God, I wish I was in New York. I'd parade you everywhere."

"You'd parade me right into the can."

"Nonsense. The cops are crazy about you, Holden. You did their work."

"They're fickle bastards," Holden said. "They can squeeze me whenever they want."

"Not without squeezing themselves. You're the prince, Holden. You'll be solving capers for some district attorney for years to come."

"I've seen what happens to princes," Holden said. "They die or become little decorative kings."

"You've been having too many lunches with Florinda. You're spoiled, Holden. Take my advice. Stop banging aristocratic ladies. Find yourself a sweet little woman."

Like Andrushka, Swiss? He'd have tossed Schatz out the window, but he couldn't get away with murder in the sixth arrondissement. He'd have to lure Schatz behind the Gare d'Austerlitz. He was fooling himself. His own bounty depended on Swiss. He was no better off than his dad. A bumper with a vice president's ticket, and he was still Schatz's slave.

"Holden, come with me to lunch. I want to show you off. We'll have duck with orange sauce. I'm meeting with a film producer and he owes me a lot of favors. You can start a career in pictures. You'll be the next Bogart. We'll cast you as a hood from Marseilles."

"Like Billetdoux."

"Has that imbecile been bothering you? One phone call, and he's out of your life for good."

"Leave him, Swiss. I'd get lonely without Billetdoux."

"Lonely, here," the Swisser said, "in your bosom town? You could have a cup of chocolate any afternoon with Andrushka. She—"

"Stop it, Swiss." Holden's ears started to whistle. He grabbed a corner of Schatz's desk. He had a touch of vertigo. That's what happened when you lost your wife.

"Can I get you something? You look pale all of a sudden."

"Don't talk to me about Andrushka, Swiss."

"Holden, you ought to give up mourning that marriage and find yourself another wife."

"That's the trouble, Swiss. Andrushka is my wife."

The vertigo was gone. Holden didn't have to grab Schatz's desk.

"Are you going to be technical about it? It's not my fault. She's a child. She's frightened of divorces. But she's fond of you, Holden. She misses your company."

"I told you to stop."

"Then don't be a savage. Come to dinner if you can't make it to lunch."

"I'm booked," Holden said. "I wouldn't want to disappoint Billetdoux. He likes to have his dinner six tables down from me . . . goodbye, Swiss."

"What if I need you? Where can I get in touch?"

"Ring Billetdoux. He's reliable. He'll give me the message."

And Holden walked out on the Swiss. Billetdoux was waiting for him in the courtyard of the church. He had a ham sandwich that looked like a poor boy from New Orleans. Holden was partial to poor boys and *croque madames* and chicory coffee and blackened fish. He'd gone to New Orleans with his bride, visited Albuquerque and Santa Fé, Tucson and Phoenix, where Holden collected a couple of the Swisser's debts. He was an enforcer, even on his honeymoon. Swiss had given him a fat book of traveler's checks as a wedding present. He'd gambled, made love, stood on the levee in New Orleans, a married man who'd gotten into real estate. Swiss had helped him finance a co-op on Fifth Avenue. He'd gone before the co-op board with Andrushka and Swiss. Swiss had rehearsed him, told him what to say about his job at Aladdin.

He was vice president of a fur company, he dressed like a British lord, and he had the most beautiful wife in the building. The whole board was smitten with Andrushka. Couldn't take their eyes off her. They loved the fact that Holden had a permit to carry a gun. They looked upon him as the building's police chief. Holden moved in with a mess of furniture that Andrushka had selected with Swiss. She attended tea parties in the building. She went to museums while Holden conferred with his rats and bumped some son of a bitch. His network grew. He'd acquired his own secret service. Andrushka felt more and more comfortable on Fifth Avenue and Holden didn't. He lost her somewhere between Aladdin and the Museum of Modern Art.

She brought him to openings of this show or that and he couldn't find the right vocabulary. He was a keeper of rats. He could talk about the insides of a Beretta Minx, but he stumbled over the names of artists and their different schools. She talked of moving to Italy and Holden was forlorn. How could he concentrate on Caravaggio when he had to protect Aladdin's books? His wife's education worried Holden and amazed him. She'd started as a mannequin who could barely spell her name. She'd slept with buyer after buyer, and now he had to wheedle and woo to get her to sleep with him. He loved her eyes, her hands, the drone of her voice, the print of her body on their marriage bed, but she'd gone out of his life with Caravaggio.

He returned to his hotel on the Place St. Sulpice. Holden was in a deep chill. He remembered his days of courtship, flowers, chocolate buns, and notes for Andrushka. Other men fell away from her and she only had him. He would have bumped all her suitors. That's how their romance flourished—in a frozen field. She took his flowers and his chocolate buns and considered his notes.

"Holden, you're crazy. How can you marry a girl you haven't gone to bed with? You might not enjoy my moves."

"What's marriage got to do with moves? I'm not one of your tricks."

"Don't you belittle my customers. They're nice men."

"Andrushka, I wasn't trying to slight anyone. I'm only saying love is love."

"Jesus, are you always this serious?"

"Yes."

And their betrothal began. It troubled Holden that he had to chase a mannequin who'd slept with half the fur market. Greek furriers whispered around Holden and twisted their napkins into horns. Holden dropped his Beretta on the floor and stared at the Greeks until the Greeks ate their napkins. The whispering stopped. Furriers couldn't poison Holden's love. And now he had to sit in a hotel room, a couple of avenues away from Andrushka. He looked out his window and saw Billetdoux. His only friend in Paris was a bumper like himself who might shoot Holden in the head tomorrow.

He went downstairs and walked along the rue de Vaugirard, with the bumper behind him. He stood outside the Luxembourg Gardens and stared up at Andrushka's windows. Holden accomplished the same maneuver every time he got to Paris, a maneuver of misery, because he felt like a stone man outside the gates of the Luxembourg, a goddamn mute.

His vertigo came back. It was the dizziness of love. Schatz had described him right. Holden was a mourner. Seven years since Andrushka, and he hadn't come close to living with another woman. He'd had hookers, fantastic ladies, light and dark, but they couldn't provide the pleasure of that twig he'd married. Andrushka was a heartless bitch, with a childhood as bleak as Holden's. She'd come out of black smoke in Wisconsin, with a stepfather who'd fondled her when she was nine or ten, and a mother who performed tricks. The seventh grade was as far as she got. Some guy who ran a ghostly shuttle had delivered her from Green Bay before she was fifteen, sold her on the idea of modeling, and turned her into a mannequin. She wouldn't declare who her savior was. Holden wondered if it was Schatz.

He blew on his hands like some dumb medieval knight bound to a crazy, impossible love. Holden had to snap the string. He was doomed, a bumper who'd gotten famous. The Mariels had a grudge against him, the Pinzolos too. But he had to see Andrushka before he was hit in the head. He crossed the street and entered her building. The concierge didn't question him. He could have been the duke of Paris. He marched up to Andrushka's floor and rang the bell.

"Qui est là?" he heard a woman call.

Holden was petrified. The door opened. "Yes?"

"I'm Schatz's partner. I'd like to see madame."

The woman at the door was a beautiful nurse, he figured, a little too heavy for his liking. But she didn't wear a uniform, and a nurse wouldn't have gold in her ear. He was the biggest dumbbell in France. His bride had filled out in seven years. It was the twig. She started to laugh.

"The mystery man. Likes to come unannounced."

"You'd have hung up if I called."

"So what?" she said. "That's my privilege . . . don't stand there. People will think you're a trick."

He followed her into the apartment, watching the girth of her shoulders and wondering if she played volleyball in the Luxembourg Gardens with Swiss. Andrushka was something of a giant. But he didn't stop loving this strange person who'd once been a twig. She brought him into a living room that overlooked the palace in the park. Schatz and Andrushka were king and queen of the Luxembourg Gardens. The girl he remembered had become a woman in the fat man's arms, big-boned all of a sudden, with an awful lot of hip under her dress.

"Sit down," she said. "You're making me nervous."

Holden collapsed into a soft chair next to the window and watched the palace roofs. The giantess frightened him a bit. He didn't know what to tell her.

"Would you like a cake or some French seltzer?"

"No," he said. "I'm fine."

The giantess sat down and seemed to gobble up all of her chair.

"Holden, how come I get the honor? You happened to be in the neighborhood, or what?"

"Swiss," he muttered. "He said it was okay to visit."

"I wouldn't trust his okays. He doesn't like you very much. He's been trying to get you killed, or are you too dumb to notice?"

"I'm his insurance policy. I collect for the man. What could he gain from getting me killed?"

"Pleasure," she told him. "It irritates Bruno that I was once in love with you."

"If it irritates him so much, why didn't he hire a boom-boom man?"

"That's vulgar," she said, like some matron of the arts, and he wondered where she kept her Caravaggios. Museums had ruined their marriage. Holden swore never to visit a museum again, though he'd hired a graduate student after Andrushka left, a kid from Yale, to teach him the fundamentals of modern art. He looked at his bride again. She wasn't really a giantess. The twig had gained twenty pounds.

"You listening to me, Holden? Swiss doesn't need a boom-boom man. He sends you out on exercises because he wouldn't cancel your career without a profit to himself. It's not his fault you run into hellholes and come out alive."

"He pays me for all the risks," Holden said. "I have bank accounts in sixteen cities. I could go to London and buy a house."

"Dead men don't need houses."

"I'm not so dead I can't see you have a terrific appetite in Paris."

"That's just normal eating, Holden, and being away from you . . . how could I finish a steak when I couldn't tell if I'd have a corpse on my hands from one day to another."

"I never caught you crying," he said, feeling more and more at Andrushka's mercy.

"I cried, all right."

"Where? In the museums?"

"Shut up about museums," she said. "You didn't want a wife with culture. You wanted me to wait at home while you were beating up on people. You would have been happy if I didn't say a word."

"That's not true. I loved it when you talked."

"Talked about what? Hats and shoes. You shivered, Holden, when I mentioned Cézanne."

"I wouldn't shiver now."

"Is that why you came around? To impress me with your progress? How could I breathe inside a coffin? That's what it was like living with you."

"You call eight rooms over Central Park a coffin?"

"Imbecile," she said. "I'm not talking about a view."

"And Swiss has culture, I suppose. He was nothing but a crook with arts and archives. He sucked eggs for a lot of generals, just like my dad."

"You're so dumb you can't see the difference. Swiss used your father to blind those generals and bleed them dry . . . Holden, did you come here to save me from the Swiss? He appreciates a woman. You didn't even know what wine to serve. And who was going to teach us? Holden, we never had a chance."

"What's so hot about a millionaire who swallows prune juice for lunch?"

"Prune juice keeps him regular. He makes love to me morning and night."

"I didn't ask for the details," Holden said.

"I'll bet you didn't." And she leapt out of her chair with lines of fury in her forehead. "Were you counting on a kinky afternoon, huh, Frog?"

"Don't call me that."

"But that's what you are, Holden. A nasty little frog. I have a husband, thank you. I don't need your gifts."

She left him in the living room, shutting doors between Holden and herself. And he was stranded with a palace in front of his eyes. He turned from the windows and began to notice paintings on the walls. Schatz had built a fucking museum for Andrushka. Holden tried to remember all the art tricks that kid had taught him. Apples and oranges. Cézanne and Miró. But he couldn't recognize a single painting.

He walked down into the rue de Vaugirard. He couldn't find his shadow. That bumper must have gone for a ham sandwich. Billetdoux. And Holden was caught in the dream of Andrushka. A man with yellow hair stepped in front of him, and Holden, who could always sniff trouble out on the street, in Marseilles, Milan, or the two Berlins, was unprepared. The man fell into Holden's arms. His body twisted around. He had a bullet in his neck. He coughed and the bullet came out. He fell deeper into Holden. Billetdoux was behind him, holding a popgun with a muffler that was half the length of his arm. The bullet must have sounded like a sparrow's cry. Holden hadn't heard a thing.

"Who is this poor slob?" Holden asked as Billetdoux stripped the popgun and dug pieces into his pockets.

"Don't know," he said.

"And you popped him? Just like that?"

"I had a feeling," Billetdoux said. "He followed me while I was following you."

Holden protested. "I would have seen him. I'm not a kid."

"Your eyes were in your ass," Billetdoux said. "Will you dance with him? People will notice he's nearly dead."

Holden held up the man, who coughed in his arms. "Billet, the guy could be a perfect stranger."

"Of course," Billetdoux said, pulling on the man's coat until a spear with three prongs dropped out of the sleeve. "Recognize that?"

It was a fisherman's claw that the Bandidos would use to destroy a man's face.

A police car stopped in front of Andrushka's building. This wasn't Manhattan where Holden could buy his way into some police lieutenant's pocket, or count on his killer attorney. Billetdoux was a bumper from Marseilles. He couldn't have had much of a rabbi on the rue de Vaugirard. But the flics didn't get out of the car.

"Walk him," Billetdoux said. "Walk him gently." And Holden waltzed the coughing man to the police car. Billetdoux opened the rear door and Holden sat the man down on the seat. There were no tattoos on his fingers. "Come on," Billetdoux said. But Holden pulled on the man's lip and saw a blue mark inside the flesh of his mouth. It was the moist little heart of an executioner. The man hissed at Holden with his eyes.

"Come on," Billetdoux said.

Holden ducked his head out of the police car. Billetdoux slammed the door shut and the car bumped along the rue de Vaugirard like some mortuary wagon.

"Billet, I didn't know you were into the police."

"I'm not," the bumper said. "Those weren't flics. They were friends of mine. The suits were rented."

"And the car?"

"Also rented. Don't worry. I didn't have to pay."

"Who's my benefactor?"

"The Swiss."

"I thought you work for Bronshtein."

"I do. But I also work for Schatz."

"Let's have a coffee," Holden said. And the two bumpers marched up to a café near the Place St. Sulpice.

Carmen

7 HOLDEN ALWAYS WENT to Muriel Spencer's when he was in despair over the twig. He didn't have to worry about any girl with a hardened look, because Muriel wouldn't tolerate a whore in her establishment, and Holden would drink a lemonade and lie with the girl for half an hour. None of the girls ever stayed longer than six months. They'd marry one of Muriel's clients or become an intern at a brokerage house. They were always young and narrowly built, and they never talked foul. Holden learned from his spies that Muriel had an exclusive arrangement with several finishing schools in the Midwest, but all the girls couldn't have come from finishing schools. A couple of them were as ignorant as Andrushka had been before she'd discovered what a museum was.

Holden hadn't returned from Paris for some polite, skinny-boned girl. He'd given up the delusion of finding another twig at Muriel's place. But he wanted to know how come the Bandidos were so eager to have him dead. Holden didn't believe it was on account of the Parrot and his mistress. They were rip-off artists from Miami. They weren't connected to the Bandidos up here. The Parrot had an isolated game. Why should the Bandidos have cared . . . unless the Parrot was related to one of them. Holden had to know.

His spies had fallen down on him. His secret service ought to have sniffed whatever danger there was. Half of Holden's income went to his rats. And some moron with a tattoo in his mouth had nearly ruined Holden's face with a fisherman's spear. He wondered what kind of secret service the Bandidos had if they could afford to send a man to Paris. He had to grab hold of Gottlieb. But Muriel cornered him in her parlor. She was as tall and thin as the debutantes she produced. Her eyes were painted aquamarine, just like a water goddess. Holden had never desired the woman. Her manner, her whole allure, seemed to have come out of a finishing school. That was charming for a girl of nineteen. But Muriel was forty-five.

"Holden," she said, with a slight pinch of her mouth that was a mark of naughtiness, "where have you been? Everybody wants your autograph."

Muriel wouldn't allow her girls to mingle with the men in her parlor. She did the selecting for you. The girls would wait upstairs in their clothes, like some banker's daughter. They always unzipped themselves and lay like dolls while they were being caressed. Muriel discouraged all signs of passion. The girls were notorious for doing very little. That's why Muriel married them off so quick. Her clients didn't have to worry about the phantom of any other man. Muriel wouldn't permit lust without marriage.

There was a lone card game in the parlor. Holden recognized Robert Infante, Don Edmundo (chief of La Familia), Edmundo's bodyguard, and another guy, that playwright Rex. Abruzzi had brown hair. He wore suspenders and a bow tie and looked like one of Edmundo's thugs. His nose had been broken and he had the small, baffling eyes of a dreamer. He was an enormous man. Holden assumed he was writing dialogue in his skull while he held cards at the table.

It was Infante who looked up first. "Ah," he said, "our man is back . . . Holden, I think Rex wants to shake your hand. You remember Rex. Fay Abruzzi's husband."

Rex stood up. He was six-five, and Holden felt like a bear cub in his presence. The playwright squeezed Holden's hand. "I don't know how to thank you."

"Lend him your wife," Infante said, and Abruzzi laughed. He had yellow teeth. The laughter traveled through him like a gigantic pipe. Holden tried to conjure up that naked woman he'd collected from Red Mike. She had big shoulders and a round face. But he couldn't remember if she was pretty.

"Holden's good at escorting wives," Infante said. "He takes

Florinda to lunch. But he's getting a little too popular, right Edmundo?"

"Right," Edmundo said, winking at his bodyguard, who was a Batista baby, like him. Edmundo had been a jeweler in Havana. He fled to Miami after Fidel came down from the hills. He disappeared into the Florida Everglades for six months and surfaced again after the Bay of Pigs. He arrived in Manhattan with his own Familia. Didn't bemoan Castro any more. He established betting parlors, dabbled in cocaine. Holden had killed the Parrot essentially for him, because the Parrot had been ripping off Edmundo and his people. But Edmundo's bodyguard didn't appreciate the attention Holden got. The bodyguard despised Holden, fancied himself as Edmundo's enforcer. But he was frightened of the Bandidos, frightened of moon, sun, and sky. He'd come out of the Everglades with Edmundo, married Edmundo's niece, could fire a machine gun, drive a car. But the bodyguard had never bumped a man in his life. He was Edmundo's little wax soldier, the family clown.

"Jeremías," Edmundo said, "be kind to Holden . . . he sends people to paradise."

"He's okay for punching women," the bodyguard said. "Edmundo, I'm not interested in your paradise man."

The bodyguard yawned into his cards. He knew Holden wouldn't slap him in front of Edmundo and start a war with La Familia. The Bandidos had kidnapped him twice, and twice Edmundo had ransomed him for much more than Jeremías was worth. Edmundo was such a king, he could afford to keep a fool and advertise him as his bodyguard. But he did have soldiers in the hallway and on the roof. Because the Bandidos were crazy enough to kidnap Don Edmundo himself, and who would negotiate ransom money for a king?

"Holden," Edmundo said, "the boy is rude. Forgive him, please."

The bodyguard crumpled a card in his fist. "I'm not a boy, Edmundo. I'm fifty-seven. I fought Fidel . . . I'm not a boy."

"But you behave like one."

"Because you dishonor me, Edmundo. You let this assassin do my work."

"Shut your mouth, Jeremías. We have a guest." And Don Edmundo smiled at the playwright and then turned to his bodyguard. "Go up to the roof and look for Huevo, eh?"

"If he decides to bother us, Edmundo, can I have him for myself?"

"Of course."

The bodyguard got up from the table, tried to uncrumple the card, bowed to Muriel, excused himself, and left for the roof as if he were on the journey of his life.

"He finished high school, but he has no manners," Don Edmundo told the playwright. "He couldn't find a career in the United States. Holden has a career. Holden is important to my family, so Jeremías suffers a lot."

"Who's Huevo?" the playwright asked.

"Nothing," Don Edmundo said. "A boogeyman for us. He haunts my family. You should write about Huevo . . . Big Balls. That's his religious name. He's one of the boat people. I adopted Huevo, fed him, and now he makes war on me."

"Edmundo, when can I meet him?"

"I told you. He's the boogeyman. Huevo has such big balls, he never goes out on the street. He sleeps with witches and rides the roofs . . . Holden, tell our friend, have you ever seen Huevo?"

"Not yet."

"But he murders my lieutenants, shoots them in the mouth. And he won't take money from me. He's not a businessman. He likes blood."

The playwright held his chin. "And what would Jeremías do if he found Huevo on the roof?"

"Scream to Jesus, I suppose . . . but we're boring Holden. He didn't come to hear me lecture on Huevo. He'd like a girl. Holden, it's my treat."

"I can pay."

Edmundo's lips shrank into his mouth. "Don't embarrass me

in front of an artist. Rex will write about us. We'll appear in his next play. I'll become the sissy who can't capture Big Balls or treat you to a girl."

"My apologies, Don Edmundo. I meant no harm."

"Ah, Holden's some politician," Infante said. "Like his dad. Holden Sr. knew how to apologize with pie in his face."

"My father loved pies. He'd always eat something with lemon meringue."

"What happened?" Infante asked. "You come home from Paris surly as hell, insult Edmundo and me, barely say hello to Rex. Don't even ask how Florinda is."

"Some monkey wanted to claw my face outside the Luxembourg Gardens. I think he was a Mariel."

"Impossible," Infante said. "Bandidos never ride in planes. They're religious freaks. Their gods wouldn't allow it. And most of the Bandidos can't spell. How would they get to the right gate?"

"Let him finish," Edmundo said. "Holden, what makes you sure it was a Bandido?"

"He had a tattoo inside his mouth . . ."

"Anyone can imitate a tattoo."

"I agree, Don Edmundo. Thought of that myself. Only why would someone go through all that trouble?"

"To bring you into our war and create worse and worse relations between the Bandidos and ourselves."

"Who would benefit?"

Edmundo laughed. "Half the world . . . or one of my lieutenants who would like to start his own family. We're talking ambition, Holden. And I'm surrounded by ambitious men . . . take Robert, for instance. He could move his Italian friends into all my boutiques."

"Fuck yourself, Edmundo," Infante said. "I'm a lawyer. I create the peace."

"But lawyers bend the language. Tuesday's peace is Wednesday's war."

"Then find yourself a Cuban witch doctor. Let him write up your articles of intent."

"Huevo has all the witch doctors. I'll hire Rex. He has imagination, eh? . . . but I was only citing an example, Robert. Don't be offended, please. I value you and trust you. We're friends. My point is that some *jíbaro* with a tattoo in his mouth isn't necessarily a Mariel. But Holden still doesn't have a girl. Mrs. Spencer, find him the thinnest creature in the house. Make her adorable, please. I haven't forgotten his wife."

Muriel whispered into a telephone, then she put her arm around Holden and accompanied him to the door. "The north room, upstairs. Melissa."

The name didn't carry much of a magic song. He wasn't even curious. He'd have to give her a perfunctory kiss, or she'd feel insulted. But he didn't climb up to Melissa right away. He went searching for Gottlieb. Holden discovered him in an office behind the stairs. Gottlieb wore a gun this afternoon. Any of the police inspectors who visited with Muriel could have picked the gun off Gottlieb's chest and buried the little bastard. The boy was seventeen and had almost as many bank accounts as Holden. He was much more sophisticated than a bumper who'd been to France. Gottlieb knew about wines and temperatures for aging cheese. He'd established his own private college near Muriel. He was a nymphomaniac about books. Gottlieb read all the time. He'd been a male hustler when Holden found him on the street, dressed in princely rags at fourteen. He could feel the boy's intelligence and Holden recruited him as a rat, placed him with Mrs. Spencer. He was a sandwich boy with the title of assistant manager. Muriel's was a haven for La Familia, for mob lawyers like Infante, for police chiefs with a little cash in their pockets, and Gottlieb was Holden's highest-paid rat.

"How can I get to Huevo?"

"You can't," Gottlieb said.

"He sent me a greeting card, a goddamn claw, and I still don't understand. The Parrot wasn't his people."

"I warned you, Holden. The Bandidos are after your life."

"Well, can't we have a meet?"

"No."

"Gottlieb, it's not nice to say no. Get me to Big Balls. I don't care who you bribe. Sell your ass."

"What if I sold yours?" Gottlieb said.

"If that's the road to Big Balls, I'll take it. Come on, you can come up with one of his witches."

"Holden, you don't fuck with a man's religious beliefs."

"I'll cross you off the payroll."

"You wouldn't dare. Holden, you taught me too much. I could hire a bumper to crack your neck."

"And what if I cracked your neck, kid?"

"You'd miss me, Holden. In your heart of hearts you'd really love to make my ass."

"I have no heart of hearts, kid."

And Holden marched upstairs to Melissa. But Melissa wasn't in the north room. Holden wondered if he could march back down and offer his regrets, declare that he wasn't quite in the mood to lie face to face with a debutante, but Edmundo might laugh at him and Holden could lose his standing in the house. Where would he go when he wanted to close his eyes and sleep with a long-stemmed beauty for half an hour? So he sat on the bed with its decorated quilt in a room that could have been designed by Grandma Moses, because Muriel wouldn't tolerate whips and boots, ceiling mirrors and garter belts on a doorknob. I'll marry Melissa, Holden decided, make love to her in a mask.

A girl came into the room. She seemed much too throaty for a debutante. Her legs weren't long enough. "Melissa?" But she was more like a girl out of a convent than a finishing school. She was dressed in black and Holden felt numb behind the ears because he was staring at Red Mike's little sister, Carmen Pinzolo, with a hammer in her hand. "I'll kill you," she said, and he didn't move. The hammer went higher and higher in the air. "This is for Eddie and Rat and Red Mike." Holden, the ice man, loved that throaty girl, loved her anger, her marvelous black hair. She was nine or ten when he'd married Andrushka. She'd scribbled love letters to him when she was fifteen.

"Carmen, I had to—"

The hammer landed. Holden heard a roar inside his head. His brains were sticky. He floated in a stupor, saw his bloody skull in the room's only mirror and socked the hammer out of her hand, said, "I love you, Carmen," and slapped her in the face.

Blood trickled from her nose.

"I'll kill you, Holden. Today, tomorrow, I don't care."

"Baby, it wasn't my fault."

"I'm not your baby now," she said, leaping at the hammer on the floor. Holden kicked the hammer across the room, seized her by the neck, and brought her out of the room with blood in his eye.

Carmen twisted and tried to bite his face, but Holden shoved her head into the stairs and walked her down one step at a time. He got her into the parlor with a bumper's crazy will.

"Hey, Muriel" he said, "does this look like Melissa?" before he crashed into the card table and scattered piles of blue and red chips.

 HE WAS IN AVIGNON with his dad. Holden Sr. wore military boots and a sergeant's coat. They climbed up the steps of the Palais des Papes. The palace was white, and Holden didn't see any popes. But he saw a bridge that stopped in the middle of the water, and he wondered what a bridge like that could bring. His dad was the handsomest guy in town. Holden Sr. had different-colored bars and stripes across his chest and the palace walls were reflected in the wax of his boots. Holden wouldn't talk French with his dad. He was an American boy. Holden and his dad were polite to all the priests and nuns who settled on the palace stairs. The priests were taking pictures. And Holden wanted one of his dad, so he could remember him in his uniform and the white gloves a sergeant major was allowed to wear. He posed with his dad for a number of priests and scratched his address on a sliver of sandwich paper, so the priests wouldn't forget to send the photographs.

The nuns had floppy capes and their stockings gathered round their knees like stalks and Holden asked his dad if these nuns were his people. Holden Sr. said God didn't wash His own underwear. He gave it to the nuns to wash and that's when Holden opened his eyes, after he heard his father's raucous laugh. "Daddy," he muttered until he realized his father wasn't there. Holden was in Muriel's north room with a fancy turban on his head. The room had become a hospital station while Holden went to Avignon. An oxygen tank like a huge green bullet stood near the bed. Another machine monitored the rhythms of Holden's heart. Jeremías, that miserable bodyguard, sat in a chair next to Holden, like some Cuban angel of mercy. Jeremías seemed glad that Holden had come out of his sleep.

"We were worried. The boss had to go and look for his hospital team. He likes you, Holden. He said, 'Brothers, don't let this man die.'"

Edmundo must have had his own anti-Castro medical corps, refugee doctors from the Bay of Pigs.

"Where's Carmen?"

"The little hammer girl? She broke your head."

"Did Edmundo hurt her?"

"I can't say."

And Holden clutched at the quilt. He had paraphernalia attached to both his arms. The heart machine made irratic cries.

"You crazy?" the bodyguard said. "Don't move."

"Get Edmundo."

"'Mundo doesn't have time for you. He's taking a bath . . . with Melissa."

"Then I'll meet him at his tub."

"Wait a minute," the bodyguard said. "Have some respect."
And he telephoned downstairs to the tub room. "Edmundo,
Holden's back from paradise . . . he wants to see you."

Don Edmundo came upstairs in a purple robe. His body was
still wet.

"What did you do with the girl?"

"Holden, do you always growl like that when you wake from the
dead? You had a terrible concussion. We had to take pictures of your
skull."

"What did you do with the girl?"

"I took her home."

"I thought she was living here."

"Not a chance. She was a part-time maid. Muriel hired her last
week. How could she tell the girl was a Pinzolo? . . . Carmen was
waiting for you, Holden. She must have memorized your routes."

"And Muriel wasn't suspicious? All her maids are beautiful like
that?"

"Holden, it's a classy house. Lots of girls come through the
door. Did you want us to keep mug shots on Red Mike's sisters, eh?"

"Don Edmundo, get me my clothes."

"Clothes, who wears clothes in bed?"

"I do."

"Jeremías, help me. Holden's delirious."

Holden shook the paraphernalia attached to his arms. "Edmundo, I swear it. I'll knock your whole little hospital down. I'm
getting dressed. I want to see how alive Carmen really is."

"Ungrateful one, who sat with you six days?"

"And took baths with every girl in the house. My clothes,
Edmundo. And untie me from this bed."

Jeremías fetched the doctors, three antiquated men, who
buzzed around Holden and untangled every tube and wire. Holden
felt like Frankenstein. A girl was summoned to give him a bath. She
had short brown hair and a boy's chest. "Who's this?"

"Melissa," Edmundo said.

Muriel had discovered one more twig. Melissa washed Holden

with a big soapy glove, the same mysterious expression on her face that Andrushka always had. Perhaps it wasn't a mystery, but nothing, nothing at all . . . or some dark dream of Caravaggio. Melissa didn't say a word. She had all the proper flourishes of her finishing school. She soaped his groin without ever looking into Holden's eye.

The doctors redid his turban, unwinding yards of bandages until the room was like one long white carrousel. Took them half an hour to dress Holden's skull. Then Gottlieb arrived with a full set of clothes. Holden couldn't be friendly with his rat while La Familia was around.

Muriel peeked into the room. Her eyes swelled with anger and alarm. "Gentlemen, is he going out on a date?"

"I've recovered."

"You'd better leave some instructions, Holden. In case you happen to die on my stairs."

Holden Sr. had suffered a heart attack at Muriel's. Died near the debutantes. Holden stood up. The ceiling seemed to press hard on his head. The mirror registered his likeness: a turbaned ghost in a London jacket. Gottlieb leaned against his shoulder until Holden stopped swaying. He arrived at the door and cured his vertigo with one deep look down the stairwell. He wasn't going to fall.

Don Edmundo had a convoy waiting for Holden in the street. Cadillacs, Lincolns, and a Rolls Royce. Edmundo didn't like to travel alone. Cousins and uncles followed him everywhere, Batista babies who sat behind bulletproof glass with 9 mm rifles. But it wasn't a simple retinue of soldiers. Edmundo had his own storyteller in one of the cars, his own priest, women from the family compound in Westchester. He'd given up Manhattan as his *residencia* years ago. But he had offices in three boroughs, at the back of a beauty shop or travel bureau. Edmundo controlled a thousand betting parlors. Every one of his daughters had been married at the Pierre. The husbands were librarians, college professors, novelists who'd never have to starve. Edmundo was establishing his own rabbinical line. He loved the idea of having scholars in his family. None of the husbands was an outlaw like himself. That's why he tolerated

Holden's eccentric tricks. Holden was a comanchero, a trader with
a gun . . .

Holden sat in the Rolls Royce with Edmundo and Jeremías,
who lent himself as the driver. Edmundo shut his eyes and listened
to Mozart on the way to Queens. He dealt with all the Italian chiefs
through his counselor, Robert Infante, but he had contempt for the
Five Families, *rústicos* without politics or art. Edmundo had become
a bandit only after the Bay of Pigs. Stuck in the swamps, trapped
like a featherless bird, without the American air support he'd been
promised, fifteen hundred exiles against the whole Cuban army. He
was wheeled through Havana in a cart, the notorious Comandante
O, who'd led one of the invasion teams. He was removed from his
own men and jailed with murderers and child molesters in the
penitentiary at Pinar del Río, where he rotted eight months, a
scarecrow in commandant's fatigues . . . until the gringos ransomed
him, returned Comandante O to Miami. People kissed his hand on
the street. Grandmothers blessed him while he drank coffee in Little
Havana. "Comandante O." But he wouldn't sit on the Revolution-
ary Council or dream of yet another invasion with air support that
would never come. He left Miami and went "uptown" to the Yan-
keeland of New York. All his lieutenants followed him, uncles,
cousins, aunts. He didn't have to fight for a living. He had his own
Familia.

And now he was taking a bumper to Queens, an assassin with
a code of ethics that Edmundo admired and deplored. Holden was
a dangerous man. Edmundo couldn't tell where the bumper's honor
would bring him. A girl brains Holden and Holden has to see that
the girl's all right. Edmundo wasn't sure how long he could afford
the luxury of such a man.

The convoy arrived at Red Mike's simple estate near the veterans'
center in St. Albans. Sometimes soldiers and sailors would drift out
of the center in their uniforms and Holden would think of his dad,
while he was having lunch on Red Mike's lawn, the soldiers staring

through Mike's wire fence, starved for company. Mike would often let them through the gate, give them food and comfort until their keepers arrived. And Holden would look for the nearest sergeant among the runaway soldiers and have long conversations on every subject.

But there wasn't a sergeant inside the gate. Holden recognized Edmundo's people. They stood on the lawn in black shoes, waiting for their commandant. Holden realized that whatever Pinzolos were left had become prisoners on their own estate.

Holden walked into Red Mike's house with Don Edmundo. He was startled to meet Mike's dad, who should have been on Rikers Island. Old man Leopardo. He was wearing one of Red Mike's suits. He must have shrunk a little in the can. Leopardo seemed much heftier a year ago. He'd come out of Rikers to preside over the ruin of his family.

"I'm sorry," Holden said. But the old guy wouldn't answer in front of Don Edmundo. Holden went with him to the window, where Leopardo loved to stand and look at all the grass his son had accumulated.

"Holden," Leopardo whispered, "I'm glad it was you and not a stranger . . . I wouldn't want my sons butchered by someone's hired hand. What the fuck happened to your head?"

"Carmen went for me with a hammer."

"She did that? I'll smash her face. She had no business mixing in men's affairs. Mikey loved you like a brother."

"Leo, he shouldn't have kidnapped Abruzzi's daughter-in-law. I had to get into the act. Mike must have known that. It became a tribal thing."

"He was a hothead, my Mike. He could have buttoned up Abruzzi. But he wanted to steal something that would humiliate the son of a bitch, make him suffer. The D.A. comes down on us like it was a blood feud or something. It wasn't fair. We contributed to his campaign. My own boys were his precinct captains. And then he dumps on the Pinzolos. Christ, we put up his name to the Democrats, we sponsored the man, and the first time we lose a little popularity, he pounces on us. Mikey didn't kill. He didn't send his shooters out. He grabbed the girl . . . he would have given her back."

"Couldn't he have telephoned me?"

"Mikey didn't want to put you in the middle."

"He should have called . . ."

"He had his pride," Leopardo said. "He took the girl and lived with the consequences."

"But Leo, it was a waste."

"Not for us. My boys had to follow it to the end. We gave Abruzzi a shit fit. That was the important thing."

"Leo, I—"

"Shh, Holden, it's done."

The old man turned away from the window, and Holden was left with that view of the grass. He could have sworn there was a soldier outside the gate, his uniform slashed by wire. But it was a phantom, encouraged by that blow on the head. Holden blinked and the soldier was there again, and he wondered what strange powers Carmen had given him. He traveled through the house looking for her. He covered room after room, cluttered with Mike's trophies and hunting guns, Rat's collection of comic books and baseball cards, like the dross of someone's childhood, only Rat was involved with comics until the afternoon he died. Holden couldn't catch a trace of Eddie in the house. A toy, a gift, a photograph? Eddie was gone.

Holden could hear voices coming from the third floor. He bumped in and out of rooms until he located Carmen and her sisters in an upstairs den. The Pinzolo girls, Dotty, Josephine, Laura, Luiza, and Carmen, lovely, dark, and unmarried in the bower Red Mike had provided for them. Josephine was a grand old lady of twenty-nine. Dot was twenty-six. Carmen was twenty and had troubled Mike the most. She'd never have returned to the house if Don Edmundo hadn't been holding her here.

Carmen lowered her eyes, but the other sisters looked at him with a certain sadness, as if they couldn't stop loving the executioner. Holden wanted to take them in his arms, but he didn't dare. He'd lost that right in Far Rockaway.

"Carmen, Mikey knew I'd have to come for him. He'd have come for me if—"

"He'd never have come for you, not Mike. He'd have told the Five Families and all the Puerto Rican dons to go to hell."

"Edmundo's not Puerto Rican," Holden said.

Carmen locked herself in the toilet behind the den.

Holden rattled the doorknob. "Carmen, talk to me."

"The only reason you're alive," she shouted from her vantage of the door, "is that the Puerto Rican said he'd kill papa if I hit you one more time."

"He's bluffing, Carmen. He wouldn't dare. He knows I love you. And he's not Puerto Rican. He's a Cuban hero. Comes from the Bay of Pigs."

"Who remembers? I wasn't even born," she said.

"Carmen?"

"Go away."

Holden appealed to the other sisters with a squeeze of his eyes. They wouldn't convince Carmen to come out of the toilet. He'd orphaned the whole family with a target pistol. Red Mike had been the real pater of the house. Leopardo was a guy who liked to strangle people. He could never control the girls. He would have found feeble husbands for them—bricklayers, bums—if Mike hadn't intervened.

Holden wandered downstairs, said goodbye to Leopardo, and joined Edmundo on the grass. "I don't want the girls kept prisoner in this house."

"We're protecting them, Holden . . . they could mutilate each other."

"That's their business."

"And what if Carmen or Luiza comes after you?"

"I'll duck the hammer next time," Holden muttered.

"It's a miracle you still have a head."

"Edmundo, I'm serious. Carmen goes free."

"I heard you. Carmen goes free."

"And how did Leopardo get out of the can?"

"His sons are dead. I got him a weekend pass."

"This isn't the weekend."

"I can't help it if the Department of Corrections doesn't keep better tabs."

"Edmundo, I want him returned in one piece."

"Why are you so considerate of your enemies?"

"He's not my enemy. I happened to kill all three of his sons."

And then Holden saw khaki checkers of cloth beyond the gate. There was a soldier, all right. Holden hadn't spun him out of the turban on his head. The soldier had green eyes. A fugitive from St. Albans. He wore a battle scarf and his regimental bands. He had a tie and a clean shirt. The only hint of disorder was his tennis shoes. And Holden wondered if the army had adopted sneakers as part of its new battle dress.

The soldier stood behind the gate and saluted him.

Holden returned the salute and got into the Rolls Royce.

Fay

9 HE WANTED TO HIDE out until his head healed. He had four apartments, under different names, where no one but Holden had a key. They were his mattress pads. It was smarter than getting on a plane, because airports could be watched, but a street in Chelsea was only a street in Chelsea. Away from the fur market Holden was as anonymous as any man. He had simpler clothes in his four apartments, a VCR, enough canned goods, bottled water, and video cassettes to keep him for a month. None of his rats knew where the apartments were. Goldie was familiar with one, Mrs. Howard with another, but he could step from apartment to apartment until all his baggage dropped and blurred whoever Holden was.

Sometimes he'd go to one of the apartments and camp there for a week. He could lay the Beretta down in a drawer, retire the silk handkerchiefs, shuck off the tyranny of Douglas Fairbanks Jr., and dress like a scarecrow, put Dietrich on his VCR. But even that wasn't much of an escape. His dad had loved Marlene, and he couldn't watch *Destry Rides Again* without thinking of fathers and sons. He'd start to shiver after five or six days, his teeth would knock inside his skull, and he'd remember the twig, that curling body on his marriage bed, the weight of loving her, the lectures she'd give him on Cézanne while they watched the Academy Awards.

"Holden, what the hell is Hollywood to you? I'm talking about a guy who structured the world with apples and pears."

"Well, I'd rather have Robert De Niro."

"That proves you're a thickhead, because actors can only act."

He should have left her a mannequin at Aladdin Furs, and she wouldn't have haunted his life. After a week of closets and walls, he'd look for his holster and handkerchiefs and return to civilization.

So he decided not to do his healing all by himself. He'd visit with Loretta Howard and the leopard girl. He arrived late in the afternoon on Oliver Street, entering the front door with his key. Holden was too tired to worry about Bandidos. Mrs. Howard didn't shriek when she saw the turban on his head. Gottlieb must have phoned in, Gottlieb or another rat.

"Holden, you have too many corpses in the closet. You'd better stop killing people and take a rest. It's lucky Carmen didn't have more than a hammer in her hand."

"A hammer's enough," Holden said. "I was unconscious."

"It did you good. Holden, you have some color in your cheeks."

"Any messages?" he asked.

"The phone hasn't stopped ringing."

"Does anyone know why Big Balls wants me dead? Jesus, I pay an army and we can't even get the fundamentals down."

"There are no fundamentals here. Nobody's established a line between Huevo and the Parrot . . . Holden, it has to be the girl."

Leopard eyes? Holden thought to himself. "She's with the Bandidos? Did you talk to her about it?"

"Yes. But she keeps insisting you're her daddy."

"Maybe I am. Can't I have a lost daughter somewhere?"

"Crawling under a table while you murder both her babysitters?"

"What if they weren't babysitters? And it wasn't an accident the Marielita was there? What if they'd kidnapped the kid?"

"Kidnapping wasn't their usual line. And would they grab a girl who belonged to the Bandidos?"

"What if they didn't know who she was? Somebody gives them a girl to hold. I come along. And now I'm the bad guy."

"It still doesn't make sense."

"But it makes more sense than worrying about the Parrot's itinerary. Mrs. H., we've got to go public with the little girl, tell some of our people that she's in our hands. If nobody claims her in a month, then she's mine.

"Where's she going to live? At Aladdin? Holden, you need a wife."

"I'll buy one," he said. "Where is the Marielita? Napping a little? I'd better not wake her."

"Nonsense," Mrs. Howard said. And they stole into the bedroom Mrs. Howard had prepared for the leopard girl, who lay with a lollipop on her chest. She had a child's even snores. And Holden didn't care how many dads materialized. He wasn't giving her away.

The girl woke and smiled at him with her leopard's eyes. Then she saw the bandages and her body shivered.

"*Querida,*" he said. "I'm okay." And he picked her up inside her little gown, whirled her across the room until he saw spots in the wall.

Mrs. Howard tugged at him. "Holden, you stop that. You'll both fall."

But he held the girl tight until the spots disappeared.

Holden lived on Oliver Street for a couple of days. He slept in the foyer, with his ankles in the air, woke in the middle of the night, went through the file cards he kept in Mrs. Howard's drawer. He sorted out the cards he had on Huevo and put a little portrait together. Lázaro Rodriguez, born in Havana on June 11, 1955, while Castro was hiding in the Sierra Maestra. He didn't have much luck when the Fidelistas got off their mountain. He was in and out of juvenile facilities after the age of ten. And turned into a regular convict by the time he was seventeen. Holden counted six prisons for Huevo. He'd lost half his teeth and converted to that jailhouse cult of African gods. He was the tattoo artist of La Cabaña penitentiary, Taco-Taco, and El Príncipe. He left his mark in every jail he visited. *Favors eagles,* the notes said. *Eagles and U.S. flags.* Huevo arrived in Miami during the fourth month of the boatlift (July

1980). First seen in New York around September. Recruited by La
Familia during the same year. Took part in Don Edmundo's policy
war with the Maf. Formed his own attack squads. Firebombed
betting parlors, burned Mafia hitmen alive. But he made a nuisance
of himself after the peace. He wouldn't stop firebombing the policy
stores. He left La Familia with some of the Bandidos. He's been
waging war on Edmundo ever since, kidnapping Edmundo's lieutenants and selling them back to La Familia. Huevo was considered a
mad dog. The police, the Maf, and Edmundo were after him. Most
of his army was dead. But Huevo survived, protected by a series of
madrinas, high priestesses who healed his wounds and hid him when
they had to. Edmundo kept capturing *madrinas*, but none of them
would give Big Balls away.

What the hell could this futile soldier want with him? Was the
Marielita Huevo's child? There was nothing about a marriage in
Holden's cards, and a lot of Changó's followers weren't so romantic
about women. Was Big Balls supposed to be a troubadour, worshipping some Doña Isabel, when he'd lived his young manhood entirely
with men?

Suppose the little girl wasn't a Marielita at all? She might have
had nothing to do with the boatlift. Some accidental child in the
Parrot's hands when Holden had come to kill him. Then what could
it be? Holden hadn't insulted the god in the red dress. He hadn't
made love to a *madrina*. What could it be?

Holden had his rest on Oliver Street and returned to Aladdin,
after Loretta changed his bandages. None of the cutters dared mention the turban he wore. Even Nick Tiel was reticent; Nick was
preoccupied with the Paris show. His eyes would glaze soon, and
Holden would have to escort him everywhere.

"Maybe you ought to go to Paris, Nick. Paris would appreciate
you. You wouldn't have so many Greeks ready to cut your throat.
You could eat with the Swisser at Maxim's. They'd kiss your
hand . . ."

"You know I never travel," Nick said.

"It's a pity, Nick, because all the French furriers swear by your coats. You'd meet a lot of your fans. Why should Swiss take all the credit? You're the designer, for Christ's sake?"

"Ah, what do I care what Swiss does? He has his haunts. I have mine. When he comes into my territories with a pair of scissors, I'll start to worry."

"You kidding?" Holden said. "He wouldn't touch your sketches. He worships every pencil mark. But he's a fucking thief."

"What did he steal?"

"My wife."

And Holden went into his office. He put on the light and saw a headless chicken on his quilt. The chicken had feathers stuffed down its throat. It was a gift from the Bandidos, but how the hell did that bird get into his office? The Bandidos were always sacrificing roosters to that god in the red dress. They'd burn the chicken and drink its blood, but Holden's bed wasn't a religious altar. He took the chicken and marched out to the nailing boards.

"How did this get into my office?"

The nailers and cutters stared at him.

"I asked you a question?"

The cutters thought Holden had gone insane. That's why he wore a turban. It was clear as a bell. Holden went around dancing with dead birds. But they started to shake, because he might just happen to shoot all of them in the head.

Nick Tiel came out of the designer's room. "What's up?"

"Nicky, who let a Bandido into my office?"

"Come on, Holden, we got alarms all over the place. No one can enter without the right key."

"Then explain this," Holden said, dangling the chicken.

"What is it? A fucking bird with feathers in its neck. The janitors were playing a joke."

"Don't say janitors, Nick. Janitors aren't into voodoo. It's a curse, meant for me."

"We've been here day and night. Nobody walked that chicken into your room, unless he was invisible."

Like Changó, Holden thought. Changó could build a wall of vapors around his red dress. Changó could have brought the chicken.

He'd gone to the Algonquin to collect money from a British furrier who owed Swiss a bundle. The furrier always traveled big. His name was Clive Exland. And he'd do a week at the Algonquin, steal whatever designs he could, and disappear. But Holden's rats always knew when the furrier arrived. And Holden meant to squeeze him, but he was waylaid in the lobby.

"Holden, over here."

Rex Abruzzi called him from that lounge at the Algonquin where all the Brits loved to have a drink. It was practically a British hotel. Rex was with his dad, the district attorney of Queens, and a woman wearing eyeglasses, a scarf, and a purple dress. Holden recognized Fay Abruzzi under the glasses and all the clothes. But she seemed slimmer, slighter in her dress, much slighter than Andrushka in Paris.

They were sitting around a table, the three Abruzzis. The district attorney shook Holden's hand. "Good to see you, Holden . . . heard about your head. Damn those blood feuds. We have some strange families in Queens. Hope you're all right."

He seemed wistful about the turban, as if Carmen were his own wayward child. He was a man of sixty, much smaller than his son, and eager to become a judge. He wore a flower in the lapel of his undertaker's suit. That's what Goldie would have called the district attorney's dark sack. Holden was dressed in turquoise today. His handkerchief was island green. His pants were the blue of tropical water. Rex had dandruff on his brown suit. He could have stepped out of the Salvation Army.

Holden had become a snob. But he knew nothing about women's clothes. He couldn't tell how much Fay's scarf was worth. He felt like an idiot who was wise in a couple of directions.

Fay wouldn't talk to him. She looked like some dreamy bitch when Robert Infante arrived.

"Hello, Rob," she said.

Infante had once worked for the D.A. He was a prosecutor in Queens until he waltzed over to the other side, but it hadn't hurt his relations with Abruzzi. Robert was even more valuable as a mob lawyer. He put one arm around Holden. "Can you believe this bum? Looks like a blue diamond. And you can't get near his tailor . . . Fay, don't be bashful. Give him a hello before he runs across the street and puts a few bad guys out of commission."

"Robert," Holden said, "thanks for advertising me to the district attorney."

"Come on," Infante said. "You're among friends. What happened to Red Mike couldn't be helped."

"Goodbye," Holden said. But Fay Abruzzi started to speak. Her mouth quivered. She lost that melody she'd had out in Red Mike's bungalow.

"Mr. Holden, I wanted to . . ."

She turned silent, retreated into her own sad song. Rex hugged his wife. "Holden, Fay's had a scare. And the television people won't leave her alone. The bastards call in the middle of the night, begging interviews. They want her opinion on crime. They want her on talk shows. We've had to change our number. It doesn't help. The bastards keep calling. But you did save her life . . . sit down with us, please."

Holden saw that British furrier slip out of the hotel, but he couldn't chase Clive. He sat down with the Abruzzis and his own lawyer.

People kept coming to the table, offering their regards to the district attorney and his daughter-in-law, and Holden wondered if the Algonquin was Abruzzi's Manhattan office. People ignored the playwright, but they smiled at Holden, curtsied to him, and he grew miserable. Everybody knows I'm a bumper. I'm the man who murdered Red Mike.

He'd lost the British furrier. But he wasn't so concerned with Aladdin's affairs. He had his own business to worry about. He'd have to touch base with the Bandidos, but his rats were stingy on the subject

of Big Balls. No one wanted to be firebombed. Holden had to trust
his file cards, which were at least six months old. There was a bumper
bar up in Manhattan north, a place where Marielitos with *"madre"*
tattooed on their hands could meet.

The bar was in Inwood, under the elevated tracks. He rode up
there with Harrington, his rat who'd brought Fay Abruzzi home
from the Rockaways. Harrington's was the one limousine service
Holden ever used. Harrington had been a friend of Holden's dad.
They'd met in the Tombs.

Harrington kept peering under the el. He had a liver problem.
He was gaunt and his face had gone yellow. Holden's contributions
to the limousine service kept him alive. But it wasn't charity. Even
with his yellow face, Harrington was the best chauffeur in town.

"Keep driving," Holden said. "I don't want the Mariels to see
you."

"But you might need a good getaway car."

"I'll walk out of this, thanks."

"Holden, you're as stubborn as your dad," Harrington said, and
he took off in his limousine.

Holden stood under the tracks. The bar had a shamrock in the
window from its glory days when all of Inwood was a huge Irish
football field. The bar was called County Clare, and the Marielitos
hadn't bothered to remove the name. Holden walked inside with his
turquoise ensemble. He didn't have prickles at the back of his neck.
The only man he'd ever been afraid of was his dad. He'd tremble
slightly in Holden Sr.'s presence. His dad was like a cold desert where
the wind rattled your skull. Holden couldn't even say what pleased
his dad after living with him seventeen years. Holden moved out
before his eighteenth birthday. He'd already bumped a man for the
Swiss and didn't feel much remorse. Bumping people was like visiting with Holden Sr.

He entered County Clare. The bumpers didn't stop talking.
They hardly noticed he was alive. But he knew he'd come to
Changó's house. Several of the bumpers wore *collares* of red and
white beads. They had eyeglasses with one dark and one light lens.

Their neckerchiefs were blood red, the color Changó adored. They wore a brown shoe on their right foot, black on the left. One man sat at the bar in a red dress. He must have been the priest of the place. Holden sat down next to him and ordered a café cubano and a cream cheese custard.

"Hombre," he said to the man in the red dress. "I'd like to meet Huevo."

"Who wouldn't?" the man said.

"He's been sending me ticklers . . . a rooster without a head."

"That's unfortunate, but Huevo doesn't live here."

"I can pay good money," Holden said.

"Don't insult us, señor. We know who you are. The paradise man. Finish your custard and get out."

Holden looked past the man in the red dress and into all those eyeglasses with the one black lens, and he didn't argue.

The barman wouldn't take his money.

"Adiós," he said. The bumpers didn't answer.

A jíbaro followed him out the door. He had a black coat that was stitched to a brown sleeve. Goldie would have liked this guy. "Hey, Holden," he said.

"Can you help me?"

"Not here, for Christ's sake."

The jíbaro led him away from the tracks and showed him a detective's shield. "I'm Nunco. I work out of the Four-one." An undercover dick from Fort Apache. Holden expected Paul Newman to pop out from behind Nunco's black lens.

"You have a lot of cojones to come in here and ask for Huevo. It's lucky they knew you. This is Don Edmundo's bar. The men are loyal to La Familia. They didn't leap when Huevo leapt. These Mariels hate that son of a bitch and are scared to death."

"Do they figure you're Changó with a brown sleeve?"

"Get outa here," Nunco said. "The Bandidos made me years ago. They tolerate my ass. They used to be afraid of cops . . . no more. They thought every cop was a jailer. But they're not afraid of our jails. They've been to Rikers. They call it the Ramada Inn.

Sometimes they talk to me like I really was a Bandido. That's how comfortable they are with my face."

"Are you wired?" Holden asked.

"Would I walk in here with a fucking microphone? They'd chop me in their kitchen and serve me as cheap steak. They're telepathic, Holden, just like a witch. They could tell if a man was wearing a wire."

"What about Huevo's witch, his *madrina?* Do you know who she is? I can lay some money on you."

"Shh, don't talk money," Nunco said. "How do I know you're not an IAD man?"

"Do I look like a cop? How could I be with Internal Affairs?"

"You're fucking untouchable. You whack this guy, that guy, and you're still on the street."

"Forget I ever talked money. Can you tell me the most logical candidate for Huevo's *madrina?*"

"There is no candidate. *Madrinas* and logic don't mix. Can I drive you anywhere, Holden?"

Nunco brought him back to the Algonquin, but the British furrier had checked out. Holden would have to grab him next season. He returned to the fur market. It was Saturday night. Even Nick's aristocratic nailers and cutters would be gone. And Nick himself? Smoking hash or lying down with a debutante at Muriel's, because Nick hated to be alone. He needed the cutters around him when he was scribbling the outlines of a coat. He'd never married. He'd choose a girl at Muriel's, be attentive for a month, and then abandon her to the fury of his designing board.

Holden took the freight car up to Aladdin, and unlocked the elevator door. The factory was dark, but Holden could smell the skins nailed to the boards. He was about to enter his office when he felt a sudden tickle. His bumper's intuition told him that his bedroom-office was boobytrapped. He expected a firebomb to explode in his face on the other side of the door. He removed his turquoise coat, held it in front of him like an asbestos cape, undid the locks, and shoved into the room with his Beretta.

A body flitted around in the dark.

"Stand still, or I'll turn your head into bumpkin soup."

The body paused and Holden put on the lights. It was Abruzzi's daughter-in-law in the purple dress.

"How did you get in here, Mrs. Abruzzi?"

"I came with Robert . . . he let me stay."

"He unlocked my office?"

"Yes. Isn't he your lawyer?"

"That doesn't give him the right of entry."

"Well, he has your keys."

She wasn't such a gloomy bitch in Holden's office. Her Rockaway melody had come back to her.

"What does the 'S' stand for?"

" 'S'?"

"On the door. S. Holden, it says."

"Why'd you come here?"

"Because I wanted to talk, and I couldn't do that with Rex around. I didn't mean to startle you. But my father-in-law told me you were badly hurt on my account, that Michael's sister tried to kill you."

"He kidnaps you and you call him Michael?" Holden said, profoundly jealous.

"What else should I call him? I lived with him and his brothers six or seven days."

Holden returned the gun to its cradle and put on his turquoise coat. "Mikey made you walk around naked. Didn't that bother you?"

"At first, yes. But I understood the reason behind it. He didn't want me running away. And where could I run without my clothes?"

"And Eddie and the Rat never patted your behind?"

"Michael wouldn't have allowed it."

"They didn't say things to you, rotten, lousy things?"

"Yes, they did, but I got used to it after a while. They were like children. It was the only kind of talk they knew . . . I'm a sociologist. At least I was before I married. Modes of speech interest me a lot."

"And you were interested in Ed and the Rat?"

"Immensely . . . I cooked for all the brothers. I mended their shirts."

"I didn't save you. I interfered with your life. You would have been happy to stick it out in the bungalow for a year."

"No," she said. "I have two little girls at home. I couldn't have abandoned them."

"Mrs. Abruzzi, Mike was my friend. I loved those boys. I might not have killed them if Rat hadn't paraded you in front of my eyes."

"He's a child, I told you. He liked the power of bossing me around."

"I suppose you would have joined their gang in another week?"

"No. But I might have continued cooking for them."

"Did you tell it to Rex?"

"Of course. He laughed about it. But he was worried . . . until you brought me home."

"I didn't bring you home. Harrington did."

"But he works for you. And he was very fond of your dad."

"Jesus Christ, did Harrington open up on the ride?"

"A little."

Holden sat down. "I'm speechless," he said. "I assume the world is one thing, and suddenly it's another. Why'd you come here?"

"I told you. To talk."

"There's nothing to talk about. I took you from Red Mike and gave you back to Rex and your father-in-law."

"But no one consulted me about it. I wouldn't have minded a few more days without my clothes . . . I liked the breeze on my body."

Holden stood up. "That's enough."

"But I'm not finished yet, Mr. Holden."

"I'm not Mr. Holden," Holden said. "I'm Holden."

"And I'd prefer it if you called me Fay."

"I can't. I mean, I talked to you once . . . at the Algonquin. You hardly said a word."

"But you've seen me without my clothes. And we did talk . . . after you shot Michael and his brothers."

"That was different. I was on the job. It wasn't a social occasion."

"It could have been. I might have cooked you a meal if you'd let Michael live."

Jesus, Holden thought, this woman had dropped her wig somewhere. "Look, I appreciate the effort. But I'm tired, Fay. I'll take you home. We can talk again."

Her eyes lowered, and he felt a certain pity for her. She'd been caught in some crazy battle between the district attorney and the Pinzolo boys, and she'd flipped out in that bungalow.

"The 'S' is for Sidney," he said. "But don't you dare repeat it."

She smiled. "Sidney. It's a good name. I'd like to call you that."

"Only in private," he said. "I have a reputation to consider. If people started saying Sidney to me, I'd have to bump them or leave town."

He managed to coax her out of the building and into a cab. She was a silent creature in a purple dress, looking out the window like a lost animal. Holden had the urge to stroke her hair.

She lived on Madison and Sixty-ninth—but when her doorman rang the apartment, Rex wasn't there—and Holden didn't feel like leaving her all by herself.

"Is your old man at the theater, rehearsing a play?"

"I doubt it," she said. "Try Muriel's. He's with all his whores."

What could Holden do? He stopped at Muriel's townhouse on East Fifty-fourth, asked Fay to sit in the cab, and entered with the key Muriel gave to her choice clients. The men in Muriel's parlor made a fuss over Holden, and Muriel herself admired the whiteness of his turban.

"God, you're handsome in that hat. It goes with all the blue."

"Where's Rex? His wife is waiting."

"Holden, you should have brought her upstairs. We could have gotten her into a rummy game while Rex washes up . . . try the south room. You'll find him."

But he found Gottlieb first.

"What were you doing in Inwood?" Gottlieb asked.

"I went looking for Huevo."

"In La Familia's own fortress? You always freak when you get back from Paris. Don't go there again."

Scolded by a seventeen-year-old boy . . . His reputation had slipped among his own society of rats.

"I can't get to Huevo without his *madrina.* And what am I supposed to do?"

"Wait," Gottlieb said.

"Is Nick Tiel around?"

"Yeah, he's doing hash in one of Muriel's closets."

"Take me to him."

"He might not appreciate that."

"Take me to Nick."

And Gottlieb showed him to a closet on the same floor. Nick was all alone with a little bubble-pipe in his mouth, sucking at the coals. His eyes were yellow, but he didn't have that frantic look he carried around with him in the designer's room. A fucking artist, Holden thought. Bleeds himself for the Paris show and he has to suck his pipe on a Saturday night. Holden was glad he couldn't design a coat. He'd have to live with patterns in his skull. He'd rather bump than caress a designer's dummy.

He marched upstairs to Rex. The playwright was lying with Melissa, the debutante of the month.

"Rex, your wife's downstairs. She's a little spooked. I think you should go to her."

Rex blinked from the pillows. "You brought my wife to Muriel's? You told her where I was?"

"She already knew."

"You could have denied it."

"I'm not a marriage counselor. Get the fuck out of bed."

"Don't you talk to me like that. My father's the D.A."

"Yeah," Holden said, tossing a stocking at Rex. "A D.A. who orders hits."

"My father never—"

"Shut up," Holden said, and took the giant by his shoulders and hurled him into the door. Rex swung at Holden like a pathetic windmill. Holden ducked under Rex's fists and socked him in the stomach. Rex sat groaning on the floor.

"Help me dress him," he told Melissa, and they got the playwright into his pants, shirt, and shoes. They didn't bother about his underwear. Holden liked this skinny girl. Muriel would find a senator for her, or some mob millionaire.

He clutched the back of Rex's shirt and marched him down to the taxi cab. He opened the door, shoved Rex inside, noticed the dark outline of Fay. She troubled him. He signaled to the driver, and the cab disappeared down the block. But he couldn't shake that image of the daughter-in-law with burning eyes in the back of a cab. Damn, Holden thought. Another leopard girl.

10 WHENEVER HE BEGAN to drift into some long mystery, Holden performed his own kind of calculus. Parrot + Mistress + Marielita = what? It had to be the little girl. She was the answer to why Huevo wanted him dead. Even if he'd become her dada, he'd still have to interview her. He arrived on Oliver Street and didn't have the heart to challenge the girl. Mrs. Howard redid his turban while the Marielita watched.

"Loretta, she has to be Huevo's daughter . . . or niece. There's no other explanation."

"Huevo's black. Does this girl look black to you?"

"He could have married a gringo?"

"He's not into that kind of marriage."

"Jesus, she talks to her dolls. She talks to you. If only we could get a name out of her. It might help."

"I got her name."

The bumper froze. "Thanks for volunteering the information."

"Holden, I've had other things on my mind. I take your calls from morning to midnight. I have to interpret some pretty weird stuff and act like a priest to some of your spies. I protect you from all that. And I have to fix a menu for the girl and wash her hair."

"What's her name?"

"Barbara."

Holden ground his teeth like his dad had always done. "We're in trouble," he said. "She could be the missing *madrina.* Don't you get it? Barbara is Changó's Christian name. She's involved with the cults. I'm telling you. The little bitch drinks chicken blood."

Mrs. Howard slapped his face. He couldn't pull a gun on a woman who was the nearest thing to a mother he'd ever had. The last time she'd slapped him, Holden had been twelve. He'd peeked at her in the bathroom, spied on her while she washed her breasts. He remembered the slow journey of the sponge, the dreamy look in her eye. He'd coughed and Mrs. Howard turned to stare at him. She came to Holden without covering her chest and slapped him. Twenty-five years ago.

"You apologize to Barbara, or get yourself another answering service."

He looked at the bitch, who hugged her doll, and Holden wondered if that doll had any of Changó's features. "Didn't mean it," he said.

"Dada."

"Mrs. H., can't you get her to increase her vocabulary?"

"You try." Mrs. Howard left him with the little girl.

"Barbara, do you remember chickens, chickens on a fire? *Gallo, gallo rojo.*"

"*Rojo,*" she said. And Holden pressed his advantage.

"How old are you, *querida?*"

"*Ocho,*" she said. Eight. So she had to have been born before the boatlift. She was a pilgrim, like Holden himself.

"Where's your mama?"

"Mama dead."

"She die in *Los Estados Unidos?*"

"*Sí.*"

"And who's been raising you?"

"Holden and Mrs. Howard."

"Before that, *querida.*"

"*La nada,*" she said. "*Querida* raise myself."

"You're a fairy child, an elf."

"*Sí.*"

Holden took a crayon from Barbara's coloring box and copied an executioner's heart in the webbing of his thumb. He crumpled the "tattoo" until most of the heart disappeared.

The Marielita laughed. "Your hand likes to talk."

He had her now. She thought he'd created a hand puppet. He blew words into his fist.

"Hello, Doña Barbara."

She giggled and tossed her head. "What is your name, señor?"

"Huevo."

Barbara eyed the puppet. "No, señor. It's Holden, I think."

"I'm Holden," Holden had to say. He was trying to destroy the girl's will. But this baby Santa Barbara was much too clever for him. "*Querida,*" he said, hiding his hand. "Do you have a friend, a *dueña* who looked after you . . . before you met Mrs. Howard?"

"*Sí.* Dolores."

"Was she skinny or fat?"

The Marielita pondered with a finger in her mouth. "Fat."

Holden kissed the girl, grabbed her in his arms, felt all her mysterious odors, set her down in the middle of her dolls, and went looking for Loretta Howard. Loretta was doing Holden's books, with a gun strapped to her side.

"We have a possible *madrina*," he said. "Named Dolores. Can you check her out?"

"I'm not a goddamn agency, Holden. I'm a gal with rheumatism. It's lucky I had a crush on you while I was living with your dad, because you drive me to distraction. Holden, you just can't win. You're out there freelancing, and you can't even tell who you're freelancing for. Your dad didn't have much brains, but at least he worked for one man."

"Yeah, the Swiss. Loretta, I work for him too."

"But he has you bouncing all over the yard. You belong to Infante. Then you're Edmundo's child. Then who knows? You mess with the Marielitos, Holden, it's like being in outer space. They got the witchcraft. All we've got is spies."

"Why are you so ornery today?"

"Because I'm worried about you," she said. "You're not even kin. You're a white man who kills a lot of people."

Holden hugged her and she started to cry. "Don't you play sweet with me. I'll find that old Dolores. Give me a couple of minutes . . . well, go on out of here. Can't I have a little privacy?"

He strolled Loretta's rooms with nothing to do, looked in on the little girl, but she was occupied with her dolls, and Holden didn't want to disturb her. She sang to each doll in a tongue he couldn't understand—neither Spanish, nor English, nor a mix of both; it was like a whisper, a constant hiss where he couldn't locate the syllables. A language a man or god might use to fool his jailors.

Loretta called him back to her code room.

"There is a Dolores. She runs a religious store on the Lower East Side."

"That's not Huevo's territory."

"But she's a witch. That's what matters."

"A hefty woman?" Holden asked.

"How the hell should I know? She has a *botánica*. She sells dust that can make a Bandido disappear."

Holden stood like a boy in front of Mrs. Howard. "Can I take Barbara to see the witch?"

"Certainly not."

"But I won't be able to tell if she's our Dolores."

"You'll have to use your head." Loretta touched a loose cotton string on Holden's turban and started to laugh. "I'm sorry. Didn't mean to make fun. But you are a sight . . . we'll take the girl together. No harm done. If Dolores throws her powder at us, we'll sneeze it back into her face."

And so they dressed Santa Barbara, allowed her one doll, and Loretta got Harrington on the line. That yellow-faced man was waiting outside on Oliver Street like some lost Mohican, and Holden couldn't figure how he had the time to get there. Harrington's garage was in Brooklyn. He must have crossed a bridge that no one had ever heard about. It spooked Holden to have a chauffeur like that. He wasn't into magic. He understood the value of a yellow face. Harrington's liver was eating him alive. Holden believed in intuition, luck, and loyal friends, but he wasn't going to be cursed by a chicken without a head.

It was only a seven-minute ride to Madison Street. The *botánica* was near a supermarket that had more aisles than Holden had ever seen. He could have traveled to Avignon along those aisles, but he hadn't come down here to sink into some past he couldn't even recall. The *botánica* had relics in the window, Santa Barbara and other saints. Flowers, shrubs, herbs, roots, medicines that could heal or make a man sick. It meant nothing to Holden, whose only voodoo was a Beretta .380 above his heart.

He went into the store with little Barbara. The *botánica* had an aisle of crazy plants. The woman who tended them wasn't fat.

"Dolores?" he asked, pulling on the little girl's hand to feel if there wasn't a bit of electricity between Barbara and the *botanista.* "Dolores?"

"What you wish?"

"A potion," he said. "A potion that can make a man appear."

The woman scrutinized him. "I have not such things to sell."

"But it's a particular man. Lázaro Rodriguez."

"I do not know him, and if I did, why would I tell a stranger?"

"I'm not a stranger. Lázaro and I share the same child."

"Please, if you are a policeman, I have nothing for you. I do not interfere . . . please"

"Can you take a message to Lázaro. I didn't hurt his child."

"Please, I am not political . . ."

There was nothing for Holden. He'd come to the wrong witch. He walked out with Barbara and began to sneeze. He had a garden in his nose.

Holden couldn't believe it. The bitch was in his office again. He wanted calm, an evening of quiet with *Casablanca* and the file cards he'd brought with him on *botánicas* and African gods, like Oyá, Changó's mistress, who borrowed his thunder whenever he was in jail. Oyá wasn't as temperamental as the thunder god. And she didn't wear a red dress. But she had her own river, the Niger, and she'd navigate it with her nose above the swell, like a crocodile. And now Abruzzi's daughter-in-law had interrupted his investigations and his dreams.

"Did Infante let you in again?"

Fay wouldn't answer, and Holden went searching for Infante, because he didn't care for uninvited guests, even if they were pretty. He found the lawyer in Swiss' old office.

"Robert, I'll take your wife to lunch, I'll sit with her in Mansions to get her out of your hair, but I don't want you dumping people in my office. I'm not your private letter box."

"It was innocent, Holden, I swear. The woman's in trouble. She came home a little loony from Red Mike's. She must have been scared shitless of Eddie and the Rat. Rex doesn't know what to do with her. She's been asking around for you, so I thought, why not? You're her savior."

"That's not how she sees it. She was honeymooning with Mike."

"It's a fantasy, Holden. That week with the brothers wrecked her constitution."

"You're wrong. It was the hole I put in Mikey's head."

"What's the difference? All her attention has gone to you. You don't have to babysit. Just tolerate her for a while . . . it'll wear off. She's a mother, for God's sake. And a professional woman . . . a sociologist."

"Well, I don't want to be studied by her, Robert."

Holden left Infante's office. The lawyer began to pick at his nails with a silver knife. And Holden returned to Fay. He noticed how curly her hair was, and the color of her eyes under the thick glass: gray like some goddess, he thought. But Oyá was black.

"I have important business," Holden said. "A Cuban bandit is after me. He throws firebombs. He's fucked an entire organization called La Familia . . . forgive the bad language, but I'm irritable, Fay."

She moved toward the door, and Holden couldn't stop looking at all that curly hair. "You don't have to go," he said. "Sit . . . we can have a conversation."

He had no armchair in his office, or a sofa, and the most comfortable place was the pillow on his bed. He hadn't mapped his office for seduction. Never even brought a woman here. He would sleep with Florinda Infante in some apartment she'd borrow from one of Mansions' many kings. It troubled him that Robert didn't seem to worry, as if Holden were a hired horse put out to service a mob lawyer's wife. Shouldn't the lawyer have been a little angry at Holden? And why did Infante have to find dates for Florinda? Couldn't she have cuckolded him on her own? And now Holden was with another man's wife. He sat cautiously on the bed with Fay, didn't want to give her the idea that he was a permanent stud in Infante's stable.

"Sidney, why are you sitting so far away? I wouldn't dream of biting you . . . I haven't been well."

He moved closer to her, and a strangeness fell off. She could have been part of the furniture, or an old friend.

"You're stuck with me, I'm afraid . . . am I awful?"

His skin was tingling, and Holden wondered if he had the flu. He followed the line of her long black stockings, from the kneecaps down. Why did the bitch feel familiar? He'd hardly ever been around a woman who wasn't a model or a whore. He'd married a whore, really. Holden didn't mind. He could chase clients off Andrushka's back. She'd stuck to him in bed, like a twig. He couldn't figure it out. Why should a mannequin from Green Bay have excited Holden and given him so much peace . . . until she discovered Caravaggio and culture.

"Am I awful to bother you like this?"

"Not awful," he said, wanting to touch her curly hair.

"I've changed, Sidney. I can't bear Manhattan after the beach. I know it sounds weird. But I wasn't naked all the time . . . with Michael, I mean. He'd give me a raincoat to wear, and we'd explore the other bungalows."

"Did you love him?"

"Yes, in a way. But it wasn't what you think. We were like children together. He'd grow serious and tell me, 'I could never kiss a hostage, Miss Fay.' It was all a game to Michael. And the game had its rules. My father-in-law hurt his people, and so he captured me. It was like a gambit in chess. And Michael was the black knight."

"And what am I?"

She leaned into Holden's arm, and it was as if a baby deer had bumped him with a horn. "Another black knight," she said. "It's because I was fond of Michael that I like you."

"But I killed him."

"That was only an accident."

He pulled away from her. "It wasn't an accident. I'd come to kill him. That was my job."

"But you told me before that you might not have killed him if I hadn't been naked."

"It's true. I loved Red Mike. And if we'd talked, if we'd argued it out, and you were in a dress, it's conceivable I wouldn't have killed him. But he'd have had to make me an offer. I wouldn't have left the bungalow without you."

She bumped him again. "Then it was like a game, with its own rules and regulations. Two black knights, and only one could win."

"That's the problem. I didn't win. Mikey's dead. And you were happier with him than you are now."

"But I am happy . . . with you."

Holden laughed, and the stitching hurt his head. "Happy with me? Take a closer look. I got death on my face."

"So did Michael."

"And Eddie? And the Rat?"

"It didn't matter. They wouldn't have survived without Michael. Killing them was a kind of mercy."

The bitch in the long black socks could have been a lawyer. She'd have danced around Infante in court, seduced judge and jury with all her clothes on. She was Oyá with a pale face.

He heard a funny, winding noise, a metallic shriek, and Holden jumped off the bed. He knew what that noise was all about. It was the factory's supersonic smoke detectors. Aladdin had alarms and systems that were as sensitive and musical as the most fabulous violin. Because the company couldn't afford a fire— Aladdin would lose the Paris show without Nick Tiel's scribbles. Nick couldn't recall the patterns that dropped out of his head. That's why Holden guarded all his scribbles, and flew with the prelims to France.

He grabbed Fay and went to his closet, wrapped her in a cashmere coat. He could feel the waves of heat. The factory was burning. But it couldn't have been an ordinary fire. The alarms would have located it, the sprinklers gone off, and half the company would have knocked on his door, standing in a pile of water. But the house wasn't wet. Someone had sabotaged the sprinklers. Holden didn't have to dig. He recognized the signature. A Cuban cocktail. Benzene and God knows what in a bottle. Huevo used the same recipe to destroy hundreds of betting parlors. There was never an explosion, nothing to warn Huevo's victims. The artist would treat his bomb like a baby bottle, pack it in salt, bring it to a gentle boil, and you'd have a fire in your lap.

Holden shoved Fay under the coat and then he opened the door with his collar up to his eyes. The heat slapped his face. There was bedlam around him. Nick Tiel's nailers ran like wild geese, clutching skins and dropping them.

"Forget the fucking minks," Holden said. "The fire door, the fire door."

Infante bumped into him. He wore a scarf around his ears. One end of it was on fire. Holden put his hands inside his coat, made himself a pair of mittens, and slapped at the fire. "Where's Nick?"

"Don't know. I didn't see him."

Holden left Fay with Infante and went into that storm. The nailing boards were on fire. The fixtures had begun to melt. Fluorescent bulbs popped over his head. Glass flew at him, but Holden had his hat. He could feel little bites in the turban.

He got to Nick's door. It was locked from the inside.

"Nick, it's me, Holden. Will you come out, or do I have to die waiting for you?"

The door opened. Nick Tiel was clutching his patterns and his clothing dummies. His eyes were terribly pale. He was in a fright. He couldn't hold on to his entire inventory. Holden grabbed the dummies, with Nick's designs pinned to them, said, "Come on," and led Nick Tiel out of the fire.

Holden's eyebrows had been seared. His face was a mask of smoke. He looked like a monkey in a Saville Row suit. But he got Nick to the far side of the fire door.

The fire chiefs had arrived. They wore coats down to their ankles. Holden had Infante handle them. He climbed down the stairs with Nick Tiel and Fay.

There was a crowd of Greeks on the sidewalk, like a bitter chorus. They stared at the dummies and enjoyed the prospect of Aladdin's ruin. But Holden hadn't lost a scribble in the fire. He found a telephone booth and called Harrington's garage. The chauffeur arrived before the last fire truck. They delivered Nick Tiel to his penthouse on Sutton Place. Holden went upstairs with Nick, boiled a cup of soup for him, put the soup and soda crackers on a tray, and walked him out to the terrace.

"Holden, your head's all black."

"Drink the soup."

He watched the tramway over Roosevelt Island, little cars in the sky, and stared out at the shores of Queens. "It's fucking gorgeous . . . I wouldn't mind living here."

"Holden, was it the Greeks? Did they set us on fire? But Infante was right there. And he owns those miserable bastards."

"It wasn't the Greeks."

"Then I don't get it."

"Nobody was after your designs, Nick. Some Marielito's been trying to kill me. The same guy who planted the chicken in my office. Huevo."

"That maniac? What the hell did you do to Huevo?"

"I'm not sure. He thinks I stole a little girl from him."

Nick had come out of his haze. He stared at Holden. "What little girl?"

"Remember the Parrot and his mistress? Well, I found a little girl under the table. I took her with me and lent her to Mrs. Howard.

"Just like that? Without telling me and the Swiss? You had instructions, Holden. You were supposed to mop up the Parrot and everything that belonged to him."

"Fine, Nick. Then you strangle the little girl."

"That's not the issue. You put us in danger, Holden."

"Could be, but I wouldn't let the Swiss know about it, because you'll have a civil war on your hands. The girl stays with me until I give her back."

"Since when do you set our policies?"

"It's not a policy, Nick. It's just something I have to do . . . I'm sorry. Take care of yourself."

Holden went down to Harrington's car. Fay shivered next to him. He sucked his teeth. She'd entered his life with that curly hair and those three killings in the bungalow. He knew he wouldn't be taking her back to Rex.

HE BROUGHT HER to his mattress pad in Chelsea. It was a risk. Because each person who came to his pad compromised him a little. Of course, he could lock it up and sneak into the storefront he had on White Street. But he'd begun to leave a trail.

She didn't collapse on his couch. She changed his blackened bandages, and Holden had one more turban. She looked into cupboards, found his survival food. There was wine under the sink and seltzer in the fridge. She prepared a tuna casserole, and they sat on the couch together, nibbling with plates on their knees. The twig had never prepared a casserole in her life. She didn't know how to cook. And Holden thought, this must be how it is to have an ordinary wife.

They hardly talked. Holden listened to her chew. He touched her hair. She smiled. He didn't ask her about her children, or the climate at the Central Park Zoo. She could have left the mattress pad, put down her plate and disappeared. Holden wouldn't have stopped her. But she'd crept inside his guts with her curly hair, and he didn't want her to go.

He couldn't remember how they'd started kissing. He hadn't reached for her. But suddenly they were lying on the floor and Fay was undressed, like she'd been at the bungalow. And he said without thinking, "Are you comfortable, dear?" It wasn't crazy of him, because she was his dear. He had to put a hole in Mikey's head to find his proper darling. He'd met all his other women in Aladdin's

showroom, or at Muriel's place. He'd looked at them, liked them,
gone to bed—even married one of them, the twig, because her
fragile toughness moved him, and how could he not love a seventeen-year-old named Andrushka? But his years of mourning her,
missing Andrushka with a terrible grief, while she lived on the rue
de Vaugirard, had dropped off Holden with the help of a .22 long.
How could he explain it otherwise? He didn't love Andrushka any-
more.

He spent five days with his darling in the house. She cooked
from Holden's cans. They watched whatever Holden had on the
VCR. She lived inside one of his bathrobes. He made love to her
in the bathroom, while she braced her arms against the toilet seat.
He watched the ripples in her back.

On the sixth day they ran out of spices, and she went down to
the grocer in Holden's overcoat and returned with pies, meat, and
gallons of ice cream. And it was then that she declared: "Sidney, I'll
need some clothes."

"We could buy them. I'll get Harrington to drive us to
Macy's . . ."

"Not new things. I'd like my clothes. I'll take a cab uptown."

"But Harrington could—"

"I'd rather not arrive in a limo. It's simpler, darling. You'll see."

His hand was shaking. "When will you be back?"

"Oh, an hour or two, if I don't have complications . . ."

"What if the children start to cry?"

She laughed. "You're worse than a husband. Tina's at boarding
school. And Adrianne's in Arizona, visiting with a friend."

She said goodbye, and he felt broken. He called Mrs. Howard.
There was a scratch in his voice he couldn't hide.

"Mrs. H., have people been asking for me?"

"They don't have to ask. They know you're with Abruzzi's
daughter-in-law. You and her are the sensation of the month."

"You heard about the firebomb?"

"That's all been fixed. Infante's had Cuban carpenters around
most of the week. Nick is back in the designing room."

"And the skins? We must have lost a fortune in sables."

"They're insured. The company stands to make half a million on the fire. We'd love to see you, Holden. Barbara's been asking about her dada. I didn't have the heart to tell her there's another woman in the case."

"I'm not her dada. Anything new on Huevo?"

"Not a bump."

"Well, I can't let him go around dropping benzene torches outside my office. I'll lose my reputation."

"Edmundo has an army looking for his ass, and that hasn't bothered Huevo at all."

"You're supposed to encourage me."

"I am."

He put down the phone, and he was still trembling. Fay's absence felt like a bullet cruising around in his head, a .22 short that dug into his ear and started to chip against his skull. Holden sat like a wounded boy and waited.

It grew dark. He closed his eyes. It was like the times he waited for Loretta Howard to come home when she was still with his dad. She'd spring upon him while he was dozing in his chair, and she'd have some tiny gift for him: toffee or hazelnuts, and she'd be dressed like a dream, with a hint of perfume behind her ears, and if his dad came home first, Holden would sulk, because he wouldn't have his hazelnuts or a hug, and he'd watch the door for Loretta, watch and wait until the lock turned slowly, and his heart would pound. She'd have to deal with his dad, soothe him before she could come to him, and he'd wish his father dead. It was that moment when his career was made. He'd become a bumper in his father's house.

He must have been snoring, because he hadn't heard his darling knock. He forgot to give her a key. He opened the door, and a kind of happiness crossed his face. His cheeks were red. The bumper began to blush. She had one small suitcase and a shopping bag filled with trinkets. It didn't seem worth a trip uptown, frightening him with her absence when he could have bought her anything she desired. "Darling," she said. "I wasn't away that long . . . there were neighbors. I couldn't cut them off. And Rex was home."

"What did you tell him?"

"Nothing much. I needed a vacation from him and the girls."

"Does Rex know about me?"

"Of course."

"And he wasn't angry? I mean, a man can run off with his wife just like that and it's okay with Rex?"

"You're not a stranger I met on the street."

"Almost. I met you in a bungalow. I shot Red Mike. That's not exactly a marriage."

"But we aren't married. I'm your sweetheart."

"Tell me," he said, taking the suitcase and the shopping bag, "have you ever run away with a man before?"

"No, not that I can think of."

"I'm the first?"

"If you don't count Michael. I didn't run away with him. He took me by surprise."

"Michael, it always comes back to Michael."

"But that week with him prepared me for you . . . would you rather I left?"

His hand was shaking again. "I didn't say a word about leaving. We were having a conversation, that's all. I'm glad you've come back."

"You don't sound glad."

"I was worried that Rex or somebody would convince you to stay uptown."

"But didn't I promise you?"

"Fay, should I tell you how many promises I've had to eat?"

"But I belong to you, Sidney."

"Yeah, now that Mike is dead. Would you be here if I hadn't killed him?"

"Probably not . . . but you might not have wanted me, darling."

It was true. His whole goddamn romance hinged on Mike's

death. He kissed Fay and his terror was gone. They explored the trinkets in her shopping bag. She had a crazy little animal with its head on backwards so it could see its tail.

"That's you, Sidney. You're so suspicious, you can't swallow without turning your head. That's why I love you. You take nothing for granted."

"My dad was a suspicious man. The United States was after him all his life. He lived in exile until a friend sneaked him back into the country."

She took out other trinkets: a cloth cat stuffed with pine cones, a jar of jelly beans, little brass pots that she arranged on Holden's windowsills, a torn doll, a pencil sharpener from her hometown in Illinois, wedding souvenirs, a sorority pin, locks of hair . . . like a history of Fay in miniature, a map that she distributed in Holden's rooms, a little circus of herself. And it amazed Holden that she could stuff her past into a shopping bag and carry it downtown. He had nothing like that, no menagerie.

She entwined her life with his and built her own contours in the apartment, a borderland where she kept her animals and her clothes. She was happy here. That's how it seemed to Holden. The mysterious lady who'd arrived out of some catacomb, appeared in Far Rockaway without her clothes, another man's wife, devoted to Rat and Eddie and Red Mike.

One afternoon while Fay napped he walked over to Aladdin. Holden couldn't believe what the Cuban carpenters had done. The whole fucking factory was restored. The nailers were at their benches. The cutters waltzed around Nick Tiel's dummies with tape measures like yellow collars at their necks. The fluorescent lights hissed over his head. His title, last name and first initial had been redone on his door. His office opened with the same old key. He still had a VCR. He could smell the fresh paint, but there wasn't a single bubble in the wall that could remind him of the fire. He went into his closet. Some of his underwear was gone. An old shoe. But his wardrobe had survived the crisis. He packed his favorite clothes and left without consulting Nick.

Holden hid out in Chelsea with his love. His apartment was on Tenth Avenue, near a seminary with a garden in the middle. Holden could see the young seminarians from his bedroom window. He'd had three semesters at Bernard Baruch, where he'd studied banking and Aristotle, and he wondered now if the seminarians were discussing Aristotle and Aquinas or Qaddafi and the fate of the world. He'd enjoyed his three semesters at Baruch. Swiss had sent him there to master the art of accounting so Holden could help with Aladdin's books. But he was much more valuable out in the field. How could Swiss have known beforehand that an eighteen-year-old kid would have such a talent for bumping people? College began to interfere with his work at Aladdin. The kid was studying all the time. Holden had to drop out. And he watched the seminarians with remorse. He envied their Aristotle. But suppose he'd become an accountant? Would he be a fat cat, like Infante, with an aristocratic wife who loved to eat at Mansions around a lot of kings?

Holden took care of a different sort of books. He collected for Aladdin. And he bumped. Fay caught him at the window, recognized his sadness, and took him in her arms. "Sidney, we shouldn't sit around like this. We have to get out."

And they went to the movies together, to the theater, to concerts, to performances of dance. Holden knew there was a danger. But he had Harrington drive him to all the shows. He searched under the seats for a Cuban cocktail. He was that animal with its head on backwards. He had to be.

He couldn't avoid Fay's old girlfriends, who'd appear at concerts and eye Holden as if he were Ali Baba in a British suit; they must have known he was the one who'd rescued Fay and killed the three bad brothers. He could feel a sexual edge to their glances. Who were these girlfriends? Had they gone to Swarthmore with Fay? They chattered about a universe Holden couldn't enter at all. Benefit concerts. Charity balls. A pianist named Vladimir. A dance company out in Brooklyn where women whipped men with their

hair. Had he seen *Pixote?* No. *El Norte? A Nos Amours?* They
weren't into *Destry Rides Again.* And Holden gave up pretending
he had the least bit in common with the girlfriends. He was Fay's
bandit lover, the vice president of a fur company who couldn't even
quote the price of Canadian mink.

But she never called him Sidney in public, and she didn't leave
him floating in a corner with the girlfriends. She stood next to
Holden, touched his arm. And whatever brought her to him—the
feud between a district attorney and wild men in Queens, her own
strange marriage, Red Mike, the barrel of a .22 long—there was
nothing tricky about Fay's devotion to her bandit.

He had to find Huevo, but he went to the theater with Fay.
He ignored little Barbara and Mrs. Howard. He wouldn't visit Gottlieb. Holden had gone off the street. He'd glued himself to Fay's
curly hair. He'd never been so passive, not even with the twig. He
forgot he ever had a secret service.

And then Holden bumped into his own tail at a temple on
Fifty-fifth. He'd arrived with Fay to watch a dance company at City
Center. They had seats in the sixth row. Holden was content. He
held Fay's hand. She never lectured him. He watched. The first
dance was about the Fourth of July. He could see the women's
nipples under their tights. It didn't turn him on. They were moon
creatures to him, dancers on a stage. Fay had been a dancer once
at college. But she didn't have that crystalline look, a body made of
prisms and planes. She was much rounder than the women in this
company. He decided that he loved round women after all. The twig
had been an accident of fate.

A figure crept out of the aisle. It was Jeremías, Don Edmundo's
bodyguard. He haunted the temple like a spook with sick eyes.
When the lights went on Holden saw half of La Familia. Edmundo
had gobbled up an entire row in the middle of the orchestra. He had
his daughters with him, his sons-in-law, his soothsayers, his wife,
business associates, and another man who turned away from Holden.
It was Count Josephus from that restaurant of kings. And suddenly
Holden's three semesters at Baruch made sense. He understood the

economics of owning a restaurant. Mansions was a Cuban front, a cashbox for Don Edmundo. The count was Edmundo's doll.

Edmundo bought champagne for Holden's darling. No one mentioned Rex.

"That tall one, Gladys," Edmundo said to Fay about one of the dancers, "did you like her elevation?"

Holden looked at the count, remembered the executioner's heart on his hand, an Albanian with a Cuban prison tale to tell. But the count never looked back.

Holden didn't have to lie. He announced to Fay that he was keeping business hours again. But first he taught her to use a gun. He had a Llama .380 in the house. He took her with Harrington to some deer park on the other side of the George Washington Bridge and had her fire into a tree.

"Darling, this is a waste of ammunition. I could never shoot a man."

"It doesn't matter. At least you know how."

He returned her to Chelsea, squeezed her in back of the car, left her with the Llama .380 and its shoulder cup, which he strapped to her chest while she laughed. "It's ridiculous. I look like Belle Starr. I'll have to get a new wardrobe to go with that gun. I won't wear it."

"You will."

"Are we going to fight in front of Harrington? . . . at least come upstairs."

"I can't. But wear the gun, Fay. I have enemies."

"I thought this apartment was a big secret."

"It's only a secret if we stay indoors. We've been hopping around. Too many people know about us. I'm a worrier, Fay. I'd never be able to leave you alone. You'd get sick of me. I'd crawl inside your pajamas."

"That's not so bad. But I'll wear your silly gun."

He kissed her and drove uptown to Mansions. Florinda Infante was at her window table, eating medallions of pork with King Alfonse. Holden saw the streak in her hair through the glass. She knocked on the window, summoned him inside.

"Say hello to Fatso," she said. "You're his hero. He read all about the mystery man who stole Fay Abruzzi from the big bad borough of Queens. I think he wants to shake your hand. Right, Fatso?"

"Indeed," Alfonse said.

"But he'll be crushed when he hears that you've been banging the lady."

"He doesn't look crushed to me," Holden said.

"That's because it takes time to penetrate. He's a king . . . Holden, you shouldn't duck out on your friends. I don't mind your liaisons. But to shack up with a housewife who's a real flake? Rex is laughing in his pants. I think he got his father to stage that kidnapping. He ought to give you an allowance. Should I ask?"

"I'll do my own asking."

"Aren't you going to sit down with us? Fatso will be disappointed."

"Sorry. I have an engagement with the count."

Florinda looked up at Holden with her aristocratic face. She had more bearing than the twig, and she was twice as voluptuous as Fay, but she couldn't move him to madness. His head wasn't occupied with the purple in her hair.

"It's funny the count never told me you were coming. He tells me everything."

"Well, his calendar got a little clogged."

Holden bowed to Fatso, kissed Florinda's hand, and went into the heart of the restaurant. The count was at a table with several other kings. Seeing Holden gave him a touch of gloom. But he wasn't fickle. He stood up and accompanied Holden to his office behind the bar without exaggerating his limp.

"Count, I don't want to discuss your imperial past. How you got from Albania to Cuba is your business. Just tell me about the jails."

"What jails, Monsieur?"

Holden grabbed Josephus' hand and displayed the executioner's heart. "Don't monsieur me so much. You're a fucking convict. You killed people, or you wouldn't have that mark."

"But I could also kill you," Josephus said.

"Not a chance. You gave up the life. You're a restauranteur. And restauranteurs are notoriously slow. Tell me, count, were you with Huevo's gang once upon a time? Be careful, because if you lie I'll come back and tear your face off."

"Yes. I was with Huevo."

"Did he fix up your hand, give you the tattoo?"

"Yes. It's Huevo's work."

"And you sailed out of Cuba with him on a boat from Mariel?"

"Holden, I'm sixty-one."

"And you really are noble, like those other lost kings who collect here. You came to Cuba without a dime. You ran a couple of casinos, I figure, and you might have switched to Castro's side, because most counts are a little crazy. But the Fidelistas found out you had your own black market in Havana, and they threw you into Taco-Taco."

Josephus smiled. "You're not a bad biographer, Holden."

"How did you earn the mark on your hand?"

"I killed for Fidel . . . and other people. My politics were very wide. I could swing right or left."

"And where did you meet Huevo?"

"In Taco-Taco. We were both politicals. They stuck us with ordinary convicts. We survived and got to America. Edmundo took us in. He'd never had a count fighting in one of his wars. He groomed me for this job. But Huevo wasn't satisfied. He wanted to start his own family. He did."

"And you didn't go with him."

The count twisted his head. "Do you know how hard I worked to make Mansions a success?"

"Yeah, you gave every king in town a free ride."

"But look what a clientele we got out of it? Customers like to eat around kings. They feel good."

"And you convinced other Bandidos to stay with Edmundo."

"What could I do? Huevo forced me to pick sides."

"How come he doesn't kill you? Or bomb Mansions?"

"We were friends a long time," the count said. "I taught him about America."

"What America?"

"You kidding? I went back and forth in the old days. I collected for a couple of gambler friends. I flattened a cop in Boca Raton. The shit started to fly. But they couldn't find me in Cuba. And Huevo? He was in love with the idea of America. I sang Gershwin to him inside Taco-taco. He had a Captain America tee-shirt. The *rojos* tore it to shreds . . . I'm like his uncle, Holden, and you don't hurt an uncle even if he's gone bad."

"Then tell me how I can get to his *madrina.*"

The count laughed and showed his silver teeth. "If I didn't tell Edmundo, why should I tell you?"

"Because you're useful to him, and he's impressed with a count. But I'll strangle you in this closet if you don't help me."

"Holden, I've bumped more people than you'll ever know."

"We're not talking about batting averages. I need a name."

The count didn't have the familiar smell of fear that was like chlorine and piss. Holden had to do something. He took out his Beretta. The count's eyes were as clear as the enamel on Holden's toilet seat. But Holden didn't point the gun. He kicked open the door. "I'll hit the chandeliers first. Then the bottles of whiskey on your bar. Then the mirrors."

"You wouldn't dare. The cops would arrest you in five minutes."

"So what? I'll plead insanity. I have a great lawyer. But Mansions wouldn't look right with gunshot wounds. And they'd start investigating you for letting desperate characters into the place. Who knows? They could discover your past . . . and your connections with La Familia. Count, I'd make a great canary."

"You're bluffing."

Holden aimed his gun at the count's central chandelier.

"Wait," the count said and shut the door. "Huevo's not a fool. He doesn't stick to one *madrina*. He'd be dead if he ever did that. But I could give you a name . . . Chepita, she has a sewing shop in El Norte."

"Where's that?"

"You don't know much, do you, Holden? With all the rats you have, you're still alone. El Norte is at the bottom of Fort Tryon Park. The real estate barons like to think Manhattan is their personal kingdom. But the Marielitos have taken over the top of the island. There's two Manhattans now. El Norte and El Dorado."

"Where do you live, count?"

"On Lexington, Holden. I'm not Cuban. I became a Marielito by chance." He wrote down the *madrina*'s address.

"You can start drawing a salary from me, count."

"Don't be stupid. I'm not one of your rats."

"What else would you call it? And pray that the *madrina*'s at this address."

Holden walked to Florinda with the count. She sat with Alfonso and touched the streak in her hair. "What have you two been conspiring?"

"Nothing," the count said. "Holden wanted to become my partner and I turned him down?"

"What the hell does he know about restaurants?"

"That's exactly my feeling."

"Holden, will you sit with me?" She scowled at Fatso, as if her eyes could shove him off a chair.

"I can't sit," Holden said, and he floated out of the restaurant, leaving Florinda with a grim face.

12

EL NORTE.

Now he didn't even know Manhattan. He was a stranger in fancy silk and wool, a frog spawned in Avignon. He'd lived with his dad in Queens until he was old enough to enter Manhattan as a bumper for Swiss. He'd rocketed over his dad in one or two years. Because bumpers were hard to find, bumpers like Holden who weren't cruel away from their work. He didn't seek partners or back-up men. Goldie supplied the guns and the suits. Harrington drove him sometimes, sometimes not. Holden didn't like patterns that an enemy could trace. But he did have a signature. A bullet hole in the middle of the head. Jeremías had been right about him. He was the paradise man. He never butchered. He dispatched you with the least amount of blood.

He'd watched his dad grow smaller and smaller while his own reputation spread. His dad became Holden Sr. all of a sudden, like he was in exile all over again, condemned to some private Palace of the Popes. He died at Muriel's, falling down a flight of stairs before Holden had the chance to marry Andrushka. To his father he was always the kid, even after he had his name on Aladdin's door. Technically, Holden Sr. worked for him. He'd found his father on Muriel's floor and couldn't cry. Hadn't he always waited like this for his father's death? He'd never have had the nerve to bump people if he hadn't hated his dad. But he didn't feel like some triumphant boy at Muriel's. He looked ashen, like his father. The bumper had gone gray.

He rode up to El Norte like a little king at the back of Harrington's car. But if it was a Marielito province Holden couldn't tell from the street. He saw one Jewish center, an Episcopalian church, a movie house with gringo films, an Irish grocery store. El Norte had all the old sinews of Manhattan. It wasn't like the Cuban zone of Miami with its Calle Ocho, its *marketas*, cups of coffee in the street. There were no Little Havanas under the elevated tracks. He didn't stop at the bumpers' bar where the Bandidos wore eyeglasses with one dark lens. He visited Chepita's sewing shop on Seaman Avenue.

When he opened the door he knew he'd found fat Dolores, no matter what the *madrina* called herself. This was the woman who'd raised little Barbara. Holden was certain of that. She looked like a heavyweight Carmen Miranda. Three hundred pounds of prettiness, with hooped earrings, eyebrows that followed a perfect line, and nails that were red as blood.

The shop had no signs of Santería. No saints in the window, no magic leaves. Just doilies and pins and the paraphernalia of a seamstress. Holden didn't believe Dolores sold a thing. He saw a curtain in the back. That was where she had her shop.

But Dolores wasn't unfriendly. And what made him think of Carmen Miranda who'd died when Holden was just a baby? His dad had kept a picture of her in his desk. Carmen dancing with Cesar Romero, her many skirts whipping around her legs like the lines of a beautiful flower. Carmen had no underpants. It was the first piece of erotica he'd ever shared with his dad. He was eight or nine when he discovered Carmen Miranda in the drawer. And he still wondered what the picture meant to a man who could have had any whore in town. He'd never discussed Carmen with his dad, but he'd seen her movies on the Late Show and remembered her legs. For twenty years the sight of Carmen Miranda in her tutti-frutti hat gave Holden an instant erection.

"Dolores?"

"I'm Chepita," Dolores said. "Do you like to sew?"

He didn't want to get into a fight with Dolores. He knew he

couldn't win. "I'm Holden," he said. "Your godson's been trying to kill me."

"I have no godsons," she said.

"I think you do . . . and I've taken something from him . . . a little girl. But it wasn't a scam. Tell him I had no evil intent. I was hired to dispose of two pests, and the little girl happened to be under the table. I'd like to give her back . . . if it's not too late. Will your godson see me?"

That big, graceful body moved behind the counter. Her nails gleamed. Holden shivered. He could have been watching *Down Argentine Way*.

"Why should I trust you? You come to me with a gun under your coat."

"Here, you can have it," Holden said, opening his blazer and uncovering his heart.

Dolores smiled. "Foolish man, your career would end if I shot you in the knees. The executioner would have to crawl home."

"But you still wouldn't have the little girl."

"And you would not be able to stand up so you could steal her again . . . come with me."

He followed fat Dolores behind her curtain. There was nothing remarkable at the back of the shop. A hot plate and a fridge, a shower stall and a can that could have been a child's throne. The can was painted blue.

They went through a door and into a big alley behind the shop. The wind blew on Holden. Bits of dust got into his eye and he had to shield his face. But Dolores' body seemed to bite back at the weather. Her hips swayed as she walked. Carmen Miranda. Holden wasn't frightened of the priestess. He'd have gone with her to Oyá's kingdom, where all the goddesses dwelled. He'd have swum the river Niger with fat Dolores. He was in her hands.

Yet he knew he'd have to kill Huevo or make peace with a phantom army that could turn off sprinklers and alarms and deliver Cuban cocktails through a wall. Was it Changó who'd come to Aladdin with the goddess Oyá and set Holden's little house on fire?

They traveled across the alley, Dolores with her light step among clotheslines and mops hanging from a window, and out to Isham Street. He could feel a whole lot of eyes on him. Was Changó wearing his red skirt behind some Cuban window?

They walked into the cellar of an apartment house. The concrete in the courtyard had started to crumble. Holden could have fallen into a hole and sat in a grave of brown dust. But he began to wonder if that god in the red dress had become his personal saint? And had Oyá declared herself Holden's mistress without bothering to knock?

Dolores had led him to a mattress pad, like his, but it didn't have a VCR. Three sullen men sat on different mattresses. Dolores' godsons, Bandidos she'd sworn to protect. If this was Huevo's army, then Big Balls didn't have much of a future in Manhattan, north or south. They spoke to their *madrina* in the same sing-song whisper Holden had heard little Barbara use with her dolls. It was prison patois.

"We would like your gun," Dolores said.

Holden unclipped his holster cup with the Beretta inside. Dolores handed it to one of the Bandidos, a scrawny black man with flecks of white in his hair. His eyes were green. He looked undernourished.

"This is Valentín," Dolores said. "He will be your guide. But you will have to pay him. He is very poor."

Holden removed his money clip.

"Don't insult him. You haven't used his services yet."

And Holden took off with Valentín, leaving Carmen Miranda with the other two men.

They walked back out to Isham Street and climbed a hill, Valentín wearing Holden's holster cup inside his pants. This was one of the Cuban hillbillies Edmundo couldn't dislodge? Valentín had tiny hands. He walked with a nervous shuffle. He had razor cuts along his neck. A scar ran down his lips like a burn of white skin.

"Can I help you?" Holden asked. He didn't know what to say to a bandit who might have been starving to death on Isham Street.

What could Carmen Miranda do for him? The hillbillies didn't even have a stove with their mattresses. "Valentín, I could give you a bonus."

"What kind of bonus?" Valentín stared at Holden with watery green eyes.

"An apartment with a fridge. Spending money. The best clothes you ever saw."

"Like this," Valentin said, touching Holden's sleeve.

"If you want. I have my own tailor."

"And how many I have to kill?"

"I never said kill. I need information. Nothing against your comrades, understand? I wouldn't expect you to rat on Big Balls. Valentín, am I clear? A simple deal. Why does Huevo want me dead?"

"I can tell you without a refrigerator. He doesn't like you, señor. He thinks you're a *puta* and a *cabrón*. He says you look ridiculous in your million dollar suits, like a *coño* with a brown tongue. He's very bitter that you murdered Red Mike."

"What's Mikey got to do with him?"

"You are a *hijo bobo*, a very stupid child. Red Mike was trying to stop Edmundo's push into Queens. He met with us two days before he died. Edmundo didn't have to look for a trigger. He had you."

"Why couldn't Huevo have talked to me?"

"He doesn't talk to shits."

And the scrawny bandit stayed quiet as Holden began to brood under the darkened street lamps. "Valentín, I'm not 'Mundo's man."

"*Puta de madre*, yes you are."

They entered Isham Park, and Holden slumped in his clothes, feeling like a brightly colored bird without brains. The black Cuban stopped in front of a bench, away from the lights of the park. A blond man sat on the bench, blond as the Parrot and his mistress, blond as the guy who'd gone after Holden in Paris with a fisherman's claw. Holden wondered if the Bandidos had organized a blond religion.

"Huevo," Valentin said, "I bring you the *puta* from Doña Dolores."

The blond man wore a double-breasted suit that must have been rescued from the Salvation Army's barrels. The skirts of the coat came down to his knees. Lincoln might have worn such a coat in Illinois.

"We didn't invite you," the blond man said. "Why did you come?"

Holden tossed the blond man over the bench. But he didn't turn on Valentín. He wouldn't bump the son of a bitch until he knew him better.

"Call me a *bobo*, I don't care. You're Big Balls, not him."

The blond man sat on the grass and reached into the depths of his coat. But Valentín signaled to him, and the blond man got up, brushed his legs, walked around Holden, and stood against a tree.

"I have to be careful," Valentín said.

"How careful is careful? You're carrying my gun. How did you smuggle the chicken into my office?"

"One of your janitors is part of our family."

"That's how you turned off the sprinklers and meddled with the alarms. Why didn't you just whack me in the head and get it over with?"

"Because in my religion you prepare a man for his death. You have stolen a child from me and you must suffer."

Holden had enough. He could rush the bandit, crack his neck, draw the Beretta from Valentín's pants, and shoot the blond man between the eyes. It wouldn't have been difficult. He'd have gotten Big Balls off his back and closed the case. But he couldn't do it. He felt a kinship with the little bastard. Perhaps it had something to do with Red Mike.

"Huevo, was the Parrot your people?"

"No."

"Then how did he get the little girl?"

"By thievery. Someone paid him and his *puta* to hold her for us, because we couldn't attend to her while we ran from 'Mundo."

"But they weren't such terrific parents. They would have finished me while the girl was under the table. Huevo, she would have seen the blood."

"It couldn't be helped. 'Mundo was murdering all my god-mothers."

"Then what is she to you?"

"She is family, and family does not concern *coños* and *putas de madre.*"

"I didn't plan for her to be there. Why punish me for what was no more than an accident?"

"We do not believe in accidents. Every life, señor, has its own string. And you have caught yourself in the child's string. You cannot wiggle away. And if you could, it doesn't matter. Because we cannot take her back. Not now."

Holden smiled. "It's not so clever to kill her guardian."

Valentín fingered the scar on his lips. "Maybe. Maybe not."

"And you're the one who told her not to talk about her dad . . . she's your secret agent."

"Señor, she is a child. And you must not discuss her motives."

"Then bump me, Huevo. This is your park. You own the grass. You own the trees."

"I am not inclined to hurt you tonight. But soon we will want the child. After we finish with 'Mundo. And then I will kill you. Because you have meddled in our religion . . . and you will strangle on my string."

He returned the holster to Holden and left the park with his blond companion. And Holden had to laugh that such an army of *bobos* would molest La Familia, which had eaten blood during the Bay of Pigs and gathered around Don Edmundo for twenty-five years.

He sat on Huevo's bench in the middle of Isham Park, with the moon in the trees. Small armies of young men bopped around him in the dark. They cursed and spat, but they didn't interfere with Holden.

"*Tío,*" they said, mistaking him for some lost uncle, a *bobo* who sat under the moon. And he was a *bobo*, because he'd come to El Norte and learnt so little. All he had was memories of Carmen Miranda.

13 HE DIDN'T SEARCH for Harrington's car. He took Broadway and traveled down Manhattan's spine, walked the length of the island like a man who'd never been to New York, followed a long line of Latino lights. Men and women sat outside *marketas* at three in the morning. A boy serenaded him with a mandolin. A baby girl sang to him from a window. "*Tío, tío.*" He was Uncle Holden, whose future was stuffed inside a chicken's neck. But Broadway wasn't like the dead boulevards of Queens, where pizza parlors closed at ten. He'd come off the prairies nineteen years ago.

He got to Oliver Street around five A.M., his head beating with Cuban coffee he'd drunk along the way. He could still hear the boy's mandolin. He didn't plan to wake Mrs. Howard. But he had to tell her about his meet with the lord of Isham Park. El Señor Huevo–Valentín. He'd sleep on the couch until seven or so, and then he'd look for the coffee pot and surprise Mrs. H. with breakfast, like he'd done as a boy in his father's house, when he'd sneak into their room, catch Loretta in her nightgown, with one nipple out, while his daddy snored, his arms around Loretta. The old man wasn't angry then. That sourness fell off his face. Holden Sr. had his heaven.

Holden got up at a quarter to eight and found the coffee pot. He loaded Loretta's grinder with beans, turned it on, and the grinder squealed at him. He worried that the noise would draw Loretta out of bed. She'd scold him for breaking into her kitchen. He measured the coffee like a rich merchant and packed it into the pot. Holden was rich. But he'd lost his appetite for money after the twig left him. He didn't even have a summer cottage. He had a hundred suits, lightweight, washable, silk, rayon, and winter wool. But the suits gave Goldie pleasure, the suits were Goldie's dream. Holden was like a mannequin with moveable arms.

He set out the milk to boil. He broke the muffins gently with his hands and lay them in the oven. He squeezed orange juice for Loretta and the leopard girl. *"Tío,"* he muttered to himself, preparing two trays. He didn't have to bump. He could have been a short-order man at one of the fur market's famous delicatessens.

He danced into Loretta's room with both trays. She was lying on the floor. Her eyes seemed to be searching the walls. She wasn't even undressed. She had her holster on. Her face was clawed. There were holes in her chest. Holden couldn't help think of the design: her blouse had become a crab of blood. He looked at her with a little bit of wonder and started to cry. Holden never cried. His father had beaten him. Friends had beaten him at school. Holden never cried.

He sat on the floor next to her, touched the marks on her face. It was Cuban work. The Marielitos. But it didn't make sense. They'd gotten close enough to scratch her and she'd never drawn her gun. She wouldn't have invited strangers into the house.

He picked up her head and put it in his lap. "Mama," he said. He'd never called her that. And Loretta wouldn't have allowed it. She was his father's whore for a while. That's all she'd say about her career with the Holdens. But in his child's fantasy she wasn't one more woman in a line of bitches. She was Loretta, the sexy mom he intended to marry.

Holden rose up on his knees in a panic. He'd left a little girl in the house. *"Querida,"* he shouted, *"venga aquí."*

But his shouts were futile. Wouldn't Santa Barbara have protected Mrs. H. if she could? He rushed into every room, whacking at the furniture, probing the little girl's dolls. It seemed monstrous to him now that he'd courted Fay, gone to recitals, made love in the toilet, under the windowsill, near the fridge, and never bothered to see Loretta and the girl.

Love always fucks my head, he muttered. Makes me into a pig. But how could he have saved Loretta if he'd been around? She'd opened the door to one of Holden's friends. Why? His bumper's instinct had failed him. Nothing would come. He called his mortician, Saxe & Son.

"I don't want to speak to one of Bernie's partners," he said. "I want Bern . . . tell him it's Holden." He waited until Bernhard Saxe Sr. got on the phone. Holden had been dealing with Bern for seventeen years. Saxe & Son were morticians to the mob. They'd held a franchise with Murder, Inc. But the firm never talked of its clients, present or past. And what good was it to know about bandits and bumpers of fifty years ago? That was like cowboys and Indians, a kid's game.

"Bern, I have a package that can't wait."

And Saxe arrived on Oliver Street with one junior partner and his undertaker's wagon. He was a conservative man with little knots of hair inside his ears. He'd dealt with Mrs. Howard on Holden's business, and he understood what that beautiful black woman with arthritis had meant to him. Loretta's murderer might have also been his client, but that didn't keep him from mourning with Holden.

"A terrible thing, a tragedy. I was talking to her last week. Whoever did it ought to lose his eyes and ears . . . Holden, should I send the bill to Aladdin?"

"Put it on my account. I'd rather not have a bill like that in Aladdin's books. I want prayers sung for her. But no flowers."

"And next of kin? We could make up a memorial card. Something very smart and simple. A notice that she passed away."

But Holden couldn't even tell if she had brothers, sisters, sons in some manger. "Bern, I'd rather not dig . . . as quiet as possible, okay?"

"It's done," the mortician said, clapping his hands. He draped a sheet over Mrs. Howard and began to put her on a stretcher. But Holden got in the way.

"I'll carry her," he said. He lifted Mrs. Howard and brought her out to the truck. She wasn't heavy in Holden's arms. He'd carried dead people before and had struggled under their weight. He'd almost gotten a hernia carrying his dad down Muriel's stairs.

"Bern, I don't have to tell you . . . this is not to circulate."

"Holden," the mortician said, pulling at a knot in his ear. "Do you want a stone with a Star of David?"

"She wasn't Jewish."

Saxe frowned for the first time. "It's quiet in the Sephardic cemetery. Less questions asked."

"But her name has to be on the stone. I don't want you picking something out of your undertaker's book."

"Initials," the mortician said. "No names. Someone's always getting nosy."

"All right, initials. And say, 'Beloved of father and son.' "

Saxe took off in his truck. Holden returned to the house. He went in to gather his file cards, but the files were gone. All he had were the cards in his pocket about the Bandidos and their gods. He didn't even have the current phone numbers of his rats. Most of his secret service had been in Mrs. Howard's drawers.

He could have taken the little girl's dolls, but they wouldn't bring luck without the girl. And he didn't need mementos of Mrs. Howard. He'd have her perfume in his nostrils for the rest of his life.

Holden marched to Hester Street. The six Chinese seamstresses sat bent over their machines. Holden could have been a shadow to them, a nonmaterial thing. They never looked up from the garments they stitched for Goldie. And Holden wandered in to see his tailor.

The maestro stooped over the plans for a suede coat. He had pins
in his mouth. He'd gone completely out of this world. He wasn't like
Nick Tiel who tailored for the love of money and the original touch
of his designs. Goldie took more delight in his counterfeit suits than
Nick could ever know. He looked up from the suede to see that
darkness Holden had, like a trigger that had gone off inside Holden's
body. "What happened?"

"Mrs. Howard's dead . . . and whoever killed her took the little
girl."

"When?"

"I'm not sure. I've been delinquent, Goldie. You heard about
the fire at Aladdin. I moved out . . . with Abruzzi's daughter-in-law.
Mrs. H. was wearing her holster when she died. She never even
pulled out her gun. She had to have let the bumper in. And there
are only two men she'd have invited into the house. Gottlieb and
you."

Holden heard a cackle come out of the tailor. "Well, you can
always cancel me and the girls in the front room would never notice."

"Are you my *tío* or not?"

"What does that mean?"

"Have you been fucking around all these years, dressing me up
like Doug Jr. while you monitored me for the Swiss?"

"And suppose I did? Does that make me a killer? Mrs. Howard
was the love of your father's life."

"That's why she'd have let you in without a thought. Goldie,
who has the girl?"

"My guess? The Swiss."

"He's in Paris humping my wife."

"You only think he is," Goldie said. "He still has his throne at
Aladdin. Infante and the Cubans sit at his feet."

"And you?"

"I'm part of the enterprise. A little part. I always was. Jesus,
Holden. Me and your dad started out with the Swiss during the
goddamn war. He was practically our teacher."

"Arts and archives," Holden said.

"He ran the show. The generals were scared to meddle with him. He was trading masterpieces with Goering's people. The Nazis wanted to invite him to Berlin."

"And what did you get out of it?"

"Don't knock the Swiss. He taught me how to forge. Half the masterpieces in our collection we created ourselves."

"And my dad got stuck in shit."

"He was careless," Goldie said. "He began boasting to a couple of the ladies about our exploits. And he wanted to give a phony Rembrandt to some bitch in Verona. We'd have all been guillotined."

"So you saved your ass and sent my dad into exile."

Goldie chewed on a pin. "Didn't we bring him out of Avignon? Got him papers and a new name."

"And who was he before he was Holden?"

"Does it matter?" Goldie said. "He's Holden and you're Holden."

"And Swiss had Mrs. Howard bumped."

"I'm not sure of that. It's a guess."

"That's why you came along with me to Red Mike's . . . you were Swiss' back-up man."

The tailor stuck out his throat. "Go on. Finish me if you believe that. The Swisser was behaving a little funny. The whole thing stank. You and Mike were almost twins. And Mike was a chivalrous son of a bitch. He took the daughter-in-law, big deal. He might have slept with her if she'd been willing. But he wouldn't have forced himself on Fay. And he had enough sense to keep his brothers quiet. Swiss could have gotten to Mike, negotiated with him. But he sent you, knowing it was a point of honor between friends. I didn't like it, Holden. That's why I came along . . . and you'd better return the bundle."

"What for? Rex doesn't seem to miss her much."

"I wasn't thinking of Rex. I was thinking of his dad, the D.A. Paul wants to wear a judge's gown. He's not going to take kindly to a scandal in his own house. First the daughter gets kidnapped, then she goes to the bumper who grabbed her from Mike. And he's dreaming of a highchair on the State Supreme Court."

"Fuck him and his highchair. It was political, Goldie. Edmundo was moving his betting parlors into Queens. Mikey stood in the way. And I'd swear the 'judge' was taking Cuban money."

"What makes you think that?"

"Paul's a clever bastard. The future was with Edmundo, not a family nobody wanted. But you still haven't told me how my dad got to be called Holden."

"It was the name of a character in a book. We had to call him something. Swiss decided on it. He was always reading. But it's not your problem. You were born with that name."

"Yeah, I'm a Swiss fable."

"You are not. You're your father's son."

"And who was my father? Swiss invented him, like he invented me."

"Don't say that. Swiss was very fond of your dad. He loved him in a fashion, like his very own child."

"That's the point, Goldie. My father stayed a child. Did Swiss ever advance him? He died a chauffeur."

"He was content. He never complained to me."

"Yeah, but you didn't live with him. Goldie, ever see my father smile?"

"The man was a little gloomy, so what?"

"Gloomy? You stole his name. He couldn't tell who he was. He drank, he whored a lot. He always had his bitches. He fucked up the one good thing in his life. Loretta."

Goldie gnawed at his own teeth. "His life was regrettable, so you think I killed your dad. I threw him down the stairs at Muriel's? I gave him the push?"

"It's worse than that. He didn't need you to throw him down the stairs. That would have been a kindness. You and Swiss created a chauffeur called Holden. He didn't exist."

And Holden left the tailor, who'd been more of a dad to him than his own dead father, who'd dressed him, taught him the art of color schemes in clothes, how to eat among civilized men, how to clean a gun . . . He called Harrington from a public phone. Harrington didn't pick up. It had never happened before. That yellow-faced man would sit in his garage, waiting for Holden's call.

Holden took a cab out to Brooklyn. He knew the script, but he had to make sure. He got off near Atlantic Avenue and hiked over to Harrington's garage on Boerum Place. The limo had been waxed by Harrington's own hand. It stood like a kind of extraordinary ship. Holden found Harrington in the trunk, with a bullet behind his ear.

"Ah, Jesus," Holden said. He called Saxe & Son. Bern arrived with a different wagon. "I'm sorry, Holden." That's all he said. There was no talk of payments. Bern disappeared with Harrington's body, wrapped in a painter's cloth.

Holden could have driven away in the limousine. But it was Harrington's car. He took a cab to Chelsea, got out, circled the block, and darted upstairs to his mattress pad. Fay was at the door, with agony in her eye. "Where were you?"

"I couldn't call."

"It's like Michael. You come, you go, and you worry your women to death."

"I couldn't call."

"I made dinner, breakfast, lunch, and had to sit staring at the food like an idiot, thinking you'd come if only I cared enough."

"Fay, we have to move."

"What?" she said, whipping at her hair until Holden, with all his regret, and with murder on his mind, wanted to make love to her, not on the bed, where they'd linger for an hour, but with Fay against the wall, arching her back, while he climbed against her shoulder and she scratched the wall.

"It's not safe here . . . two of my people got killed. What happened to the gun I gave you?"

"I forgot to wear it," she said.

The bumper couldn't help himself. He slapped Fay. It had the violence of a kiss. She didn't move. "I'll take you home," he said. "It's better."

"No," she said. She found the holster and put it on.

"Fay . . ."

"Shut up. We have to move."

She packed her things and Holden grabbed the suitcase, marched out with her, and locked the door. She looked at him. "You left a closet full of clothes."

They took three cabs and ended up on the other side of the seminary, a block from where they'd begun. She didn't ask him about the ritual of that ride. She could have charted it on a curve, the paranoid loops of a gunman. The longer the ride, the nearer the destination. That was the logarithm of Holden's life.

His new apartment was exactly like the old. A couch, a bed, a kitchen table, a VCR. All she had to do was stand in the middle of the room, and the apartment was hers.

"I missed you, Sidney. Lie down with me a little."

"Can't," he said.

"I could take off your clothes."

"I wouldn't let you."

"What if I pulled out the gun I'm wearing?"

"That wouldn't work. I know you'd never shoot. Look, if I'm not back in forty-eight hours, get into a cab and run uptown. Understand?"

"Yes, I hear you, Sidney."

She fiddled with his scalp. She went under his holster, inside his shirt. She was crazy about Holden. She'd lied to him, of course. Michael had made love to her. But if she hadn't got used to his wildness that week in the bungalow colony, his long silences, his gentle way with his brothers and with her, she wouldn't be here with Holden.

He turned her to the wall, hugged her like a delicate ape.

He was lost without Loretta. Could barely make a fist. He was like an infant gone out into the world. He went to Muriel's, marched up the stairs. The debutantes sat in a corner. It was a slow time of day.

Muriel's eyes had little moons in them. The moons weren't for Holden.

"Where's Gottlieb?"

"He took a leave of absence."

"Mind if I look?"

He searched in all the closets. Gottlieb had emptied his bureau. The kid must have gone to Singapore. But Holden discovered Rex coming down the stairs. The playwright was wearing one of Muriel's best silk robes. The robe was ridiculously small. His genitals hung out. Holden grabbed the giant, pinched his face until Rex's lips made a sucking sound.

"Aren't you going to ask me about your wife?"

Rex's mouth stretched like a horrible mask across his face. The giant began to shiver. Holden stopped pinching his cheeks.

"Don't you ever touch me again."

"Why? Going to tell your dad?"

"Listen to me, Holden. Forget about Fay. She always comes back. She's been having a breakdown for years."

Muriel arrived with a pocket pistol, a silver Le Francais that could have shot his eyes out. "Holden, you're disturbing one of my clients."

"Where's your loyalty? I have longer standing in this house."

"Not any more. Holden, you're not welcome."

He didn't care if the bitch was Annie Oakley. He plucked the silver gun out of her hand and hurled Muriel across the room. The debutantes fell on Holden. Begging and screaming, they knocked him to the floor. He had to crawl out from under their thighs.

He got to the street with his jacket hiked up above his shoulders like a humpbacked clown. Six men were waiting for him. They weren't bumpers he could recognize. Their suits had come from a suburban mall. One of them wore pink socks. "How are you, lovey?"

Shooters from Chicago wouldn't dress like that. They were some kind of gang from Queens. Now he remembered. They wore prairie clothes.

A Cadillac stood at the curb, a sleek black job, good for a

civilian general. Had Fortune 500 come after Holden with goons in pasty pants?

They shoved him into the car. Holden landed on the floor, near the polished brown shoes of the Queens district attorney.

Paul Abruzzi patted the cushions and smiled. "Hello Holden. Be a good boy and sit down."

14

THEY DROVE across the Fifty-ninth Street bridge in Abruzzi's Cadillac. Holden's brains weren't right. Should have figured that the goons were from the district attorney's own detective squad. He was prince of the city, their Paul. He went to the opera with his voluptuous daughter-in-law. He spoke at bar mitzvahs, weddings, and in front of the bishop of Queens. He was more popular than any politician. He rode out of the Criminal Court Building in Kew Gardens and made war on mobster families. He was merciless. His own Fay had been captured in the fight. He could have run for governor, but he preferred a nice, safe seat on the bench. He was a widower, and he didn't intend to marry again. Holden understood. He didn't like to go to the opera without Fay.

They brought him to a shack in St. John's Cemetery. It had one comfortable chair, for the D.A. Holden had to sit on his fists.

"I'll be blunt," Abruzzi said. "I didn't mind a little fling with Fay. She's a stormy woman. And my son hasn't been much of a husband to her. I let you have your games. But it's time to give her back."

"It's too late, Paul. I'm in love with her."

The detectives bunched around Holden and banged him with
their shoulders.

"Send them away, Paul. We're having a discussion."

"Get out," Abruzzi said, and the six detectives moved over to
the door.

"Paul, the best woman my father ever had is killed. My chauffeur is killed. Muriel gives me a funeral face. Why?"

"You were getting too popular. This town doesn't like bumpers
who are on the hit parade."

"But who put me there? I had your consent to get Fay and deal
with the Pinzolo brothers."

"There was nothing on paper," Abruzzi said. "I didn't sign a
death warrant."

"It comes to the same thing. I couldn't have gone into the
Rockaways without a nod from you."

"You could still be hit with a homicide rap. Infante's not going
to save you."

"I'll get another lawyer and subpoena your ass . . . Paul, you're
a son of a bitch. You draw Red Mike into your own web. Why would
he have figured on Fay unless you made it clear that she was your
prize? Who the hell would kidnap a district attorney's daughter-in-
law?"

"You're sick, Holden. And I'm taking you off the street."

"Handcuff me," Holden said. "I'd love to wear your cuffs. You
can make the arrest yourself . . . are you going to kill me on the way
to Kew Gardens?"

"You're really disturbed. I could have you committed, Holden.
I know a couple of doctors who'd declare you insane."

"That's even better. I'll have time to write my memoirs in the
crazy house. It will have Edmundo on the first page. I'll tell how you
let the Cubans into Queens. Isn't that what your feud with the
Pinzolos is all about? Cuban money under the table."

Abruzzi rose up from his chair to punch Holden, while the
six detectives held Holden's arms. "Don't you ever call me a thief.
This is a cemetery, Holden. Or haven't you noticed? Think of the

reputations my boys could make. They'll tell their grandchildren how they took out the lights of the great desperado as he was trying to threaten the district attorney."

He punched Holden again.

"Fay might not stick to that story . . . if she loves me enough," Holden said.

His nose began to bleed.

Abruzzi pointed to the detective with the pink socks. "Go on, Dimitrios. Wipe him. I can't stand to look at all that blood."

Dimitrios held his handkerchief to Holden's nose.

"Get smart," Abruzzi said. "I'm the last ally you have left. I can deputize you, give you a little work, and no one would ever dare harm you . . . just send Fay to me."

"I can't," Holden said, with the handkerchief against his nose. "When I'm in love I'm in love. She can still go to the opera with you and all that. But she has to live with me."

Abruzzi sat down again. "You're a bumper. You couldn't hold her very long."

"Then what are you worried about?"

Abruzzi laughed with his detectives around him. "The man is silly in the head . . . take his shooter and let him go."

"I have a carry permit, Paul. It's a licensed gun."

"Take his shooter, I said."

Dimitrios took Holden's gun with the same bloody handkerchief. Then Abruzzi and the six detectives walked out of the shack. And Holden had to climb across that cemetery all by himself. He wondered if Saxe & Son did any business at St. John's. He got to Metropolitan Avenue and found a gypsy cab. His nose was still bleeding.

He slept with Fay that night, held her, listened to her breathe, and started to prowl at four A.M. He tore a Beretta Minx out of a hole behind the tub, where it had been wrapped in an oily rag, toyed with the gun, because he didn't have Goldie to fix it, and went back to

sleep. Fay undid his turban after breakfast while Holden sat in front
of the mirror. He had a purple dent over his eye where Carmen's
hammer fell. He couldn't afford to wear a turban out on a kill. That
white hat made him too much of a target. Even with a purple dent,
he was just another man. But a whole city could recognize him in
a turban like that.

"Dear," he said, buttering his after-breakfast toast. "I met with
Paul yesterday. He misses going to the opera with you."

"Paul loves the ballet."

"Well, you don't have to give the old man up on my account.
Call him. But not from here. And don't let him bring you back to
Chelsea. If it's Lincoln Center or something, you get on a bus. You
ride ten blocks. Then you get off and wait for me. I'll bring you
home."

"Sidney," she laughed. "It'd hardly worth it. I mean, I admire
Paul . . . he's been good to me. But I can't turn every little occasion
into a nine-hour marathon. He's only my father-in-law."

"He likes you," Holden said. "Meet with him . . . next week."

"What about us? I want to go to the ballet with you."

"We can't sit in public together. It could get you killed."

"Then it's breakfasts and baths and late night films on the
video. Sidney, what happened?"

"I lost my base and I have to get it back."

"That tells me everything," she said. "You're as devious as
Michael."

"Don't mention Red Mike. It hurts."

"Then what should we talk about? *Destry Rides Again?*"

Holden had a dream of the future. Fay would become another
twig, a woman who could twist his insides with a couple of words.
She followed him to the window. "I didn't mean it, darling . . .
Sidney, I have an uncontrollable tongue. I never used it on Michael.
I didn't have the chance. But that's why Rex ran away from me. He
couldn't write at home. He had to take an office. And once it
happened, we didn't have much of a marriage. He'd wander from
one whorehouse to the next . . . he couldn't even stand a proper

affair. I know Rex. It would have been like taking a second wife. But it's peculiar. He can't write a line without being married. It comforts him, the idea of having a wife. He loves our daughters, Sidney, but fatherhood doesn't turn him on."

Holden climbed into his pants. He searched the house for a holster cup that would go with the Beretta Minx. He wore a charcoal blazer.

"You're not even listening," she said.

"I heard. Rex can't survive without a wife, but the wife has to be far away. I'm different."

"Then trust me. Tell me why when we had to move we moved around the corner?"

"Because," he said. "No one would expect you to move around the corner. They'd think you'd gone to Italy . . . or Siam. That would be the logic of a move. Or maybe into another borough. No one would tour a neighborhood twice if they figured you were far away."

His bumper's logic had returned. Gottlieb was still in town. The kid would feint, leave a lot of smoke, but he was married to Manhattan. Holden kissed his darling goodbye. She clutched at his charcoal blazer.

"What would happen if my father-in-law kidnapped me after the ballet?"

"I'd get you back," he said.

"Suppose I didn't want to come. Suppose I was tired of having husbands. Suppose I wanted a life of my own."

"Then I'd have to convince you," he said.

And he was gone. Fay saw the charcoal wash into the hall. He was like a phantom, Holden. But sweet. She felt like some prehistoric crust that had attached itself to his rhythm. It was his eyes. She'd been in a trance when he shot Michael. It was finished before she could open her mouth. But he didn't have mean little eyes. They didn't tighten with each blow of the gun. He seemed as startled as Fay herself, astonished that Michael, Eddie, and the Rat should fall. He didn't covet her nakedness, compare her tits with every other woman in the neighborhood of Brooklyn and Queens. She'd missed

Michael, yowled inside her head, felt sorry for the Rat who would have given up whatever fortune he had for a feel of her, but it was as if her memory had gone, not with the pistol blows that rattled the windows, not with Michael so instantly dead, but with Holden's eyes, beseeching her, like that poem out of the sixteenth century she remembered from her survey course at Swarthmore.

"Come live with me and be my love . . ."

Now, twenty years away from her professor's dull reading, his idiotic, sentimental drone, she understood the poem. Her college had to come from a corpse.

He was worried about the gun. Because what if Paul lent it to the Cubans, and La Familia shot up some Bandidos in one of their wars, and ballistics could prove the bullets had come from Holden's gun? Holden would get his ass kicked by the cops. And so he stood in a booth on West Twenty-eighth Street and dialed the district attorney's office.

"Paul Abruzzi please."

"Mr. Abruzzi's in conference," the clerk said. "Who's calling?"

"Danford Cohen. Mr. Sidney Holden is my client."

"Hold the wire."

Holden had to wait a couple of minutes but Abruzzi took the call.

"Yes. This is Paul Abruzzi."

Holden disguised his voice as little as he could. Goldie had taught him that trick, not to overplay. Holden discovered the world at Goldie's knee. "Hello. Dan Cohen here."

"What firm are you with?"

"Geist and Cohen. We're entertainment lawyers."

"I don't understand," Abruzzi said.

"We're negotiating the rights to Mr. Holden's life story. We've been talking to De Niro. We're hoping he'll play Sidney."

"Who's Sidney?"

"Holden, sir. He asked me to call. We'll need a release."

"For what?"

"That marvelous scene in the graveyard. Our guys are writing it in."

"Is Holden around? I mean Sidney . . . is he there?"

"Just a moment." And Holden handed the phone to himself. "How are you, Paul?"

"Holden, what the hell is going on?"

"Congratulate me, Paul. I'm getting rich. Hollywood is going to do my life story. They have crazy guys out there. They were looking for a bumper to reveal his life. And you know how it is. With all that publicity about the kidnapping, the guys got to me."

"Did Fay put you up to this? Is it Fay's idea? She and Rex used to run with a gang of Hollywood producers."

"No it wasn't Fay."

"How come you didn't mention it when I saw you?"

"I had no reason to mention it . . . until you took my gun."

"So it's funny business, huh?"

"Call it whatever you like. But have your boy Dimitrios meet me at Thirtieth and Tenth in half an hour with my gun."

"Pretty sure of yourself, aren't you, Holden? What if he doesn't show?"

"He'll show."

"How do you expect him to make Manhattan in half an hour?"

"You've got a siren on your pretty car. Let him use it . . . and if the gun's been fired, Paul, you're in deep shit."

Holden left the booth, swiveling with his eyes, because he had no sense of camaraderie out on the street. He was a bumper without expectations. He approached the fur market, walked into his bank, went down to the vault, took his safety-deposit box into a closet, opened the lid. All his cash was gone. Swiss had a key to the box. The money came from Holden's corporate account. Any of Aladdin's officers could have captured the box. He returned it to the vault manager. The Swiss had left him without money, without wheels, without Loretta and an avenue to his rats.

He strolled toward the river and into another bank, where he

kept a box under the name of Whitey Lockman, a ballplayer his
father had loved. Whitey Lockman had a social security number, an
address (one of Holden's mattress pads), and filed his tax returns.
Holden removed twenty thousand from the box in hundred-dollar
bills. Then he marched out of the vault to meet the district attorney's man, that detective in pink socks.

He stood in a hallway at Thirtieth Street until he noticed the
Cadillac with Dimitrios inside. The Cadillac stopped at the corner.
Holden leapt out and knocked on Dimitrios' window. Dimitrios
opened the door. He was a fleshy man with thick fingers. He handed
Holden an envelope.

"Did you have fun with my shooter?" Holden asked.

"What are you talking about?"

"How many shots did ballistics fire into their cotton box? I'll
bet Paul had a hard-on when he looked at my bullets under the
scope?"

"He never touched your lousy gun. Paul's a prince. He wouldn't
dirty himself with a bumper like you."

Dimitrios drove off and Holden went into a diner on Tenth,
where the waiters left him alone. He took his Beretta out of the
envelope, checked the serial numbers, and sniffed the barrel. It was
a tainted gun, wiped and cleaned by the district attorney. Paul had
Holden's "prints" on file, the particular grooves each of his bullets
made. He drank a cup of coffee, stripped the gun, and dropped
pieces of his Beretta into different garbage pails. Only a god like
Changó could reassemble that gun.

He went into a hobby shop on Thirty-ninth. The owner, an
Iranian Jew, often supplied him with props. Holden paid a thousand
for a hot detective's shield and a Ku Klux Klan mask.

"Fardel, I want your book."

The hobby-shop man avoided Holden's eyes. "What book?"

"On every four-star male clinic in town."

"Holden, I haven't compiled such a book.

It was Gottlieb who'd told him about Fardel's talents as an
encyclopedist. But Fardel hated to part with his specialty items.

They were for his Iranian friends. "Fardel, I could put on the mask, shoot your eyes out, and who would ever know? Klan masks are pretty common on Times Square."

He put his Beretta Minx next to Fardel's eye. Fardel gave him the list. It was a one-page address book of the most exclusive male bordellos in town, not baths, or nightclubs and waterfront bars, not hotels, or the interiors of restaurants, but houses like Muriel had, where a man could keep his own "chicken" for a month.

"Fardel, give me your key. Can't have you calling those clinics the second I'm gone."

Holden carried a chair into the toilet, tied Fardel to the chair, sealed his mouth with tape, shut him in the toilet, fashioned a sign that said CLOSED FOR THE DAY, put it in the window, and locked the store.

He'd have to get lucky to catch the kid. Because if he mooned around too long in each bordello, one would warn the other. And Gottlieb might really be in Singapore.

The first bordello Holden visited called itself a psychotherapy center. Holden used the badge to get in. The boss of the therapists knew more about the police than Holden did. But Holden still had the badge. He didn't find Gottlieb in the therapy rooms. The place was deserted. Holden apologized and ran.

He had a big fight with husky men at the second "clinic." But he managed to peek into every room. He discovered more beautiful women than he'd ever met at Muriel's. The third clinic was run by a woman who looked like the Duchess of Windsor. Holden couldn't take his eyes off her. Goldie had divulged the story of the duke and the duchess. Holden's hero had been King Edward, who'd given up his titles, his moneys, his land, and the throne of England to marry an American bitch. He'd served out his life as a duke. Goldie had recited Edward's abdication speech, and Holden remembered the lines about a king who couldn't sit without the woman he loved. She'd been divorced, and the Brits wouldn't have her as their queen. Goldie was on the king's side. "Bloody aristocrats," he'd said. "Serves them right. Edward's always been my king. The house has fallen since that man. It'll never be the same at the old castle."

And Holden stared at the duchess' twin. "What squad are you with?" she asked.

"I'm with the IAD," he said. "We think one of our detectives is honeymooning upstairs."

"But you don't have a warrant."

"I'd rather not deal with a formal complaint. It might be bad for business."

"Can you tell me who you're looking for?"

Holden started up the stairs, considering that king who'd lived in exile with his lady. Holden agreed with Edward in matters of love. He'd have kissed twenty thrones goodbye for the twig. And twenty more at least for Fay.

He couldn't find Gottlieb.

He was sick of showing a badge and giving explanations. He arrived at the fourth brothel wearing his mask. It was a townhouse in the West Eighties. He herded everyone on the ground floor into a closet. "Just scream," he said, "and see what you'll get."

Gottlieb was in the attic with a soldier. The soldier was neither handsome nor tall. He shivered a lot and Holden had to wallop him once to keep him quiet. The soldier slept on the floor with a sweet expression.

"Who are you with?" Gottlieb asked. "Who are you with? Don't hurt us. I have money. I'll pay you ten thousand dollars."

"Sweetheart," Holden said under the mask. "You can pay a lot more than that. I know your finances. You have half a million in the bank."

"Holden?" the kid said, staring into the eyes of the mask.

"Who'd you expect? A different bumper?"

Holden took off the mask. The kid was naked. He crept into his underwear.

"Gottlieb, did your new masters tell you I was dumb?"

"What are you talking about?"

"You set up Mrs. Howard. You knocked on her door and let the killer in. You get one answer. Who was it?"

"Jeremías."

"Edmundo's bodyguard? He's infantile. Did he come alone?"

"No. He had a couple of *jíbaros*. Just in case."

"Did you enjoy it, Gottlieb, watching Mrs. Howard die? . . . I asked you a question."

"It had to be done," Gottlieb said, looping the buttons on his shirt. He'd caught the wrong buttonholes. He looked like a scarecrow with his collar incorrect.

"Had to be done, huh?" Holden rearranged Gottlieb, ripped the buttons off his shirt. "Tell me why it had to be done."

"Because of the little girl," Gottlieb said. "The Bandidos consider her some kind of saint . . . I don't know. It's religious shit. Edmundo was worried you'd give her back to Huevo, and he'd have nothing to bargain with."

"Did Goldie tell him that Mrs. Howard had the girl?"

"It wasn't Goldie. It was Nick Tiel."

"Nick? I saved his fucking life."

Gottlieb sat down on the bed. "Holden, I have to say it. You're an asshole. Nick was never on your side."

"And you? I picked you off the street. A kid of fourteen selling himself in Bryant Park for a couple of dollars. You owe me your blood, Gottlieb. What the hell did Edmundo promise you? More money? Jesus, what other kid your age has half a mil?"

"It wasn't money," Gottlieb said.

"Did they threaten you? I'd have fixed it. Why didn't you come to me?"

"I couldn't. You were getting blind . . . a freelancer who walked around in circles and fell into Don Edmundo's pants."

"It was 'Mundo who had you wait outside Mansions and tell me the Bandidos were after my ass."

"Mundo and the Swiss."

"Then they weren't really interested in the Parrot. They knew he was minding the girl for Big Balls."

"No. That was a trick of fate. But they knew about the girl, that she was precious to Huevo. They'd been trying to grab her for a year, but they always missed."

"That's why they killed all the *madrinas* . . . to get the girl. But how did Huevo figure I was the one who took out the Parrot?"

"Come on. It had your trademark. Who else would have gone into the Parrot's apartment without a gun? But that's where it got interesting. Huevo figures you stole the girl for La Familia. He blows up betting parlors like mad, and it bothers Edmundo, because a six-man army ought to retreat. And Huevo is widening the war. Edmundo sends out his spies. But that man was in the dark until you told Nick Tiel. He starts to laugh. 'Perfect,' he says. 'Let Holden keep Santa Barbara.' And he covers Oliver Street, front and back, with an arsenal of Cubans in case Big Balls gets wise to the caper."

"I never saw a Cuban near Loretta's house."

"That's because you're always changing taxi cabs, you can never see what's in front of your nose."

"If 'Mundo had the place surrounded, why'd he have to hit Loretta?"

"He was getting worried. He didn't like you looking for Huevo. If you didn't bump each other, both of you might start to talk. Edmundo took the girl."

"But why'd he have to kill Loretta?"

"Wake up, Holden. She was the one person in the world who was loyal to you. She wouldn't have given up the little goddess."

"Put on a tie," Holden said. "You're going to help me get back the girl."

Gottlieb shoved his head out at Holden. "*Bobo,* finish me here. Because I can't help you."

"You belong to me, kid. I didn't trade you to the Cubans. Where's the girl?"

Gottlieb was silent. Holden twisted the collar of his shirt. "Where is she?"

"With Jeremías. In a house . . ."

"That's kind of you. What house?"

Holden had to twist until Gottlieb got blue in the face. The kid started to cough. "Holden, can't you see why I had to turn? It's dangerous around you. You're like a bomb. You sleep and then you explode."

"The house, Gottlieb, where's the house?"

"In Riverdale. It's a fortress, Holden. You'll never get in."

"Not without you. You're the lucky charm I found in the street."

"And if we produce the miracle, what happens? La Familia is after me for life."

"Then you'd better stick close. I'm all the papa you'll ever have."

15 HOLDEN COULDN'T RUSH up to Riverdale without wheels. He went to Fardel's hobby shop with the kid, let the trader out of the toilet, and bargained with him, while Fardel looked at Gottlieb, searched for signs, because he knew that Holden had been hunting for the kid. But the kid showed nothing. Gottlieb was Holden's rat again. He had the menacing eyes of a street urchin who'd made good. He hadn't grown soft at Muriel's. He could have lived off the rust on a sewer pipe, sold his ass to men and women on social security. Gottlieb didn't care. He'd stroked women with whiskers, men with breasts. He was a little bit in love with Holden, and to Gottlieb that love often felt like hate.

"Come on, Fardel," Holden said. "I don't have time to bargain. Get me a Dodge with good plates."

"It'll cost you double the price. I suffered in that toilet. Somebody's got to pay."

He was performing for the kid. He knew Holden wouldn't harm him in front of Gottlieb. Fardel belonged to Gottlieb's own secret service. Holden could never understand the social customs of Thirty-ninth Street. He was a hick from Queens.

"I want five thousand on deposit, and four hundred a day."

"That's fucking robbery," Holden said.

"It's my rate for people who tie me to toilets."

"Get the car."

Fardel returned with an '86 Dodge.

"Does it have air conditioning?" Holden asked.

Fardel looked at him with disgust. "I don't chisel. I rent deluxe." He handed Holden the car's registration and insurance coupons.

"Fardel, are these papers clean? I don't want to be chased by motorcycle cops. We have important business."

"If they bust you, I'll waive the fee."

"That's generous, Fardel, but if it's a dirty car, you'll remember your sit on the toilet as one of the happiest moment in your life."

"Holden," the kid said, "can't you have a conversation without threatening people?"

"I'll try," Holden said, collecting the car keys. And he took off with Gottlieb in their virgin Dodge. They arrived in Riverdale without a map. And Gottlieb had to recall the route Jeremías had taken with Santa Barbara. They were on a country road that circled around itself, as if it could bite Holden's tail. And he thought of that animal Fay had, with the look-around head. But he'd never been to Riverdale before. He'd never bumped at the edges of the Bronx.

They'd come to Blackstone Avenue. They got out of the car, which overlooked one of La Familia's compounds, not where Don Edmundo lived, but where his vassals were, like Jeremías, the bodyguard who labored at a distance from his lord. Edmundo had to protect Jeremías, keep him from getting kidnapped, because the ransoms he paid for Jeremías were a sickening price.

"Where is she?" Holden asked.

"Jeremias has her in the shed."

The kid pointed to a gardener's shack behind the main house. "Is he nice to her?"

"Jeremías? I don't know. But Edmundo hired a *madrina* for the little goddess. The girl's valuable to them . . . but I did hear her cry for you and Loretta."

A fury rose up in the bumper. He saw black and red. And for a moment he considered pummeling Gottlieb into the ground. But he couldn't get in without the kid. Gottlieb was crucial.

"You'll drive in," Holden said, "and park where they tell you to park."

"I'm seventeen. How the hell could I grab a license?"

"Gottlieb, they're not clever enough to figure that out. You're only one more kid with a Dodge."

"But I've never driven a car."

"You'll have to teach yourself," Holden said. "I can't give you lessons. We don't have the time."

And Holden crept into the trunk. The kid could have locked the trunk and run away, or delivered Holden to Jeremías. Edmundo would have given him a reward, and he'd be rid of Holden, once and for all. But Gottlieb couldn't do it.

He stepped into the car, got behind the wheel, let the Dodge rock like a gigantic cradle, and drove right up to the gate. The sentry saluted him. His name was Punto, and he had a 9 mm automatic wedged into the back of his coat.

"Is Jeremías expecting you?" Punto asked, behind a mouth of gold and silver teeth.

"No. I came on a whim. I want to see *la santita.*"

"It's all right, kid. But I'd better check, or Jeremías will chew my ass."

He dialed from the cordless phone at the gate. "*Si* . . . It's Holden's whore. He invited himself, Jeremías. I think he has a present for *la pequeña* . . . okay . . . okay." Punto got off the phone. "Come on in. You know where she is, eh? Park in front of the little house."

The kid felt like he was driving straight down to the Hudson.

The water was blue-green, like the jackets Holden sometimes wore. "I'm not gonna leave this place alive," Gottlieb said, with his hands on the wheel. An hombre stood in front of the shack, wild as Pancho Villa. One of the good Bandidos, Gottlieb reckoned, the guys who'd remained loyal to La Familia.

Gottlieb parked a piece away from the Bandido, so Holden would have a chance coming out of the trunk. The Bandido winked at him, and Gottlieb went into the shack. The *madrina* stood around with Jeremías, trying to coax the little girl, who sat in the corner with her dolls. And Gottlieb began to remember what he'd done. Knocked on Mrs. Howard's door. Said hi. He'd come with a doll for the little goddess. He played with her, while Mrs. Howard was in her coding room. Then he wandered off, unlocked the back door, returned to chat with Mrs. H., said goodbye to the goddess, kissed her dolls, and Mrs. H. walked him to the front door, while Jeremías and a couple of his Bandidos crept in through the back . . .

"Hello," Jeremías said, "will you talk to *la santita?* We spoil her, but we can't make much of an impression." Jeremías seemed genuinely glum. And what was Gottlieb? The finger man who brought death into the house, death and a doll. He had to force himself to look at the goddess. She was pale, like one of Holden's handkerchiefs. The skin was drawn around her eyes. He'd fingered men and women before Mrs. H., surrendered a couple of Holden's rats to La Familia, gotten them permanently off Loretta's line, because the rats had been a little too valuable, their information a little too correct, and might have compromised Edmundo and Infante. But he'd never had to deal with the residue: a little girl and her dolls.

"*Chica,*" he said, "don't you like your new dad? Jeremías is nice to you. He buys you toys."

"I'm more than nice. Didn't I kidnap Felisa just for her?" he said, pointing to the *madrina,* who looked as unhappy as the girl. But Gottlieb didn't believe it. The godmother had been bought, like the Bandidos and himself. They were all Edmundo's children. Holden too, but he hadn't figured that out. He'd fallen into the scheme of

La Familia, no matter how many bungalows he shot, or rats he had under his control.

The *madrina* had a milky eye. The little goddess was afraid of her. She clung to Gottlieb.

"Is it fair?" Jeremías said. "We exhaust ourselves entertaining her, and *la santita* comes to you. Can I help it if she's a holy girl? The Mariels are crazy about her . . . *santita,* come to Jeremías."

But she wouldn't go near him, and Jeremías was mortified. "You know how much I spent? Gottlieb, she's an expensive baby. She costs me as much as a *putita*. It's humiliating, no? I give and give and give and get nothing back."

He began to rock in front of Gottlieb and the girl. "I—"

Holden arrived in a great blur, like some forest animal, and Jeremías' eyes bulged as he was caught in the middle of his dance when Holden socked him in the throat. He crumpled to the floor, coughed, and started to cry. The little goddess rushed at Holden, but Gottlieb held her.

"You can't come in, Holden. This is my house," Jeremías said.

Holden lifted him up. "You should have thought about that, Jeremías, when you visited Oliver Street."

"I didn't visit. Your whore let me in."

"It amounts to the same thing," the bumper said and broke Jeremías' neck. The *madrina* pounced on him with a knife. He stepped out of her path and dug his hand into the shelf between her eyes. She collapsed with a hissing sound.

"Dada," the little goddess said, breaking out of Gottlieb's grip and grabbing Holden's leg.

"I'm your *tío*," he told her. "Nothing more."

"Dada."

"Holden," Gottlieb said. "Jeremías is finished, but the *madrina* is a little alive."

"Gottlieb, I didn't ask for a body count. Let's go."

They crept out of the shack. Pancho Villa lay with his head in the grass. Holden carried the girl into the trunk with him, and Gottlieb steered the Dodge up to the gate.

"Did you have a good time?" Punto said, but he didn't open the gate. He pressed the buttons on his phone. "I have to get Jeremías. That's the law at this estate . . . hello . . . hello?" And suddenly Holden was behind him, slapping Punto's head with the cordless phone.

"Gottlieb, open the gate."

And they drove off with the bumper behind the wheel.

They stopped in El Norte. Holden went looking for Dolores while Gottlieb sat in the car with Santa Barbara. But Dolores' sewing shop was gone. Gypsies sat inside the window, beckoning to Holden. He drove around the block to Isham Street. But there wasn't a body or a mattress in Dolores' mattress pad. Holden wondered if the *madrina* and her favorite godson staged their seances in different parts of town.

He drove to Chelsea. Gottlieb had to suck in his bowels, because he still believed Holden meant to kill him.

"Do you have a pad?" Holden asked. "Someplace where the Cubans won't find you."

"I'll get one."

Holden slapped a key into the kid's hand. "It's a storefront on White Street. A few blocks from the river. You can't miss it. It's got black window blinds. You stay there. It's equipped. I'll come and collect you."

"Where does the girl go?"

"With Fay and me," Holden said.

"The Abruzzi bitch."

"What about it?"

"Nothing," Gottlieb said.

"It doesn't feel like nothing on your face."

Better walk, Gottlieb muttered to himself. The bumper's letting you break free. But like an imbecile he had to prove to Holden his worth as a rat.

"She's Paul's girl."

"I know that. The district attorney's daughter-in-law."

"I didn't say daughter-in-law, did I?"

Holden's temples tightened into a pyramid. He sat the little girl in the car, so she couldn't listen. "What did you say?"

"Paul's been jobbing the bitch."

"Stop it," Holden said. "That's like incest."

"Almost."

He touched the kid, not to menace him, but as if to reassure himself with the feel of flesh. "How did you know about them?"

"Holden, I'm your rat . . . but it wasn't such a secret. Mikey knew. He wanted to hit Abruzzi where it hurts."

"They were having a number, Paul and Fay?"

"The old man was crazy about her. That's why he couldn't run for another office. The pols would have crucified him with the tale of his daughter-in-law. Holden, he went everywhere with her. He kept a room at the Algonquin . . . for him and Fay. I saw them kissing at some government ball."

"What were you doing there?"

"I was with Edmundo. A thousand-dollar-a-plate deal. And Abruzzi was behind the curtain, with his silver hair in her neck."

"He stole her from his own son?"

"Rex doesn't give a damn. He's into his plays and Muriel's girls. He's a real collector."

"And I was in the dark about the whole shebang."

"You're too busy bumping, Holden, that's your problem. You're always making plans."

"But I had a goddamn intelligence team," Holden said. "You ran it with Loretta."

"I can't give you everything. It would have clogged the pipes."

"Who told you not to tell me about Paul and Fay?"

"Infante. You wouldn't have gone to fetch the bitch if you'd known about her and Abruzzi."

"All right, it's established. Paul kissed Fay behind the curtain. But why does Infante send me to tickle his wife?"

"Shit, Holden, I'm not sure."

"But that can't be a bigger secret than a district attorney and his daughter-in-law. You have to have some opinion on the subject."

"He hates you, I think. Because you're private, like your dad."

"You never met my dad," Holden said.

"But Infante did. He's setting you up for a long-range kill. But I could be wrong. Infante never trusted me much. Maybe he figured I'd always be your rat."

Holden marched up the stairs with Santa Barbara. He'd have to get her a new set of dolls. But he couldn't concentrate. He imagined Paul Abruzzi hugging Fay. Holden didn't have silver hair, like the district attorney. And suddenly Paul didn't seem old or out of fashion in his undertaker's suit. A distinguished gentleman. Mature. And Holden was a boy clutching his own death certificate. His color schemes weren't right. He should have gone around in black or gray, wearing a mourner's melody.

His darling was at the door. She'd heard him twist his key in the lock. Her eyes went from Holden to the little girl. She didn't seem surprised at Holden's gift. He might just as well have brought a poodle.

"Barbara," Holden said. "Meet Barbara. She's a friend I have to guard."

His darling took to the girl. Holden wouldn't have to worry about two women fighting behind his tail.

"Have you eaten yet?"

"No. I had to get her out of a jam."

And Fay prepared some tortellini in a red sauce. It was Red Mike's favorite dish. Mike was a genius at cooking all kinds of noodles. Holden sulked at the table while the leopard girl gobbled with a pair of forks. His darling sat with a glass of wine, her skirts bunched around her thighs.

"Sidney, your hand is shaking."

"It's been a rough afternoon. I had to sock a whole lot of people."

"I'm sorry," she said.

"There's nothing to be sorry about. I got Barbara back."

They finished eating, and Fay put the girl to bed in a cot.

"Dolls," Holden said. "We have to get her dolls and lollipops."

"What's wrong?"

"I heard something. About you and Paul."

"Sidney, don't duel with me, please. What did you hear?"

"That you kissed him at a banquet, at a government ball. That he kept a room for you at the Algonquin. That you married Rex and made love to his dad."

"It's not as—"

"Did you kiss him behind the curtain, or not?"

"Is that all you care about? The yes or no of a kiss?"

"Well, it'd be a start. I'd have a piece of information."

"Yes. I kissed him behind the curtain."

"At a thousand-dollar-a-plate dinner? In front of all the pols?"

"I can't say who was watching, and I don't care. We kissed."

"And that's why Paul grabbed me off the street. It wasn't politics and it wasn't ballet. He wanted you."

"It doesn't matter what he wants. I'm here. With you."

"But I'm not your black knight. And I never played chess. I know Paul. He'll try to get me bumped."

"He wouldn't dare."

"Dare? He's the district attorney. He can dare day and night. How did it start? . . . you and him?"

"I told you. We went to the ballet. He'd lost his wife. He was lonely. Rex wasn't around. Paul was gentle with me. We didn't kiss for months and months. He barely held my hand. We'd talk for hours . . . and then he kissed me one night. He was trembling. It was like his body had started to scream. I'd never sensed that in a man. And I didn't care if he was my father-in-law or not."

"How long did it go on?"

"Years," she said.

It was like Carmen's hammer all over again, a knock in the head. "Years?" And Holden had a thought. "Did Red Mike ever see you and Paul together?"

"Once. At a restaurant in Brooklyn. Gage & Tollner. Paul liked

it because it was near the federal courthouse. And Michael came in.
He stopped at the table and looked at me . . . that's all."

"And that look cost him his life," Holden said.

"I couldn't stop him from looking, Sidney."

"It's like a big ballet. And Paul is the director of it, moving
bodies everywhere. Some of the bodies are alive and some are dead."

"But I didn't ask Michael to pull me into his car and ride me
out of Manhattan under a rug. I was going to my dentist, for God's
sake."

"But tell me, dear. Did you look back at Michael in the restaurant?"

"A little. He brought me a flower from another table. He
smiled. That was it."

"Jesus. I can't say who was the trigger and who was the gun.
Paul has to get rid of Mike, because Mike is a threat to the Cuban
machine. He can arrest the simple son of a bitch, but Mike would
go to his lawyers and dance right out of court. So he picks at Mike's
family, gets him mad, and what else can Mike do? He's probably half
in love with you by now . . . what kind of flower was it at the
restaurant? A white rose?"

"It could have been. I can't remember."

"You remember," Holden said.

"Yes. It was a white rose."

"I grew up with Mike. I know his habits. He wouldn't go
courting without a white rose."

Holden turned silent and the telephone rang. The bell startled
him, because this telephone wasn't meant to ring. He'd installed it
under the name of Lucky Jack Lohrke, another ballplayer his father
had loved. Fay went to the phone.

"Don't touch it," he said. "Let it ring."

"Suppose it's important. Life and death."

"It doesn't matter. Let it ring."

They sat there while the bell sounded ten or eleven times. "Fay,
did you give the number to anybody? I mean, the butcher, or
somebody like that."

She wouldn't answer him. The phone stopped ringing and started again. Holden felt trapped by the bell. It could have been the noise of his own existence. He picked up the receiver. "Hello?"

He heard that familiar static of France.

"Holden, are you there? . . . don't play possum. This is costing me money."

"I wouldn't irritate your pocketbook, Swiss. How are you?"

"That's not the question. You've been doing damage, Holden. I don't think we can afford you much longer."

"It's funny, Swiss. I was thinking the same about you."

"I'm quite sure of that. But you're a little leaguer, Holden. You have no sense of structure without us. Aladdin made you."

"I made Aladdin too. How did you get my number, Swiss?"

"Who else would have a listing under Lucky Jack Lohrke? Your father worked for me, Holden. I haven't forgotten any of his passions. Baseball. Women. Wine. You've disturbed our Cuban friends. That wasn't nice."

"Swiss, I'll be flying to Paris one day soon. Watch for me."

"I will. But before you get to Paris, I'd like you to sit down with Don Edmundo."

"Why? So he can turn me into cat food."

"Don't be morbid, Holden. Meet with him. At the office. Bring a dozen bodyguards. 'Mundo doesn't mind. Tomorrow, Holden. Tomorrow at ten."

And the Swisser rang off, leaving Holden as he always did, with a dead wire in his hand.

Oyá

16 HOLDEN BROUGHT the leopard girl under his own blanket, and she slept with him and Fay. He could have gone with them to another mattress pad, but the telephone would ring, and he'd have to chat with Swiss in the middle of the night. He put a couch in front of the door, screwed down the window guards, and got into bed with his Beretta Minx.

He woke to the clutter of Santa Barbara in the kitchen with his darling. They were frying bacon together, singing songs like a couple of grandmas who'd been together fifty years. It's women, Holden muttered. They get along without men. All he needed was Andrushka on the other side of the kitchen table, and he'd have a regular chorus.

The two women insisted that he eat in bed.

"Hey, hey, I'm on the go."

But they wrestled him into the blankets and Holden started to laugh until he remembered Paul Abruzzi. His face went dark. He felt miserable. His darling was everybody's catch, like some chicken of the sea. He chewed his breakfast, watched the two women, got into one of Goldie's velvet jobs, and then decided to dress Santa Barbara and bring her to his office. She was safe around Holden. How could he trust that darling of his after what he'd learned about Paul? He stood near the door, kissed Fay and hugged her, his jaw twitching half the time.

"When will I see you, Holden?" she asked.

His name sounded broken to him, after she'd started calling him Sidney. But he didn't answer. He walked down the stairs with Santa Barbara and traveled north to the fur market. Aladdin was filled with Edmundo's men. They picked their teeth around the nailers and cutters, stared at Nick Tiel's dummies, but they all turned to look at Holden and the *santita*. Some strange carpenters were with them, wearing blue hats and pants rolled up to their knees; not one carpenter had socks or shoes that matched. They were sanding the edges of an enormous wooden box. Holden had never seen a crate like that at Aladdin. It could have housed oranges, furs, or a dead man.

The carpenters were shy around the *santita*. They took off their hats. But she wouldn't flirt with them. She held Holden's hand. He went into his office and waited with the *santita*. Don Edmundo knocked on Holden's door and wouldn't come in until Holden said so. The Batista babies had unbelievable manners. They were grandees in a fur market that thrived on oils and fats and specific delicatessens. Edmundo didn't have Holden's tailor, but he liked to wear suits from Saville Row. He was bald, with a big round head. He'd earned his bones at the Bay of Pigs, the mysterious soldier who sat in Castro's jails until he was ransomed with American medical supplies.

"Ah, you brought the *santita*," Don Edmundo said. "That's kind."

"She's not for you."

"But I could steal her, Holden. What would ever stop me?"

"Swiss. He said I could bring as many bodyguards as I wanted."

"So she's your bodyguard. You've chosen well . . . I have no need for her now."

"Why's that, 'Mundo? You went to an awful lot of bother killing someone I loved to get the little girl."

The grandee blew on his fingers, opened the door, and pointed to the carpenters and the wooden box. "Have a look, Holden . . . come on." Holden walked out among the carpenters, who shoved back the lid of the box. Huevo was lying in a bed of straw. La Familia had built him his own manger. He had marks under his eyes. His lips were puffy. It seemed to Holden that someone had taken a bite out of his face.

"It's finished," Edmundo said. "Our game with Big Balls. He got careless. He abandoned all his nests and went looking for the *santita* in Riverdale. But he wasn't as lucky as you. He got lost with a hook in his head."

Holden felt a body flit around his arm. Santa Barbara had come out of his office. She had to stand on her toes to see inside the box. There was no alarm in her eyes, no loss. The man in the manger could have been a shipment of minks.

He returned to the office with the little girl. It was Holden who raged, who wanted to hurl Edmundo into the straw. "Beautiful. My stepmother gets killed, you grab the *santita*, and Huevo falls into your lap."

"Stepmother?" the grandee said. "I never knew your dad had married Mrs. Howard."

"They didn't have to marry. She was around long enough to qualify."

"But I didn't ask Jeremías to hurt Mrs. Howard. Only to take the *santita.*"

"You're a liar," Holden said.

Edmundo scratched his chin. "I could have your tongue cut off. But I like you. I always did. That's the reason you're still alive. You remind me of a monk. You have your craft . . . and no family, nothing."

"Your whole family stinks," Holden said.

Edmundo scratched and scratched until his jaw turned red. "Yes, I had the woman killed. And your Brooklyn chauffeur. And Jeremías marked her face, so you'd think the Marielitas had done the job. But I told Jeremías it was futile. You'd smell Gottlieb behind it. And I took a risk. Because Gottlieb was a perfect spy. But now he's not so perfect and he'll have to suffer."

"You didn't want the Parrot, did you?"

"What? We were talking about your whore."

"Someone must have tipped you that the Parrot was holding the little girl. And you had me grab her for you, like some kind of a dummy. You knew Huevo would come after me, and that was good for business, because he wouldn't burn so many of your betting parlors. You were hoping I'd bump him in the end. But it didn't happen."

"Holden, I would never have trusted the *santita* with you. She was much too important. And a man like you has to see conspiracies everywhere he goes. It's your craft, and your craft is killing you. But you took Jeremías, and I have to get even. Give me your whore, and everything will be all right between us, Holden. I have to have him. As payment for Jeremías. How can I let Jeremías go unavenged like a dog? He was with me twenty-five years."

"You can't have Gottlieb. He belongs to me."

"But he's worthless. He betrayed you, Holden."

"It doesn't matter. Gottlieb is mine."

"I'll catch him," Edmundo said. "You don't gain by not giving him up. And what should I tell my family? That the paradise man would rather die than be without his whore? They won't consider it funny. Holden, I cried when I saw what you did to Jeremías' neck. When Big Balls kidnapped him, I paid whatever was asked. I can't desert him only because he's dead. If you're not a gentleman, it's out of my hands."

The grandee called in his men. Tridents dropped out of their sleeves, silver prongs, like the haberdashery of a pirate. All Holden could think about were the scratches on Mrs. Howard's face. He felt a fist tighten in his hand. He'd forgotten about the *santita*. She whirled in front of him, faced Edmundo's men, hissed in that Creole tongue of hers, shut her eyes, and the Bandidos grew forlorn.

Edmundo appealed to one of his lieutenants, called Arthur, a grandee like himself, who hadn't come out of Mariel with a flotilla of convicts. "Arthur, she's just a little girl . . . what can she do to us? Take her from Holden."

Arthur moved deeper into Holden's office, and Holden had his chance. He grabbed one of the tridents and tickled Arthur's throat with a silver prong. " 'Mundo, I want you and your army out of my life."

"Let Arthur go."

"And I get a hook in the head, like Big Balls. No thanks. I'll kill him first."

"What will you accomplish? If you hurt him, Holden, my men will hurt you."

"I'm not so sure of that. They're in love with the *santita*."

The little girl swayed with her eyes closed, and the Bandidos began to shiver. Holden had never seen a bunch of murderers behave like that. "*Santita*," they said. She opened her leopard's eyes and the Bandidos marched out of the office, staring at the grandees, who were alone with the bumper and the little girl.

"I could avenge Huevo," Holden said. "I'm wearing the hook . . . get out of my office."

The two grandees left, and Holden had a problem. How could he question a saint? She seemed normal again. A girl in need of a doll. She took Holden's hand. "*Santita*," he said, because he didn't know who she was or where she'd come from. Oyá must have possessed the little girl Holden had found at the Parrot's feet.

La Familia was gone. The murderers and the grandees had fled from Aladdin, with the carpenters and their crate. Holden tossed the trident into a garbage barrel and shoved around Nick Tiel's cutters and nailers with the little girl. The designing room wasn't locked. Holden entered Nick Tiel's little kingdom. Nick was scribbling numbers on a paper sleeve. He hardly noticed the paradise man.

"How are you, Nicky?"

Nick Tiel looked up. His eyes focused on the tiny fist in Holden's hand. "I'm fine, Holden. Fine."

The son of a bitch is still in a designer's dream, Holden muttered to himself. He let go of the *santita*'s fist long enough to gather up Nick's notes. Nick stood in the corner with a crayon in his hand. Holden swiped the paper sleeve. He rolled up Nick's designs and carried them under his arm. "You're out of business, Nick. Swiss has your prelims, but they don't mean all that much. You'll never be able to duplicate what you have in time for the Paris show. You're too fucking meticulous."

Nick Tiel didn't make a move. "Holden, why are you doing this?"

"Nicky, get out of the shit storm you're in. You betrayed me to the Swiss. You told him about the little girl. Why, Nick? I risked my ass pulling you out of a fire. Saved your precious designs. Now I'm keeping them for my own collection."

"You don't have a collection. You're a bumper."

"Maybe I'll go into business with the Greeks."

"They wouldn't touch my work. Infante is their lawyer."

"Then I'll give them to the Swiss' Paris competitors."

"Holden, they'd never live to mount a single coat."

"It doesn't matter to me," Holden said. "I'll have the pleasure of fucking you and Swiss out of the Paris show. And pleasure is all I've got."

"Holden," Nick Tiel said, like the most rational creature in the world. "You'll be fucking yourself. You're still on the payroll."

Holden nickered like a horse. "That's generous of him when he's been pulling all the money out of my money box. I'll use your designs as money . . . Nick, I've been watching over you for years. The Greeks would have busted your skull if not for me. You have Infante. I'm glad. But there'll always be some hungry kid who'll want your paper. You dream a lot, Nick. Your own cutters will steal you blind."

"Holden, I had—"

"Tell it to the Swiss."

Holden walked away with the *santita* and Nick Tiel's designs. He went into the mailroom and pulled an envelope out of his box. It was his salary for the month. Ten thousand and change, after all the deductions. He had a health plan that could hold him in a hospital for years and years without ever having to pay the rent. He had a pension from Aladdin that would let him live out his life at the grandest hotel in Greece, where he'd never bumped a soul. His check was signed by the Swiss, who robbed Holden, payed Holden, and collected Holden's wife. Aladdin had become an empire beyond Holden's measurements and means.

He rocked across Manhattan and arrived at White Street in his fourth taxi cab. His pockets were swollen with change. He allowed the *santita* to tip all the drivers. She was free with Holden's money. The cabbies fell in love with a little girl who counted quarters in their palms. "One, two, five," she said. Holden adored her arithmetic. He'd send her to Bernard Baruch when she was ripe for it.

He tapped on Gottlieb's window. The kid peeked out at Holden from the storefront's black blinds. He looked like he was walking in his sleep. He roused himself and let the bumper in. He kept staring at the *santita.*

"That girl's unlucky, Holden. People start dying around her. Will you drop her off somewhere? Give her to the Bandidos, for God's sake. Let them worship a little."

"Gottlieb, you'll have to get out of here. Edmundo's after you. And the Swiss seems to know an awful lot about my mattress pads."

Gottlieb shrugged, and in spite of money, murder, and all the sexual gambits, he looked like any other seventeen-year-old brat.

"Where should I go? I didn't bring my bank books. And 'Mundo's probably watching all the banks. I'm a pauper again."

Holden handed him five thousand dollars from his personal kitty. "Haven't I supported you?"

"But I had two incomes," Gottlieb said, "when I was 'Mundo's rat."

"That's because you were such a greedy kid. If you hadn't been greedy, we might not have gotten into this mess. Now you'll have to haul your ass back to Bryant Park and hide in the bushes."

"With all the drag queens? I'm too old for that."

"It's your forest, Gottlieb. The Batista babies know uptown and downtown, but they could never get into the riddle of Bryant Park. You'll be all right. You can operate near the library lions. You're my only network."

"How can I help when I don't even have an office?"

"We're wanderers now. Your office is your head . . . and you'll have to keep this for me."

The kid found himself with a bundle in his arms. "What the hell is it?"

"Nick Tiel."

All the sadness went out of Gottlieb's face. "You took his paper? Holden, it's a masterpiece. I'll stuff those sketches into my pants."

"Not your pants," Holden said.

"I'm resourceful," Gottlieb said. "Trust me. I'll build a hole for Nick's paper."

"Where will you live?" Holden asked, alarmed that Gottlieb suddenly seemed so sure of himself.

"Holden, I was born on the street. I'll manage."

"How will I find you?"

"Just come to Bryant Park."

Gottlieb returned Holden's key, clutched Nick Tiel's designs to his chest, and started uptown.

"Wait," Holden said. "We'll share a cab."

"Forget it," the kid shouted from behind his back. "I don't sit in cabs with you, Holden. That's part of my policy. I'm not going to ride in three directions to get to one place. Goodbye. And be careful with that *santita*, huh? She could start growing some very long teeth."

And Gottlieb was gone.

Holden stopped off on Canal Street to buy the girl a doll. It was at a warehouse of stolen merchandise that he liked to visit. It was called Stumfel's and it doubled as an export-import firm. His dad often took him there when Holden was a boy. They'd go searching for a baseball glove and Holden would walk with his dad among a mountain of mitts. The salesman looked as if he'd never come out of the dark. His eyes were greasy, Holden remembered, greasy as Stumfel's walls. And Holden Sr. would say, "Benjamin, I'd like a Bobby Thompson for the kid."

Benjamin would climb up onto that mountain, use the gloves as stairs, whistle to himself, scratch his behind, and bring down a yellow mitt with Bobby Thompson's signature burnt into the skin.

This Benjamin was no longer alive. But the mountains were all in place. Mitts, pajamas, bow ties, dolls . . . Holden searched among the dolls with Barbara and a much younger salesman, whose eyes seemed to scratch at the dark. The salesman brought her dolls that she didn't like. The dolls were enormous. They could have been dressed and designed by Nick Tiel. The salesman kept returning to the mountain for another doll until the *santita* decided to choose for herself. She walked up to the mountain, sang a song in Creole, shut her eyes, and pulled out a doll that was dirty and ragged and without an arm. Its features weren't distinct. The doll could have been a boy, an old man, or a grandma in a pair of pants. Holden understood. She was mourning Huevo with a broken, savage doll.

"How much?" Holden asked.

"Nothing," the salesman said. "That's a throwaway. It's not even supposed to be in our inventory."

And Holden left the warehouse with the *santita* and her doll. They rode for half an hour. The girl loved to change taxi cabs. They walked two blocks to the mattress pad and Holden felt a shiver in his blood. He recognized Paul Abruzzi's Cadillac across the street from the pad. He was dizzy with anger and dread. The *santita* held him tight. Holden waited, waited, like a shy, shivering dog. He wanted to howl at the moon, but there was no moon. He'd arrived at his pad in the middle of the day.

His darling waltzed down the stairs. Fay had become her own leopard girl. Her calves held a sudden power. She could have bought and sold Manhattan with her stride. Abruzzi's man, fat Dimitrios, got out of the Cadillac and opened the back door. Holden watched the red smear of her mouth as she climbed into the Cadillac. She hadn't worn lipstick with Holden or Red Mike.

The Cadillac drove along the seminary's north wall and disappeared. Holden stood with the *santita*.

17 HE COULD HAVE GONE up to the Algonquin, found Paul Abruzzi's love nest, and bumped the D.A. and his daughter-in-law. Holden didn't care. He'd have gone to court, danced before the judge in Goldie's finest wool, and told the jury how he'd killed for love. They'd declare him insane. Bumpers weren't supposed to fall in love. He'd probably get a mattress at Bellevue. He'd sit for a couple of years, enjoy the scenery, and survive his fortieth birthday. He'd borrow some yellow candles, have a little party, invite all the bumpers to Bellevue. But he couldn't afford to sit too long without the *santita*. Who would buy her dolls and help her brush her teeth?

She cooked him a crazy omelette with spices that couldn't have come from the mattress pad. She must have gone shopping with Fay. She drank wine with Holden, sang to her injured doll, groomed his silly features, until Holden felt that Huevo was here with him in Chelsea.

And then his darling returned. Her mouth wasn't smeared with red any more. She'd wiped the lipstick from her face. The *santita* jumped up to show her the doll. And Holden wanted to leap out the window. He knew she'd been with Paul.

"Had to go out," she said, staring at the *santita*'s strange doll. "My heel broke. I was at the shoemaker's and—"

"You were with Paul. I saw you get into the Cadillac."

Her eyes seemed to explode like a gigantic breathless fish. "My heel," she said. "Paul's man took me to the shoemaker."

"That was only the start of the trip." He slapped her in front of the *santita*. She fell down, sat on the floor, her knees wide apart. And Holden despised himself. He'd never slapped a girl at Muriel's. He'd never slapped the twig. And this was the second time he'd slapped Fay.

She stood up and wandered a little. Holden wanted to touch her hair, but he couldn't forget about Paul. "You went up to his room at the Algonquin and you made love with him. Then you took a bath. I can smell the soap."

"I didn't take a bath," she said, blinking as she wandered about Holden's pad.

"You never stopped being his mistress . . . did Paul ask you to seduce Red Mike and me?"

"I loved Michael," she said, and he almost slapped her again.

"You gave Paul this address. That's how the Swisser got to me. Paul's been monitoring my life ever since I took you out of Rockaway. How much is he paying you . . . or are you doing it for love?"

"He said he'd kill you if I didn't come to him."

"So you went up to his room on account of me. That's what I call devotion."

"He begged me," she said. "He wanted to talk."

"Talk about what?" Holden asked. "His son's next play? Mike's insurance policies? Or the shoemaker?"

He shook her so hard, her head whipped around, and she could have been one of the dolls on Stumfel's mountain, a doll that the *santita* might have picked. He let her go.

"We talked about you," she said, with curls in her eye. "He had a thousand ways to have you killed. I let him kiss me."

"Fay," Holden said, "does it always have to be some fucking fable? You're attached to the old man. You're his silver bullet . . . he arranged our romance. He asked you to come to Aladdin. Infante let you into my office. And I was one more piece of furniture you could ruin."

"No," she said. "I loved Michael and I love you."

"But Mike's dead. And Paul has my keys in his pocket."

"He won't harm you now . . . he swore to me. On his life."

"Yeah," Holden said. "As long as you go on being his whore."

"I'm not his whore. He loves me. He always has."

"But I don't want you riding up to the Algonquin in a Cadillac just to save my skin."

"I couldn't refuse him, Sidney."

His legs were in trouble. He thought his ankles would break off after she said Sidney. "Don't call me that. You were with another man."

"I kissed him, Holden, that's all."

"Paul wouldn't have let you go with one kiss."

"It was more than one," she said. He would have strangled her if the *santita* hadn't been around. No. He couldn't have borne it if her face turned blue. He'd rather rush into the toilet and hang himself from the shower curtain. He didn't want to imagine what more than one kiss meant. But his skull beat with questions. Did the D.A. fondle his darling, take off her clothes? Were they standing, sitting, or lying down when they kissed? It was like a goddamn anatomy lesson. Fay's body had become the whole fucking world. And Holden was a kid again, worshipping Loretta's underpants, following her around, dizzy with the smell of her. And now he had this tall blonde darling with the curly hair, and he'd have to give up all her underpants and all her perfumes, because she had her own headquarters at the Algonquin with Paul Abruzzi.

"I'll forget the kisses," he said. "But I'd like to know how Paul got this address."

"I gave it to him."

"Just like that? You called him and said, 'Hey, that bumper from Aladdin is lying low in Chelsea somewhere. He's a little eccentric. When he moves, he moves around the corner.' Is that what you said?"

"No. Paul's a possessive man. I wouldn't go anywhere without giving him my address. He'd have sent all his detectives after you if I didn't tell him where I was."

"How many times have you met him since you've been living here with me?"

"I never counted . . . it could have been five or six. We had lunch. We went to a matinee at Lincoln Center. We—"

"That's enough." Holden searched for the *santita*. He couldn't find her until he realized she was standing next to Fay, with her head in Fay's hip. And he wondered what kind of secrets the two women shared. He pulled the *santita* away.

"You don't have to worry about us. You can go to every matinee in New York. You can live at the Algonquin or in Paul's Cadillac."

He started to leave with the girl. Fay clutched his arm. "Holden, I'm not in love with Paul. He's nice to me."

"And you're nice to him," Holden said. "Too nice." He took the *santita* to the door. She watched Fay with a finger in her mouth and clutched at her doll. And Holden couldn't tell if he had a tiny river goddess on his hands, or just a leopard girl.

"Holden?" he heard Fay ask. "When will you be back?"

But he had nothing to say. Because he was running out of mattress pads. And he was crazy about the blonde bitch, crazy to hug her, crazy to hold her hand. And he wasn't even sure why he preferred Fay's underpants, which weren't so special, or why he had the wish to draw her into the toilet and make love to her while she held the wall.

He went downstairs with the *santita*. He sniffed the street. He didn't have a single holiday left. Or a plan that made sense. Should he confide in his tailor? His tailor had come out of arts and archives with the Swiss. And Holden had been their biggest forgery. The boy with a name picked from a book.

He kept opening and shutting the doors of taxi cabs with the *santita*. He offered the little girl a lunch of lollipops and discharged his fifth cab a couple of doors away from the Algonquin. He decided to watch . . . and wait for Abruzzi. He sat in that Englishman's hotel in his forged English suit with a girl who could have been a bigger forgery than Holden himself. He was on a couch where he could see the elevators without being seen.

The *santita* had a dessert that was two stories high. Holden tasted crushed chocolate and bananas and ice cream. But no matter how hard he dug into the dessert with the Alginquin's silver spoon,

it didn't lose the shape it had, the shape of a chocolate lamp with
dark swollen sides. Holden was like an infant with candy he couldn't
devour. And while he chipped at one side of the dessert with the
santita's help, he noticed a face among all the other faces near the
front desk. It was the twig. He'd come here looking for a district
attorney, hoping to confront Paul, and he found Andrushka. She was
in a silverfox coat Nick Tiel had made for her, and there was a
curious silence in the hotel when Andrushka walked. She was just
as beautiful with all her added weight. And he almost shouted,
Andie, it's me. But he was a bumper and not a clown with a dish
of sculpted chocolate and ice cream. Swiss had sent her. She'd come
to lure Nick Tiel's designs away from Holden. He wondered if she
carried a knitting needle under the coat, like the Parrot's mistress.
He slumped deeper into the couch until Andrushka left the Algonquin. And then he sucked on his own hand.

The leopard girl continued to eat. Holden had half his fist in
his mouth. He should have known that Andrushka would end up in
Swiss' armed camp. He paid for the *santita*'s chocolate paradise and
marched out of the hotel. He went to Bryant Park with the girl. It
was odd to Holden. The park had almost became a country manor
since he'd found Gottlieb in the bushes three years ago with a pack
of lowlifes. The kid had been whoring for nickels and dimes. He slept
with any old man who'd have him, and an occasional woman too.
He had startling eyes, and he wore a ragged brown suit that made
him look like a young seminarian in search of a flock. He was
fourteen, and the apostle to every pusher and transvestite in Bryant
Park. Holden had been on a job. He was following a Greek furrier
with a fondness for boys. The furrier liked to nose around in the
park. His name was Andropolous. His heart was set on Nick Tiel's
designs. He'd been acquiring agents who might corrupt any of the
people close to Nick. And Holden had to stop him. He'd been
circling the park for weeks, studying the terrain, watching Andropolous and that boy in the brown suit. And suddenly he was more
interested in the boy than in the Greek. He could always frighten
a furrier. But it wasn't so easy to recruit the services of a rat. He
waited until he caught Andropolous in the bushes, fondling the boy,

and then he pounced. He slapped the Greek's buttocks in front of the boy.

"Andropolous, it's just a warning. You'll get much worse if you don't lose your appetite for Nick Tiel's paper."

The Greek started to cry. "I hear you, Holden."

"I want you to dismiss every fucking agent you have. If I catch one more snoop on Aladdin's premises, it's the end of the line . . . walk away from here."

The Greek crawled out of the bushes, and Holden was left with that fourteen-year-old boy, who stared up at him as if he were some kind of a god in a dark blazer who paddled people's behinds.

"Kid," Holden said. "From now on you work for me."

"What do I have to do?"

"Never mind that. When it's time to tell, you'll learn."

He took the kid on a sightseeing tour—Holden was touching his usual corners in taxi cabs—and deposited him at Goldie's to be fitted for a suit. He gave the kid a thousand dollars.

Gottlieb pointed to Goldie and whispered in Holden's ear. "Do you want me to kiss the old man?"

"Don't be ridiculous."

He huddled with Goldie, and then decided to leave the kid with one of the madams he knew. Muriel. He never found another kid like that in the bushes. And now the bushes were much too manicured. The park had given up its wild character. A country estate. With book stalls and a little garden restaurant. But he couldn't seem to discover the clientele. There were no squires around. A couple of cops, and a black preacher with a little mob of men. The preacher sang to an empty sky about some fall from paradise.

No one seemed interested in the preacher's songs except the *santita*, who sucked on a lollipop and listened to him with her leopard's eyes. But the *santita* wasn't enough. The preacher drifted off without his little mob of men. And Holden saw Gottlieb appear from behind a tree. He didn't have that high polish he'd picked up at Muriel's. He'd become an urchin. He was as camouflaged as the street.

"What gives?" Holden asked.

"Who knows? I'm trying to build a second career."

"As what?"

"A survivor," Gottlieb said. "You were wrong about Edmundo. His boys have been around with their stinking hooks."

"Then we'll find you another home."

"I don't need another home. The morons never noticed me."

"Well, did you put your ear to the ground? Get any tips?"

"Jesus," Gottlieb said. "I just arrived. But I can tell you one thing. Ditch the *santita*. There's no way you can be anonymous, holding her hand."

"That's not the point. She's my protection. The Bandidos are scared to death of her."

"Shame on you," Gottlieb said. "Hiding behind a little girl . . . Edmundo might not have to depend on his supply of Mariels. He could be interviewing a few other bumpers."

"What other bumpers? He'd have a civil war if somebody touched the *santita.*"

"That somebody wouldn't have to touch. All he'd have to do is steal her from you . . . Holden, I'd better run. I can't afford too much of your company. I have my own life to consider."

Gottlieb returned to his tree. Holden continued downtown. He didn't get into a cab. He was sick of circuitous routes. His fate was buried somewhere at Aladdin.

He entered the fur district. All the Greek cutters stared at him. They knew about his problems. He was a bumper without guarantees. He had no backers now. But they still nodded to Holden. This was the fur market. And there wasn't that much stability behind a mink coat.

Holden arrived at an empty house. Aladdin's big metal door wasn't locked, but the factory was deserted. There were no nailers, cutters, or skins around. Holden stared at Nick Tiel's dummies in the dim light. Nick hadn't gone back to his paper. He'd closed the shop, sent his cutters into early retirement.

Holden locked himself and the *santita* inside his office. He took a bath while the *santita* played with her doll. He'd have to get her some clothes. He heard footsteps on the factory floor.

Holden got out of the tub and grabbed his Beretta Minx. He hid the *santita* under a table. And he had to smile. Would another Holden come for him, the way he'd come for the Parrot, and find a little leopard girl under the table?

He opened the door. A woman stood in the gloom. Andrushka. She'd declare her love to Holden, tell him it was like old times, if he returned Nick Tiel's paper. She couldn't tempt him now. He was in love with that big blonde bitch. But he was still scared to look at Andrushka's face. He'd lived in the same bed with her for two and a half years. He'd fall asleep touching her neck, wake up, listen to her breathe. It mattered to him more than the kisses . . .

Wasn't Andrushka. He recognized the purple streak in Florinda Infante's hair. Hadn't she threatened to come to the office and undress him on the office couch? But he wasn't one of her fat little kings whom she could bully. He'd decide who could undress him and who couldn't. But she didn't have that dazed smile of seduction. He saw worry in her aristocratic face. She didn't have shoes. She must have left them outside the door. She was his own barefoot contessa, an inch taller than Holden. He'd never have gotten into trouble if he didn't like tall women. Wouldn't have married the twig, slept with Florinda, or gotten involved with the district attorney's daughter-in-law.

"Can I come in?" she asked, tentative with Holden for the first time.

"Yes," he said.

"Can't you put that thing away?"

Holden was clutching his Beretta Minx. He shoved it into his pocket and welcomed Florinda into his office.

"Is that the little monster?" she said, looking at the *santita* and the *santita*'s doll. "She caused a whole lot of killing."

"She's a girl," Holden said. "God knows, seven or eight."

"She's still a monster."

"Be friendly," Holden said, "or get the hell out."

"I am friendly," Florinda said. "That's why I'm here . . . Holden, the pack of them are at Mansions, figuring out your fate. I couldn't stomach it."

"Who's at Mansions?"

"My darling husband, with Nick Tiel, Don Edmundo, Andrushka, and Schatz."

"The Swiss is in town?"

"He came with Andrushka. They're sitting at Count Josephus' table, deciding the best way to end your life. It has something to do with a gun. Your gun."

"Did they mention Paul?"

"Paul?" she asked, with thick lines in her head.

"Paul, Paul, the district attorney. He took my shooter, but he gave it back. I checked the serial numbers . . . damn him," Holden said, "he pulled a Swiss. Doing Rembrandts with my gun."

"Holden, will you talk an English I can understand."

"Paul put his gunsmiths to work. He made a double of my shooter. Don't you see? He returned the wrong gun. He can lend my shooter around. Some poor slob gets killed, and they'll look for Holden."

"I still don't understand."

"Paul's playing parlor tricks. He'll dump me in the can whenever he feels like it."

"But why?"

"Because he's partners with Edmundo, and Edmundo's partners with the Swiss. He's also in love with Fay."

"That's nothing new," Florinda said. "He's been crazy about her for years. You're no threat to him. No matter who she's with, she sticks to Paul. It's a cozy combination. The district attorney and his daughter-in-law."

"She once loved Red Mike," he muttered.

"The woman has a Ph.D. What could she have found in Red Mike? He took off her clothes, and she enjoyed it."

"Who's been telling you so much about Red Mike?"

"My husband, that's who."

"He's slippery," Holden said. "He keep asking me to take you to lunch."

"That's because Robert's in love with himself. He calls you his peon. He thinks you're saving me from all the studs in town."

"Wait a minute," Holden said. "He's my lawyer. And who's a peon? I'm vice president."

"So what? You work for Aladdin. And why are we arguing? You're in danger. Let me have the little girl. I'll watch her while you run."

"Not a chance," Holden said. He kissed Florinda on the mouth, touched her purple streak with more love than he could have imagined, because even if she'd set a trap for Holden, she'd come to him alone, she'd risked her long neck, and she'd told him about the abracadabra of Paul Abruzzi's gunsmiths. "Where are you going?" she asked.

"To Mansions," he said.

18 THEY WERE SITTING like lords at some Last Supper, six of them near Mansions' far wall. The count, Nick Tiel, Robert Infante, Swiss, Edmundo, and Andrushka. Holden had come in wearing a cream-colored coat from his closet. His slacks were brown. His tie was made of priceless silk. He looked like a man who was dressed to do damage. He sat across from Andrushka and the five men. He ordered lentil soup for him and the *santita*. He saw Bandidos in the kitchen, rubbing their teeth. His first impulse was that they'd poisoned his soup. But he drank it anyway and asked for a second bowl.

Count Josephus arrived at his table. "How are you, Holden?"

"Good, considering there's a lot of people with murder on their mind. And they happen to be in your restaurant."

"That's because you're a troublesome boy."

"I'm not a boy, count. I've got gray in my hair. And I'm a bumper, like you. But I don't sit in restaurants with kings. And I wouldn't let thugs into my kitchen."

"The old man wants to see you."

"What old man? Swiss? Tell him to come to my table. I'm busy drinking soup."

"Holden, you have business to discuss . . . please."

"After my soup," Holden said, ordering a third bowl. He drank it and then walked over to the Swiss' table with the *santita*. The count provided a chair, and Holden sat with the girl on his lap and her damaged doll.

The Swisser started to laugh. "Holden, forgive me, but that dolly stinks."

"It's meant to stink. It's Huevo, Swiss. That's how a little girl mourns."

"Is she mute?" Schatz asked.

"Not at all. She just doesn't like to talk to shits."

"Keep insulting us," Edmundo said. "You already have a terrific future. And don't forget. Your ex-wife is at the table."

"She's not my ex," Holden said. "She's a bigamist. But it happens I have a lousy lawyer."

"Moron," Infante said, "who's kept you out of jail all these years?" He searched the restaurant with his nose, sniffing for traces of his wife's perfume. "Did anybody see Florinda?"

"I thought you sent her to me, Robert, like you always do."

"Shut him up," Infante said.

"Why?" Edmundo said. "He makes a good parrot. Let him talk. He has one foot in the grave. And the other foot isn't smart enough to know where to land. He's sinking fast, our paradise man."

"Not so fast. I have Nicky's paper . . . right, Nick?"

Nick Tiel blinked, without looking at Holden. He was on his own planet, where patterns could never be made. He couldn't seem to recover from Holden's robbery. Another month, Holden thought. And Swiss would have to put him away.

"Don't exaggerate your bargaining position," Schatz said. "You have the paper, but we still have Nick."

"Try him," Holden said. "See if he can sketch a cuff."

"A temporary crisis," Schatz said. "Nothing more."

"How temporary is temporary?"

"We'd rather not get into that," Schatz said. "We'll give you half a million for all the paper you have on hand."

"Half a million? When your empire is already rotting without Nick. You're a cheapskate, Swiss."

"All right, we won't haggle," Schatz said. "Five million for the sleeves and the cuffs. Is that fair?"

"Yes, Swiss. It's a sweet price. But you can't have the paper. You shouldn't have gotten Mrs. Howard killed. A chauffeur is one thing. But she was family. And that I can't forgive."

"He's suicidal," Infante said.

"No, he's like his dad," Schatz said. "Spirited and dumb . . . the paper's useless to you, Holden. You can't sell it. We'd murder whoever bought it from you. Everybody knows that."

"I don't intend to sell. I'm keeping it . . . for sentimental reasons."

"Then we have no choice," Schatz said. "If we can't have the paper, we'll have you."

"That's pretty good logic, Swiss. But be careful . . . you might get bumped instead."

"Did you hear that?" Infante crowed. "Threatens the man who gave him his living."

"And my name," Holden said. "Tell me, Swiss, who was my dad before you turned him into Holden?"

"Does it matter that much? If I give you the name, do we get the paper?"

"No," Holden said, staring at the twig, who sat in her silverfox coat, and he knew she'd have to come into the calculations somewhere. Schatz was a man who didn't waste moves.

"What if we put Andrushka into the package?" Swiss said.

And Holden smiled. Now he knew they really meant to kill him, because Swiss wouldn't have returned Andrushka for all the cuffs, sleeves, and yolks Nick Tiel had ever designed. But Holden had to enter into the Swisser's little game. "How'd you get her to agree to that?"

"It was easy. She's fond of you. She always wanted to go back to America. She gets lonely in Paris."

"Lonely for what, Swiss?"

"Fifth Avenue. Bendel's. The park."

"And me."

"Something like that," Swiss said.

"Let me hear it from her."

But the twig said nothing. And Holden liked her for that. Loved her, almost. She'd come here in the silverfox coat, sit at the bargaining table, but she wouldn't lie for her old man.

Holden stood up with the *santita*. Andrushka was like a marble mask. He could see the small blue veins in her neck. He'd kissed those veins, felt them beat like a tiny heart.

"Wait," Edmundo said. "You haven't finished with me, Holden . . . you're my property now."

"You have it wrong, 'Mundo. You're the first sucker on my list."

Holden picked up the leopard girl, held her under his arm, with the doll dragging against his stomach, and said to all the magi at the table, "Don't count on Paul. He may have my shooter, but if he fucks me, Swiss, I'll cross counties and sing to the other four D.A.s."

"Hopeless," Infante said. "The man is hopeless. He must enjoy signing his own death certificate."

"Robert," Holden said, reaching out across the table to grab Infante's tie. "Don't talk death certificates. Bump a couple of guys first, and then see how it feels."

The Bandidos came out of the kitchen, looked at Edmundo and the little leopard girl, looked at Holden and the tie in his fist, looked at Andrushka, and returned to the kitchen.

Holden relinquished the tie and left the table. He had to pass a gallery of kings, kings who turned their eyes away from Holden. He walked out onto the street, still hugging the *santita*. And then he saw Billetdoux, the bumper from Marseilles with all the seams in his face, and Holden understood what the Swisser had in mind. Billet stood in front of the restaurant with a pair of twins, the Castiglione brothers, Jean-Paul and Jupe. Holden remembered their histories. The twins had carved up half a hotel in Avignon three years ago, looking for some pathetic local gangster. They were short and mean and wore tropical suits, as if the world only had one season, and all weather began inside the Old Port at Marseilles.

"Billet," Holden said, "I'm disappointed. I figured the Swisser might send you . . . but not with your two chums."

"They're tourists, Holden, that's all. They've never been to America. It's a big thing to them. And what harm can they do? They don't understand a word of English."

"They didn't need English in Avignon."

"Shh," Billet said. "You mustn't anger them. They have no conscience and they have no shame. And they're not booked, Holden. They have an open agenda. They might harm the little girl."

"You shouldn't have said that, Billet. I like you. You saved my ass in Paris."

"I like you too. But I had to bring the Castigliones. Swiss wants his paper back."

"If you touch the girl, you'll have the Bandidos on your back. They consider her a goddess, Billet, a very sacred being."

"I'm used to goddesses," Billet said. "Besides, we'll be in and out. Today it's New York, and tomorrow we're gone. Holden, you can't win. Help yourself. Negotiate with the Swiss."

"Come on. You'd bump me anyway. With or without the paper. That's why those two homicidals are here."

"I have some pull with the old man," Billet said. "He listens to me. Give me the paper, and I'll drive Jupe and Jean-Paul to the airport."

"And then you'd come after me. I know the Swiss. I was valuable to him as long as I didn't hit on a vulnerable spot. Now he'll always have to worry about his Holden . . . I'd hate to bump you, Billet."

"Bump me, kid?" And Billetdoux started to laugh. The seams swelled along his face. "We have you three to one."

"But this is my city. And I have the *santita* on my side."

"I told you. She doesn't belong to our church. She can't melt guns and grenades."

"She doesn't have to melt anything," Holden said, and he shoved around the three men, clutching the *santita*. He would waltz across town, get rid of them one by one, with his fist, his mouth, or his Beretta Minx. He'd deal with the butchers of Marseilles, lead them on a lovely chase in Manhattan. It was like the merry-go-round he remembered from his boyhood on the plains of Queens. He'd ride the same wooden horse with his dad. It was one of Holden Sr.'s rare pleasures. His dad would take him to the amusement park that assembled once a year on an empty lot across the street from Holden's house. He'd climb up on the horse with his dad, turn with the music, and escape the other riders. Women in gaudy gowns. Men in toupees, holding the sides of their heads in that wind the horses made. Kids like Holden, laughing, crying, clutching their moms and dads. And the young dukes of the block, with their hands under a sweetheart's skirt. Holden recalled the length of a thigh, skin so pale against red, red underpants. The girls always seemed to swoon while the horses rocked along their circular path. And Holden had the deep wish that his dad could take the wooden horse out of this narrowing path and into some other merry-go-round, where he and his dad would be the only riders.

He didn't know the Castigliones very well, and he hadn't counted on their lunacies in the middle of Lexington Avenue. Jean-Paul shot him in the side with a little Spanish beauty, an automatic with its own blue muffler. A .22 short. It was as if the bullet had never torn through the cloth of his coat, but simply entered Holden and started to travel. He could feel it twist under his shoulder blade. His knees dropped a little and he felt a band of pain, like a taunt ribbon inside his body.

Jupe got closer to him. But Holden wasn't in some kindergarten class. He swerved away, bumping that mean little man in tropical clothes against the window of a lingerie store. Holden discovered a pair of lace pants that he would have liked to see on his darling. But he couldn't imagine too much. He had a bullet inside him and two homicidals at his back.

He led the *santita* into an atrium that was swollen with plants. The plants were much more spectacular than any tree. He'd entered a jungle between glass cuttings and walls. And those bumpers from Marseilles followed behind him. Billetdoux held back a bit. He was fond of Holden, Holden could tell with that .22 short sitting under his ribs. There was hardly any blood. And Holden didn't have to grab his side. He held the *santita,* because he wouldn't allow Billet's two homicidals to touch the child.

Jupe approached him again, crooning with delight about the hole his brother had made in the paradise man. *"Mon vieux,"* he called Holden. *"Mon vieux."* He had sweat on his lip. His face was square as a box. He could smell the kill. And Holden turned like some extraordinary dancer and punched Jupe between the eyes. It wasn't with his customary force. He was carrying a bullet. But Jupe was stunned. He stood under the glass sky, with his hands in his face, and Holden started to strangle him. Men and women stared at Holden, as if he were part of some mime troupe, performing in the atrium.

"Jupe," Holden whispered, *"je t'aime."*

But that other lout of a brother was nearly upon him, and Holden shoved Jupe into Jean-Paul, and continued down the promenade with the *santita.* His strength was gone. And Holden started to suffer. It wasn't his own death that bothered him. He was lucky he'd survived as long as he did. His bumper's intuition had carried him in and out of dark rooms. He could have been whacked in the head years ago. Some lost, forgotten saint from Avignon, the mistress of a pope, had nourished Holden, watched over his life, blessed him once or twice. But there were limits to what a saint could do. And as he drifted with the bullet, he could no longer protect the leopard girl.

"Barbara," he said. "Run . . . come on," he told her. "Go find Dolores."

But the *santita* wouldn't release his hand. It was all simple to Holden. He'd shoot Jean-Paul with the Beretta Minx, and Billet would have to disappear. Because Billet couldn't afford a wedding with the New York police. And how many more times would Holden have to be shot before he gave Jupe a permanent sore throat? But he had to save the *santita*. He couldn't fall down until he sent her away to that *madrina* in El Norte, the *madrina* who must have raised her.

His eyes darted in his head. He saw Jean-Paul again with that little Spanish shooter. "*Vaya*," he told the leopard girl. Because he intended to blow out Jean-Paul's brains along a promenade that was like an indoor jungle, and he wanted to give her the chance to run. Holden didn't know a thing about the little girl. But he loved her with that crazy animal love of a man who'd been wild all his life.

"Go on," he said. "Do I have to give you a slap?"

She took Holden's fingers and led him through that jungle and back out onto the street. Holden was lost. The bullet in his lining had ruined his sense of direction. The *santita* was his compass. She started to wail in her Creole tongue just as Jupe and Jean-Paul arrived from the atrium. It was a ferocious song. And Holden realized that Oyá, the African goddess, had possessed an ordinary little girl from Queens. The *santita* swayed her hips. And Holden was still alarmed. Because a goddess could go in and out of a girl's body and abandon her to some kind of orphanhood.

They were on Vanderbilt Avenue. Jupe and Jean-Paul were a couple of noses away. The *santita* danced and sang. But she couldn't sing up an army. And Holden would have to find his own dark river in Manhattan. He took out his Beretta Minx and aimed it at Jean-Paul. The twins were furious. They hadn't expected an American bumper to behave like that. Jupe and Jean-Paul stood across the street. And Holden entered the Yale Club with the *santita*. He'd fleeced a couple of businessmen inside that club. The businessmen had gone to law school with Robert Infante. They'd borrowed money from Aladdin and were hoping that a couple of Yalies didn't have to repay an old debt. But they hadn't counted on Holden. Holden trapped them in the toilet. They scribbled checks on the toilet wall. But he hadn't come to collect markers today. He sat on one of the couches near the reception desk. He looked like a Yalie. But his college was Bernard Baruch. His side started to sting.

The doormen were dressed like admirals. Goldie would have admired their blue coats. And Holden had a touch of nostalgia for the Yale Club. He remembered the marble sink in the men's toilet. There were combs on the sink in a jar of pungent blue water. The stalls had doors with wooden slats. There had been nothing like this at Bernard Baruch.

Jupe and Jean-Paul entered the club like a couple of kids from Provence, but they had a problem with the doormen. They couldn't seem to grasp the Yalies' dress code. The twins weren't wearing neckties. They would have shot their way past the doormen if Billet-doux hadn't been behind them. Billet understood the consequences of killing doormen at the Yale Club. So he counseled the twins and also calmed them. But Holden knew it was a question of time. Billet would wait outside the club while the twins went around the block to the nearest haberdashery store.

Holden wondered what species of necktie the twins would wear when they returned to the club. He'd have to give them both a bumper's special between the eyes. But there were too many Yalies in the room. How would Barbara escape if Holden started whacking people?

Barbara grabbed his hand and led him to the telephone booths. She couldn't reach the phone. Holden had to lift her and look for quarters in his pants. Barbara talked into the telephone in that

Creole tongue of hers. She didn't say much. A word or two and she
stared at Holden. "Dada, what's the name of this palace?"

"It's not a palace. It's the Yale Club. On Vanderbilt Avenue.
Used to be a golden address."

"Yale Club," the little girl repeated into the telephone, and
then they returned to the couch. Holden's side was killing him.
Should he sneak the girl into the men's toilet and ambush the twins
from one of the stalls? He wouldn't have felt right taking the *santita*
into a toilet. "Go on," he said. "Hide. Can't you see. The bad boys
are coming."

But she wouldn't hide. Should he give her to one of the doormen as a package to hold? But she'd wind up in some shelter for little
girls. Holden didn't like that. He'd rather keep her and suffer the
consequences. If he stood close enough to the door, he could whack
both homicidals and run. Run where? The bumper could hardly
move. And he had spots in his eyes, like coals on a leopard's back.

Lord, he begged, please don't let me drift. But he couldn't even
tell which Lord he was praying to. His father didn't believe in any
Grand Seigneur. Holden Sr. was a bloody atheist. And Holden
himself never had much use for God. But he prayed.

Lord . . .

And Holden had to smile. Because the Lord had a funny appa-
ratus. Men with white hair had come into the Yale Club, Mariels.
They were impeccable this afternoon. Wore neckties with their
quilted suits. It didn't matter that each Mariel had one brown shoe
and wore glasses with a missing lens. None of them had violated the
club's strict code.

Barbara got off the couch and danced over to the men. And
Holden could afford to dream. Billetdoux wouldn't have messed with
Bandidos inside the Yale Club. The bumper closed his eyes, thinking
of palaces, popes, his darling, and his dada's dead mistress.

Frog

19 FAY DREAMT of red shoes in the window at Fausto Santini. She'd been waltzing down Madison Avenue like a fisherman's wife, searching for shoes. It was almost three months ago. She'd stopped at Vittorio Ricci. But the red was too red, and it didn't match the gown she had to wear at the lieutenant governor's ball. She hadn't been out with her husband in such a long time. She'd forgotten the nature of his eyes. Green, but how green? She'd been hanging around with Paul. And people trembled at the sight of her. Paul Abruzzi's date and daughter-in-law. They held hands at the lieutenant governor's table. And she didn't care what all those assemblyman's wives thought of her. They were frightened of Paul. A district attorney could dig into anyone's past. And she'd come to a den of thieves. Fat wives with jewels on every finger. Hubbies with gold money clips. She drank matzoh-ball soup in the land of beg and borrow. College deans, assemblymen, bankers, crooked lawyers and their cronies would line up and pay homage to Paul. They bent so far, Fay could see their bald spots. They brought her flowers and boxes of Godiva mints.

"Where's the great author?" they asked.

"He's busy," Paul would growl. "Busy writing plays."

People stopped mentioning Rex. And she didn't have to make excuses. She was with Paul in a pair of red shoes from Fausto Santini. She'd stroke his neck while some grubby little man was at Paul's feet, asking for favors. But she didn't love Paul. She admired him, liked him, fed off his power, but she'd never have run away with Paul. She ran away with Sidney . . . to Tenth Avenue. Sidney could shake her blood. He didn't fondle her in Cadillacs, take her to the lieutenant

193

governor's ball, see her in red shoes. Paul liked to belittle Sidney and say, "Sidney's a gentle psychopath. He has no more brains than his dad." But she hadn't been introduced to his dad.

"I knew him," Paul had told her at the lieutenant governor's table. "The man was an ape. He belonged in a textbook on abnormal psychology. The son's like his dad . . . only he's had more of a success. He's good at killing people."

"I care for him," she'd said.

And Paul had slapped her in front of a thousand people. The lieutenant governor's wife peeked out at her from under her husband's armpit. And all the other wives started to sneer. Fay could have written a treatise on assemblymen's wives and the jewelry they wore. The relationship between gold in an ear and the lack of sex. But she wasn't a sociologist any more. She didn't have to weigh lives in terms of silver and gold. She ran from the table and Paul shoved assemblymen aside and followed her to the door.

"You can't go," he said.

"I am going."

He seemed much more passionate than Rex, who liked to slouch in pajamas with a pencil in his hand.

"I won't let you," he said, and he had eyes like a little boy. She could have done anything with Paul, undressed him, sat in his lap, stole his handkerchief, delivered a speech at the lieutenant governor's table about assemblymen's wives and their rubbery tits. But he turned sullen and played district attorney when he should have rubbed and kissed her where he'd slapped her face. "Come back . . . you can't humiliate me like this."

And she walked out on him and went to live with Holden. Holden gave her a pistol to wear. It was the oddest romance, because he was hardly ever around. He could have been fighting in some foreign war. But she was crazy about his silences, because she'd been with men who talked all the time. Rex had courted her with speeches out of Pirandello, until she wondered if she'd married Pirandello's ghost. And Paul had opinions on every ballet in the land. Holden didn't have opinions. He drank in whatever performance she took him to. He dressed like a British lord. Nothing was accented, nothing stood out. His voice was soft. He never shouted.

He had an angular look, like he was searching for something. A pair of red shoes? His mouth was strong. His eyes sat deep in his head. She'd wanted him the moment she saw him in Far Rockaway, in Michael's wretched hut. He'd killed the three bothers as silently as he'd looked at her, without even savoring her breasts. No man had ever sized her up with such polite concentration. Michael's brothers had stared at her bottom, their brains exploding with big ideas.

"Godiva," Michael had called her after his brothers took her clothes. But her hair wasn't long enough to cover her ass. She was settling in with Michael, having a good time, a holiday from her husband and Paul, when Holden arrived like some figure out of Pirandello. Sad and doomed. She could tell he didn't want to kill Mike.

She'd never asked for Holden, and there he was. She'd fallen under his curtain of doom. She belonged to Sidney, not through marriage, not through the shared birth of a child, or the practice of fathers-in-law, but through some elemental song, like a nursery rhyme she might have discovered at three or four. He was her dark, silent partner–prince, her playmate, and it had nothing to do with kissing her, or how practical he was at touching her parts. Michael had driven her insane in that hut. She'd screamed until the walls began to rock like the waves outside her window. She hardly ever screamed with Sidney. But she dug under his arm as if they'd been sleeping together thirty years.

And still she thought of those red shoes. The toes stuck out like a canoe. The heels were thin as wire. She was the tallest cunt at the lieutenant governor's table. She flirted with the politicians, destroyed their wives with the most ordinary smile, because they didn't amount to much with all their silver and gold. And she was Lady Godiva in her red shoes. Poor Michael had guessed right. She was a woman who loved to prance without her clothes. She'd have stood on the table at the lieutenant governor's ball, slapped her hips, and danced with nothing on but her red shoes, and no one would have disturbed her. She'd come with Paul.

Now she was hiding, but she didn't know who she was hiding from. Sidney had told her to shoot if a man or mouse pushed through their door. She understood eating habits in Melanesia, mating in Manhattan among rich and poor, blue-collar crime . . . but she couldn't even say what Sidney had done. She drank soup in his absence. She thought of Michael's brothers staring at her body. She dreamt of red shoes, supposing that if she conjured hard enough, Sidney might appear.

She heard footsteps in the hall. Her first impulse was to darken her eyes for Sidney, so he'd think of her as his own big blonde cat. But she didn't rush into the bathroom for her eyeliner, because it wasn't Sidney's steps she'd heard. She removed the pistol from that leather stocking near her heart, aimed it at the door. Someone knocked. She didn't like the sound of knuckles on wood.

"Who is it?" she asked.

"Paul."

She unlocked the door with her left hand, because anyone could come around and impersonate Paul, and she wasn't taking chances. Paul was astonished to see a pistol in his face. "Did Holden give you that?"

"Yes," she answered, without inviting him inside. "He taught me how to fire. We had target practice in New Jersey."

"Put it away," Paul said. "You don't need a gun. I'm the district attorney."

"But you told me it's dangerous." Every time his chauffeur had come for her, and she'd gone to the Algonquin to visit Paul, he'd said how dangerous it was to live on Tenth Avenue, how she could get swallowed up, or disappear, and he was kissing her all the while he said that, standing in his undershirt at the Algonquin, and she could sniff Eau Sauvage on him, because he had aristocratic tastes for a district attorney, and she didn't trust him on the subject of Sidney Holden.

"It is dangerous. This is Holden's craphouse. And his enemies might mistake you for his new secretary . . . can I come in, or should we have a little chat in front of Holden's neighbors?"

"There aren't any neighbors," she said. "I haven't seen a soul."

But he'd already stepped inside and he took the gun out of her hand and undid that leather stocking as if he were removing her bra. He sat her down at the kitchen table with his Christian Dior perfume and she served him crackers that must have been in storage for a year, because that's how Holden lived, like a man who went from bunker to bunker, and she preferred those crackers to steak au poivre at Mansions or Mortimer's. Paul chewed the crackers. He didn't mention the Algonquin, didn't declare his need for her. He hadn't come to kiss her in his Cadillac.

"Holden," he said. "You can't stay here."

"I don't understand you, Paul."

"He's gone."

"Did you hurt him?"

"I made you a promise. I'd protect your little frog."

"He's not a frog," Fay said, but she understood the world according to a district attorney. Paul would pounce on Sidney soon as he could. But he couldn't pounce and keep her. So he planned Sidney's destruction in his offices, mapped whole routes for getting at Sidney, but the routes were no good, because he couldn't work Fay into his plans.

"You'll have to go back to Rex," he said, like a father-in-law who hadn't dug under her dress in the back seat of his Cadillac.

"I'll wait for Sidney here."

"He's wounded . . ."

"Take me to him."

She clutched at Paul.

"I can't take you," he said. "Holden's with some African priests. They sacrifice chickens, drink the blood."

"You can find anybody, Paul. No one escapes you and your squad."

"We're talking about madmen," he said, "Mariels. They have tattoos inside their mouths. They'll blow your head off if you look at them the wrong way."

She had no idea what Sidney did outside of killing people and collecting bad debts. "What's Sidney doing with Mariels?"

"He was guarding one of their saints."

"Barbara? She's just a little girl. Sidney didn't talk about her much. I thought she was some kind of a niece. She helped me with the cooking. She sang to herself . . ."

It was beginning to start, the nervous chatter that possessed her when she was excited or upset. She'd talk like that in the Cadillac, and Paul must have known that her mind was elsewhere, not with him. "I'm waiting. Sidney will come back."

"I told you. He's gone. And his enemies are prowling all over."

"Then it's simple," she said. "Have one of your detectives sit with me. I'll be safe."

"I can't get involved. I'm not a small-town sheriff." His mouth twisted into a sad grin. "And you're a mother. You have two children at home."

Good old Paul. He couldn't use the children against her. "They're in Arizona," she said. "Adrianne is. I forgot where Tina went."

"They've been home for a month."

"Rex can feed them. We have a maid."

She was the cruel one now. Paul was crazy about the girls. He chauffeured them everywhere in his Cadillac, delivered them to department stores with his siren on, stood them in front of mirrors while he proceeded to buy out the store. It was Paul who dressed them, Paul who took them to the dentist, because he loved them and he had this terrible guilt about his courtship of their mother in the Cadillac.

"If you don't come with me," Paul said, "I'll bring Adrianne and Tina on my next trip to Tenth Avenue. They'll love Sidney. He can take them on target practice, go with them into the woods . . . if he ever comes out of Cuban country alive."

"And what should I tell them about their grandpa? That he paws me in hotel rooms, puts his hand on my ass while we're listening to Beethoven."

His hand started to shake. It wasn't some kind of miserable palsy. It was punishment for loving a woman who couldn't love him back. "Fay," he said, "either you walk with me, or you get carried."

She watched herself in Holden's mirror. Her face curled like an enigmatic cat. And Paul couldn't interpret her looks, even if he'd had all his pathologists in the room.

"Carry me, Paul. Carry me down into the street, shove me into your car and put me under the rug, like Michael did."

"What Michael?"

"Michael. Red Mike."

"I won't discuss that son of a bitch."

"Why not? Sidney thinks you set it up for Michael to kidnap me."

"I don't care what Sidney thinks."

"He says it was your way to get Michael killed."

"He's a psychopath. I could have had Red Mike on my own. Why would I have risked your skin?"

"Because you're always scheming . . . and you hate me almost as much as you love me, Paul."

"I don't hate you," he said. "I don't." She'd complicated his life until he'd arrived at some border he couldn't bear. If he stepped across he'd be in a phantom town, like the Mariels who had her Sidney. He was the chief prosecutor of an enormous village, but he spent his days at the Algonquin, dreaming of her. She started to pack, found her red shoes at the rear of Holden's closet. Party shoes. But she wouldn't be going to another lieutenant governor's ball. She'd felt the language that seemed to loom under the table, like a dry and bitter storm. Paul should have been the next governor. But he'd ruined his chances courting Fay. He'd rather bite her hair in a hotel room than sit in Albany on some wooden throne.

He watched her clothes fly about. Paul could get excited by the cotton engineering of a bra.

"I'm ready," she said, putting on those party shoes.

He looked at her, wondering, she supposed, if it was a trick, a means of seducing him out of Holden's hiding place and locking herself back in. But it wasn't a trick. She left with Paul and didn't even lock the door.

He brought her down into the Cadillac, shoving her suitcase under the jump seat. He signaled to his man, silent Dimitrios, who always drove her to the matinees. And she knew Paul could feel her flesh, her perfume, the polish on her nails and feet, the redness of her shoes, and suddenly, without warning, he held her hand. She didn't resist; they drove uptown like that, the district attorney and his daughter-in-law.

20

"FROG."

Holden stirred. He was on a cot in a room he couldn't recall. He didn't panic. If he'd found a VCR, he would have closed his eyes and considered himself a happy man. He had an ache above his groin. He looked down and saw a black lotion, thick as pudding, on that side of his body where Jean-Paul had shot him in the street. The pudding stank. Holden wasn't lost. He'd taken a holiday among the Mariels. But he still couldn't understand who the hell was calling him Frog.

"Dada. Froggy the Frog."

He searched between his legs and saw those leopard eyes under a table. He wondered about his wound. What if the bullet hadn't stopped twisting yet and couldn't find its home? It was like a satellite that went from station to station in Holden's guts and could trigger little time explosions. He'd come to kill the Parrot again. He'd discovered a leopard girl under the table. He'd brought her to Goldie . . .

"Frog."

"Stop that," he said. Holden started to get up, but the pudding leaked and he lay down again. "Barbara, is that you?"

But those animal eyes crept deeper under the table until Holden saw a darkness he'd been used to all his life. He could have been born under a similar table in Avignon. He was the leopard, not the little girl. He'd stalked from the age of two or three. But he hadn't really become a hunter until he arrived at Aladdin's door. It was his own father he pursued. He'd been weaving designs around Holden Sr. He was the bumper his daddy should have been. His rise to vice president was like some kind of revenge on the house of Holden. No matter what he did, he couldn't get close to his dad.

"*Querida*, come to me."

A voice boomed at him. "She's frightened. You've been saying things in your sleep." Holden was surrounded by flesh. He stared into the tiny, tiny eyes of Huevo's godmother, Dolores, the fat *madrina* who must have applied the pudding to his wound. Dolores occupied half the room. She swayed with a melodic lilt. Holden's Carmen Miranda.

"What did I say in my sleep?"

"Wild things. You asked everybody to call you the Frog. You shouted at the little one. You were merciless with her."

"I'm sorry," Holden said. "I shouldn't have shouted at the girl. I love her."

"I know," Dolores said.

"Where am I?"

"With Changó," she said. "You are in our lord's house."

"But where?"

And the priestess smiled. "He has many houses, Holden. And it's not so gracious to ask. He has tended your wounds. Our lord takes care of melancholy people like yourself."

"I smile when I have to smile," Holden said in his own defense. He looked around for chicken heads, cauldrons, and mounds of rust, but there were no signs of the god. Changó had a cot and a table in his room.

"You must be in mourning," he said to the *madrina*.

She laughed so loud, the table shivered. "Why?" she asked. "Do I look like a melancholy person?"

"You've lost your son."

"I've lost many sons," she said. "And I will lose more."

"I understand. But Huevo. He was—"

"Special to me? Yes, Holden. Like my other godsons. And he was arrogant and foolish. He disobeyed our lord."

"Mother," Holden said, because he didn't know how he ought to address a *madrina*. "Huevo wanted to get the *santita* back from Don Edmundo."

"What *santita* are you saying?"

"The little one," Holden said, "the little one who's under the table."

"She is a girl, señor."

"Then why do all the Mariels piss in their pants when she rolls her eyes at them?"

"Because they are sinners and she has holy powers."

"But where does she come from?"

"She comes from Queens."

"You talk like a district attorney," Holden said. "Mother, I killed a man and his mistress. I slapped them silly and I found a little girl under a table. No one wants to tell me what she was doing there."

"Playing," the *madrina* said.

"Yes, without a mom and dad. And when I asked her, she said you had raised her."

"I?" the *madrina* said, her enormous body tightening into a screw until it looked like Carmen Miranda was about to dance. "I did not raise her."

"Pardon me, but she said Dolores, fat Dolores."

Dolores punched her own chest. "See. I am Chepita. I have a sewing shop and a room for homeless men. I love the saints. And I am in the service of our lord. But I did not raise this child."

"You're Dolores," Holden said. "And you heal gunshot wounds. The homeless men in your room are bandits and bumpers . . . like me. Don Edmundo's been after you for years. But you disappear in thunder and smoke."

"You have the thunder," she said. "I was only a nurse."

Holden felt satisfied. The circuits began to connect. The pudding hardened while he chatted with the *madrina*. "And you were Barbara's nurse."

"For a little while," the madrina said.

"What about her parents?"

Carmen Miranda pulled a bitter face. "Bad people. A barber from Havana and his wife. They were mean to the little one. They lent her out to parties. They forced her to sing in a white dress and wear a bride's veil. Old men put their hands on her, touched her under the dress. The barber hired me to escort his child. He didn't want anyone to steal her. So I became her bodyguard. Because I was the godmother and the friend of Big Balls, Lázaro Rodriquez. And Lázaro was a thief for hire, without a conscience, subhuman, like all the Mariels. Why would Lázaro complain? He was wanted by the police. The barber could have him for a couple of pesos. A convict, Castro's filth. But he was a murderer, Holden, not a pimp. We brought the little one to the party in a truck. It was January, and Lázaro wore a white suit. He loved winter in New York . . ."

The *madrina* was an enchantress, and Holden was like her child. He lay on his cot and listened. Winter, the *madrina* said. The party was in the penthouse of a Cuban lawyer. Lázaro stood in his white suit, a wanted man, among lawyers and doctors who'd never been to jail. They fed him wine and asked him about Taco-Taco and other penitentiaries. Then the little girl sang, clutching candies and flowers and a doll Lázaro had made for her with pieces of wire. She was passed from lawyer to lawyer, like a great stuffed doll, and her

own dolly was lost under the heels of an admirer. The lawyers never
noticed the blue veins in Lázaro's head, where the guards at Taco-
Taco had kicked him for tattooing convicts without paying them
their usual fee. The anger swelled in Lázaro until his skull was like
a dark blue lamp, but he allowed the lawyers to fondle the girl. He
wouldn't interfere. He'd been paid to do a job. He took the girl home
to the barber and his wife, and while the *madrina* watched, he hissed
into their eyes.

"She is not our child," the barber said. "We borrowed her from
an aunt."

And Lázaro had the barber shave his own head and the head
of his wife, then he removed his needle and his dyes from a little
sack and decorated their skulls with a swan, the mark of a child
molester. The barber delivered his savings to Lázaro. "A dowry," he
said. "For little Tita."

"Tita? Was she born with that name?"

The barber shrugged. "I don't know, señor. We called her
Tita."

And he ran to East Miami with his wife. Lázaro had a daughter
all of a sudden. He lodged her with Dolores. "We will call her
Barbara," he said.

Santa Barbara was the Marielito saint, the protector of bumpers
like Big Balls or Holden and Billy the Kid. Whoever was frightened
of thunderstorms or wished for a happy death prayed to Barbara. She
was Changó's Catholic "sister," his womanly side. And the *madrina*
warned Lázaro that he should not burden the little one with Barbara's name, or Changó might grow jealous.

"It will be a secret," Lazaro said.

"But you cannot fool our lord," Dolores told him, while the girl
went to live with the Mariels as Changó's sister saint. She learned
prison songs. She sat down during certain ceremonies, where the
heart was ripped out of a rooster and blood was sprinkled near the
statue of lord Changó, who had a man's shoulders and a woman's
hips, who laughed with his eyes closed, loved to wear bracelets on

his arms and seemed to enjoy the company of little girls. The Bandidos noticed all that. The little girl would sway her hips like Dolores and go into a trance in the middle of a song. And pretty soon she was never absent from a ceremony.

Lázaro made her lots of wire dolls. He put on a disguise and took her to the circus. There were Bandidos in the audience, and they recognized the little girl. They bowed to her ten or fifteen times. They brought her garlands of candy until a fort rose in front of her feet. But Lázaro had to stop attending circuses.

Edmundo's men began slaughtering the *madrinas* around Lázaro. They set fire to Dolores' little estates. And Lázaro had to run from hole to hole. He worried about the little girl. He hid Barbara with families that had nothing to do with the war. And because he'd tempted Changó, the *madrina* said, because he'd mocked their lord by making the little girl into a *santita*, one of the families farmed the girl out to a cousin, and the cousin neglected her, left the *santita* in her apartment with a pair of crooks, the Parrot and his mistress, and it was Holden's luck to find the Parrot with the *santita* under the table.

Lázaro destroyed the family that had rented his child, and he would have destroyed Holden too, but he was concerned that a kind of divinity might be attached to Holden, that Holden was one of Changó's children, because the god was known to have dozens of brats, and a few of them were pink, like Holden, and Lázaro couldn't afford to anger the god, so he tested Holden, taunted him, but he couldn't solve the question of Holden's divinity. And when he met the bumper in El Norte, looked into those wistful eyes, Lázaro was as confused as ever. He went up to Riverdale with Changó's red and white *collares*, certain he had a god's thunder in the firebombs and the pistols under his coat, and landed in a dark field.

"Big Balls," Holden said from his cot. "He had a lot of character, like Red Mike."

"He was a fool," the *madrina* said. "He died chasing Changó's tail. I have met this Red Michael. Another fool."

"Mother, I grew up with Mike. But where did you meet him?"

"In a room."

And Holden remembered the pact Lázaro had made with Red Mike to keep Edmundo out of Queens. And now Edmundo had the borough to himself, with Paul Abruzzi's blessings. And Holden was the monkey who'd murdered Red Mike and led La Familia to Big Balls. His thunder belonged to Aladdin. He was as much of a chauffeur as his dad had ever been.

"What about the little one?" Holden asked. "Will she ever leave her hideout?"

The *madrina* started to coo in that prison patois the Mariels talked among themselves. The *santita* came out from under the table. She was clutching the mutilated doll Holden had gotten for her off Stumfel's mountain.

"Froggy," she said, and Holden frowned.

"All right. I'll make an exception. I'll be your frog."

Had he been dreaming of Avignon? He promised himself that on his next trip to Paris he'd take the bullet train down into Provence and visit that city of popes. But he'd lost his concession in France. Billetdoux would clop him the minute he got off the plane.

"Mother, how long have my lights been out?"

"Which lights?" the *madrina* asked.

"Lights," Holden said. "How long have I been asleep?"

"Eleven days, on and off. We've had to move three times. We're traveling light. Holden, this is all we have."

Dolores pointed to the next room and Holden saw two sickly men whose hair had been dyed white. Living among Mariels, he understood that inventory of white hair. White was one of Changó's primal colors. The white in the eye of a thunderstorm, the red of a rooster's throat. Dolores' last two soldiers wore red shoes. But Holden couldn't stop thinking about white hair. The Parrot and his mistress must have worshipped Changó, with or without *collares*. They couldn't have been complete strangers to that god. Had they appeared at one of Dolores' *revocacions* where Changó was adored with chicken blood? . . . met the *santita* and begun to worship her a little? Dolores would never tell. She didn't like to talk about chicken blood.

"Any messages?" he asked, forgetting that he wasn't on Oliver Street with Loretta Howard.

"One message." And she handed Holden a little pewter animal with its head on backward.

"Where did you get this?"

"From a blonde," the *madrina* said. "She was looking for you. Said she was your sweetheart. But I couldn't take the chance."

"How did she find us?"

"Holden, we found her. She was wandering in one of our alleys. She had no business there. She could have been killed. Is she your sweetheart?"

"Sort of," he said. "Did you tell her I was all right?"

"I said nothing. I couldn't give our position away. It was damaging enough that I accepted this little toy from her. She was an unfortunate woman, speaking so loud, calling you Sidney."

"Is she safe?"

"I don't care. She could have been a decoy."

And the madrina walked into the other room to cheer up her two soldiers. Holden was left with the little girl whose frog he'd become. He'd leapt out of Avignon to live with his dad on the plains of Queens. And he'd have to leap out of here.

"*Querida,*" he whispered, "find my clothes."

But she wouldn't conspire with him. "Froggy," she said. "You're sick. Stay in bed."

He grabbed the pudding above his groin, kicked out his feet, and fell into Avignon. He wasn't a tourist come to suck blood out of a city. He was a kid of three, on a stroll with his dad. A wind blew on his face. The pebbles at his feet were green, yellow, blue. It was like walking on a sea of stones. Avignon was a great picture puzzle. The popes had built a wall around the city to keep out strangers and French kings. But the wall was bitten in a hundred places. Junk and garbage lay outside the city. The French kings had their own castle on a hill across the river, and the kings could spy on the popes. That's what his daddy said. The popes had built a tomb for themselves. The tomb came with a palace. His daddy took him there. The roof was full of points, like a wall wearing a bunch of hats. Animals seemed to pounce from furrows in the wall. They were the stone leopards of Avignon, put into the palace wall to discourage and frighten French kings. Holden asked his daddy what side of the war he was on.

I'm with the kings, his daddy said.

21 HIS CLOTHES WERE GONE. He didn't have his watch or his shooter. The pudding had hardened, and Dolores had to pick at it with her hands. The two soldiers were asleep. He listened to them snore.

"Mother, I have to get out of your inn."

"But how will you fight Edmundo's dogs? You have nothing."

"I'll need a pair of pants."

The *madrina* returned with a pair of red pants. She strung Changó's beads around his neck.

"I'm not a worshiper," he said. "What good will it do?"

"The lord might pity a man with *collares.*"

And the Frog had to rise off his cot in *collares* and red pants. "Mother, please don't lose the girl . . ."

Dolores keened at him with all her flesh. He'd disappointed Carmen Miranda. "I am not in the habit of losing daughters. And she is my daughter now."

"That's true," Holden said, like some philosopher in a dunce cap. Jean-Paul's bullet must have driven the charity out of him. He picked the leopard girl off the ground, hugged her and her doll. It was like having Huevo's image in his hands.

"*Querida,* I'll be back for you."

"Holden," Dolores said. "You shouldn't promise when you have *collares* around your neck."

"Mother," Holden said, kissing Dolores while he held the girl. "I can't become a saint overnight."

And he walked out of the *madrina*'s mattress pad. He had no concept of the neighborhood. It was Queens, that's all he knew. He was familiar with the flatness. Holden hailed a cab. He rode in a rough circle, looking for landmarks. Some candy store he'd broken into with Red Mike? A ballroom where he'd gone dancing with Mike and his brothers, Eddie and the Rat? The shooting range Mike had discovered inside the old Hebrew cemetery? The creek behind the golf club where Eddie and the Rat loved to swim in the raw? But Holden couldn't find any of these stations. The landmarks had disappeared with the brothers themselves.

He'd been sailing across Queens for almost an hour when Holden suddenly remembered his finances. He didn't have a nickel in his pants.

The cabbie took him straight to Hester Street, and Holden had to run inside to borrow sixty dollars from his tailor. The tailor didn't smile when he saw Holden. He looked forlorn, like a man who recognized a cadaver in red pants.

"What's wrong, Goldie? Did Schatz tell you I was out of commission?"

"No," the tailor said. "I knew you were alive. It's your trousers. I didn't think I'd ever see you look like a ponce."

"I get corrupted, Goldie, when I'm away from Hester Street too long. I'll need a Duke of Windsor special."

"Right now?" the tailor said, with a pair of scissors in his hand.

"I'm not greedy," Holden said. "I'll wait."

"I can't cut a suit while you're sitting here."

"I'll take one of your prototypes," Holden said.

The tailor began to squeeze his eyes. He kept his prototypes under key in a closet. They were six suits his own agents had managed to steal from the Duke of Windsor, while Windsor was alive. His agents had gone into hotel rooms in Paris, Monaco, and Cannes, bribed certain night porters, and come away with the suits. There wasn't even a price Goldie could attach to the suits. They were outside anything anyone had to offer. He wouldn't have traded them for the entire wardrobe of Douglas Fairbanks Jr. No one knew of their existence outside Holden and the agents themselves. Half of Holden's suits had come from one of the prototypes. He was exactly the duke's measure. And Goldie could cut a "Windsor" for Holden in a day and a half.

"Will you open your closet? Or do I have to meet with the Swisser's men in rags?"

"You must be having dizzy spells. Swiss' men aren't in a meeting mood." But the tailor opened his closet with a tiny silver key. The Frog felt a pungent odor escape. It was the perfume of a tailor's life. He took out a blue pinstripe Windsor had worn in Cannes and then he turned around and discovered a silk shirt and silk shorts on Goldie's chair, as if some elf had made an offering.

He undressed himself.

Goldie saw the *collares* and the dark little welt above his groin. "You must have had a good surgeon."

"The best."

"Holden, you ought to give Nicky back his paper."

"What would it prove?"

"Lots of things. The Swisser might forgive you."

"No, he wouldn't. It was planned this way. Or he'd never have sent me to bump Red Mike. Goldie, my goose was cooked."

The Frog stepped into his silk shorts and then Goldie took over the job of dressing him. Holden liked the feel of his tailor's hands. He stood in front of the mirror in Windsor's coat.

"Fits like a glove," Goldie said, rummaging among the pairs of shoes he kept around for Holden.

"Goldie, I've been having dreams of Avignon. And it's a laugh.

I see leopards in a wall. How could I have remembered that? I was a pisser the last time I saw Avignon. Two or three."

"I was there once at the end of the war."

"And did you find leopards shooting out of a wall?"

"Leopards? Yes. I think there were leopards."

"Then I didn't make it up. And my father must have told me about the city's stone floor, and the leopards, and a crazy wind."

"The mistral," Goldie said. "People shoot themselves every time it blows."

"But why can't I remember my father telling me? Did somebody make him stop talking about Avignon?"

"Ask the Swiss."

"I might if I could get near him. Goldie, I'll have to ask you. Maybe my dad didn't have such a bad time in Avignon. Was he in exile, Goldie, like you said? Or was he on a caper for you and the Swiss?"

"Jesus," Goldie said, staring at Holden's image in the glass. "For a minute you looked just like the duke."

"I'm not Windsor. I just happen to wear his pants. Goldie, I want to live long enough to learn about my dad. He wasn't hiding in Avignon. He was American. And he was moody. He would have stuck out. You sent him there. Why?"

The tailor touched his chin. "It was the Germans," he said. "They had their own arts and archives section in Avignon. They buried a fortune of paintings under the street. A frog called Deladier worked in that section. He knew where the paintings were buried. Swiss got that from a captured German general. So we sent your father in after the war. A handsome GI. He knew a couple words of French. We got him a cover bride, a lady frog from Avignon, to give him a reason to settle. But your damn father took it seriously. He wasn't supposed to sleep with the bitch. We hired her to walk around Avignon with him and carry a shovel, so he could dig up the streets. But she got big in the belly and couldn't carry a shovel for him. And while she starts to swell, he's out cultivating that frog, Deladier. Buys him drinks, butters him up. And the baby's born.

You. Your father's getting nowhere. He's dug up half of Avignon. That's why he could recite the colors of different stones. He knew every path in Avignon. He strokes Deladier another year. Then they have a fight. Your father hits him with a shovel. No more Deladier. And the bride? She wants to blackmail your dad and us. That's how it was. I mean, we couldn't let her go alive."

Holden stood in his Windsor suit. "He killed my mother."

"Don't look at it like that. She was a whore, a tramp we bought to play his wife. But we got him out of Avignon. And all of us adopted you. Swiss, me, and your father. You were like our own flesh."

"Goldie, wasn't my father a military policeman before he got to Avignon? What did he do?"

"He bullied and bumped for arts and archives. When some thief would bother us, we gave him to your dad."

"Then why was he a chauffeur in Manhattan?"

"We couldn't afford to give him much of a profile. There'd been a stink in Avignon. Two murders."

"And so you groomed me. That was clever. You figured homicide ran in the blood."

"Nothing of the kind. It happened that way. You were good with a gun."

"And my father strangled on his own guts for murdering his wife . . . and depriving me of a mom."

"No, no," the tailor said. "It's the wrong interpretation. She was never a mom to you. She was a slut who decided to get pregnant, so she could have a piece of the caper. Your dad would have ditched her, no matter what."

"Goldie, what was her name?"

"I swear to God, she was a local bitch. We never bothered to ask."

"What was her name?" Holden said, a dark stitch developing under his eye.

"Nicole, I think. Nicole. But it was a rotten deal all around. There was no treasure under the streets of Avignon. That German

JEROME CHARYN 213

general had lied. Swiss found him seven years after the war. Sitting with millions in a Hamburg bank."

"I don't care about your general. What did my mother look like?"

"Holden, I hardly saw her. She was a tart."

The Frog turned from the mirror. Half his face was dark. And Goldie knew he couldn't dismiss Holden's mum like that. "She was a pretty girl. Young. Had a bit of a tuck with the Germans, I hear. Took a fancy to some lieutenant in arts and archives. It was all on the sly. The Germans handed her over to us. Because we had a partnership, you see. Rembrandt wasn't picky. Art is art."

"My mother, was she short or tall?"

"She was regular, I'd say. And slim, with brown hair and brown eyes. Like you, Holden."

"And my father loved her?"

"You could call it love. But he didn't have a choice. The bitch was blackmailing us . . . I mean, your mum decided to make a profit on our hard luck. We were all in jeopardy. There were generals involved. We couldn't have her blow the whistle, could we?"

"Shut up," Holden said. "Loved Nicole and killed her. And he never bumped another person in his life."

"Yes. That's a good summary," the tailor said. "Back in America he discovered how much he liked to drive. He drove the Swiss. Everywhere. He was almost the Swiss' companion."

"Goldie, you sit on your ass in a tailor shop and you judge the world. You pissed my father's life away in Avignon, had him dig for paintings, paintings that were never there, and then you brought him home to live and die like a dog. Goldie, what was my father's real name?"

"Mickeljohn," the tailor said. "That's Scotch. Your dad's people came from Aberdeen or Dundee. I don't remember. They worked the land for some kind of laird."

"A laird like Swiss. Or you."

"I was never one of the bosses. I can hardly keep up with my bills. I'm a stinking tailor."

"A tailor who supplies guns."

"It's a hobby, that's all. I promised your dad I'd look after you."

"Goldie, give me his whole name."

"Ah," the tailor said. "I'll have to think." He hunkered low as if he could draw names out of a pocket. "Sidney Michael David Hartley Mickeljohn."

"And I'm little Sid."

"Don't say that. Sidney Mickeljohn is wanted for murder. We had to erase whoever that was. It cost us plenty. Holden was a good name. It held him for thirty years. We didn't sink your dad. Swiss was loyal. Swiss brought him out."

"And built a grave for him at Aladdin Furs. It's my turn now."

"I could ask Swiss for a truce. It's not too late. The man listens to me. We produced a lot of masterpieces together. Some of the Rembrandts they're auctioning now came out of our workshops in Rennes. We had twenty geniuses around. All refugees from arts and archives. But the French police were coming down on us. I mean, you can't do a Rembrandt a month and get away with it for long. We had to scatter."

"And you went into suits."

"Suits were my first love. I'd never have done Rembrandts if it hadn't been for the war. We seized an opportunity. We all did."

"And now you'll seize something else. You're going to help me bump the Castiglione brothers."

"Couldn't do that. It would be disloyal to the corporation. I still have my scruples."

"Look at me, old man. Who's going to win?"

"You are," Goldie said. "Swiss has you fifty to one. But you're a lad who always defied mathematics."

"What shooters do you have in the house?"

"I wasn't prepared," the tailor said. "I didn't go shopping. But I have a Walther PPK I assembled last month."

"Red Mike used a PPK. You didn't send your ghouls out to raid his garbage cans in Far Rockaway?"

"It's an altogether different gun," Goldie said.

"I'm glad, because I wouldn't want to steal thunder from Mike."

Goldie found the PPK with its holster cup and helped the Frog slip it on under the Duke of Windsor's coat. There was a tiny bulge that Goldie smoothed down with his palm. "Done," he said. "What's the program?"

"First I have to settle with the twins. Goldie, where are Jupe and Jean-Paul?"

"Jesus, I'm not a tattler. I can't compromise Swiss. It's one corporation."

"You owe me for sentencing my dad to all those gray years."

"I didn't sentence him. I was his friend. I looked after both of you. I made you meat pies when you were a boy."

"And you reported all my moves to the Swiss. You put a gun in my hand. You dressed me up. Where are the twins?"

"Camping on Oliver Street."

"In Mrs. Howard's flat? Whose idea was that?"

"Mine," the tailor said. "I can't help it if I'm a thinker, Holden. It was the best place for them to be. The premises were unoccupied. And Swiss didn't have to pay the rent."

"You are a thinker, Goldie. And if you're planning to call the Swiss after I leave, I'd forget about it. I'm wearing magic beads. I'll feel your message, Goldie, honest I will. And I'll visit you with my PPK."

"I wouldn't call the Swiss," Goldie said, with a glint of his teeth. "I never betrayed you. I never steered you into a trap."

Holden left the shop, wondering how much the tailor had lied. Goldie was a forger. He could have invented Nicole and Sidney Michael David Hartley Mickeljohn. But Holden did have a couple of factors. He wasn't born under a table. He had a mum. A tart, Goldie said. With brown hair. And his dad had strangled this Nicole to keep her from telling about a fortune under the streets of Avignon. He imagined his father with a shovel, chipping at the stones, while his mum carried him in her belly. That's how he arrived on Oliver Street, with images of a mum he'd never met. He walked around the back, to Loretta Howard's yard. Her pigeon coops were empty and there wasn't a creature in the cat barns she'd built. Civilization had fled from Oliver Street.

It was one in the afternoon and Holden waltzed up to Loretta's back door. The curtains were down. The rooms seemed dusty to him. The door was locked. But Loretta wasn't there to tighten the window guards. Holden tried a window, toyed with the frame, and let himself into the house. He found one of the twins in the *santita's* room, sleeping near her dolls. Jupe in pajamas. Frog broke his neck with a couple of pulls on his jaw. There wasn't even a whimper of surprise. Or the little moans of an unfortunate dream. A bone cracked behind Jupe's ears. His head shivered. A drop of spittle appeared. And he was dead.

Jean-Paul was in Mrs. Howard's room, snoring with a blanket on his chest. Frog stood over him and smothered Jean-Paul with Loretta's favorite pillow. He scavenged through the pockets of both twins and found very little cash. The Castigliones had thousands and thousands in thick bundles of traveler's checks. Holden could have traded in the checks and gotten fifty cents on the dollar, but he didn't want to advertise his hand. Any one of the fagins he used might have hollered to Edmundo or the Swiss. So he settled for the cash and said goodbye to the brothers when he heard the doorbell ring. He could have scampered out the back, but he was curious about the bell-ringer. He crossed half the house and peeked out a window near the front door. He thought angels had been whispering some tunes, because his mortician had arrived. Bernhard Saxe.

Frog opened the door, and the mortician could barely hide his amazement. "Come in, Bern," Holden said. "Come in." And the mortician stepped inside.

"How are you, Holden?"

"I don't like riddles, Bern. Who sent you and why?"

"Edmundo asked me to wake up the Castiglione brothers."

"Are you a traffic cop? The brothers were after my skin."

"Holden, how long have we worked together? Fifteen years. I run a funeral parlor. I can't afford to take sides."

"But I never heard of a funeral parlor that does wake-up calls."

"I was picking up some extra change."

"At my expense, Bern. You shouldn't have figured me for dead."

"Holden, the man has an army out there. Put yourself in my place. What would you figure?"

"That you don't fuck one client to help another . . . I'm recruiting you, Bern."

"Holden, the man will kill me."

"He might . . . where's Edmundo?"

"At that cafeteria for kings. I called him from my chapel. He said, 'Wake up the twins.' "

"They're beyond waking, Bern. Come with me."

"Where are we going?"

"To the cafeteria," Holden said.

"You're crazy. I can't be seen with you."

"Bern," the Frog said. It was almost a whisper. *Bern.* And the mortician caved in. He led Holden out to his funeral truck. Both of them crept into the cab and sat with Bern's assistant, Lionel, a boy of twenty, who must have been aware of Edmundo's business, because he looked at Holden in Windsor's suit and started to weep. The bumper felt embarrassed. He hadn't provoked the boy, menaced him with the PPK. He took a handkerchief out of his pocket, with Windsor's own mark in the corner, stitched in blue, and handed it to the boy. "Here, wipe your nose."

Lionel took the handkerchief, patted his face with it, and returned it to the Frog. "Mr. Holden, please, I don't want to die."

"Wouldn't hurt my undertaker," Holden said. "Drive."

Lionel brought Holden up to Mansions. Two of Edmundo's bodyguards stood outside the window. Holden could feel the boredom in their eyes. They'd stopped reacting to the terrain. And Holden could have walked into the cafeteria all by himself and there was a fifty-fifty chance that the bodyguards would have mistaken him for just another lonely king.

He got out of the truck with Lionel and Bern, stood behind them half a step, in a slight crouch. The bodyguards recognized Bern. "Hey, did some old guy drop in the toilets? Who are you taking out?"

"It's a social call," Bern said, and the bodyguards laughed. Holden could have been a shadow, some third mortician. He entered the cafeteria with the other two. He saw kings near the window, feasting on cabbage pie. He recognized a princess who'd sat in her corner table ever since Holden began arriving with Florinda Infante for lunch. Florinda's friend, King Alfonse, stopped him as he skirted around a table with Lionel and Bern.

"Holden," Alfonse said, with a pity in his eye only a king could have. "It's not safe."

"Thank you, Fatso. I'll be all right. Just don't sit near the wall."

And then he saw Edmundo at the center table, with his mistresses, cousins, uncles, fortunetellers, veterans from the Bay of Pigs, captains, lieutenants, Florinda, and Count Josephus. He was in the midst of revealing one of his invasion plans, how he would grab Cuba back from Fidel with his own family members.

"Brothers, we won't touch Fidel. We won't pluck his beard or exhibit him in a cage. We'll fly him to New York and let him scream on the 'Today' show. He'll be the new Groucho Marx . . ."

The Batista babies laughed. *Groucho Marx.* They were dreaming of old Havana and Calle Ocho in that Cuban village of Miami. They had one prince, one father, one king. Don Edmundo. They wouldn't have noticed a mortician and two other men. The Frog wasn't supposed to be out on the street. It was Florinda who saw Holden, whose mouth puckered in the middle of a smile. She took in his form, the contours of his suit, and seemed happy the bumper was still alive. She was helpless. She couldn't warn him to go. And Holden was grateful to Florinda. He should have been kinder to her during those long, long lunches when his head would ache with having to deal with so many kings. That purple streak in her hair didn't mean she was a whore.

"I promise you," Don Edmundo said, "we will have our fun

with Fidel." He ate fish eggs on a cracker. He stood up to ruffle the hair of a nephew and a niece. He had his family around him, mistresses, bankers, fools.

He was puzzled when he saw the undertaker. But then he thought, why not? Bernardo has come with a message for me. He likes champagne in the afternoon, even if he lives in a funeral parlor. "Bernardo, did you wake up the two Frenchies? They have to find that other little frog. It's important. I'm losing face while Holden breathes. He can't hide forever under the dress of a fat witch."

But the undertaker didn't answer. And then Edmundo saw the hombre behind him. He wasn't a *bobo*. It was the señor himself in his British suit, and for a moment, Edmundo thought that Holden had come to apologize and make peace. And the señor could have some champagne and be part of the family again, because Edmundo admired that crazy bumper. The bumper had a pair of balls. He was like some kind of crusader, killing people in a holy war, but nobody could remember what the holiness was about.

Holden, would you like a drink? he started to say when he saw a twist of red and white beads over the bumper's necktie, and Edmundo knew he was lost. The witch Dolores had summoned her god Changó in one of Holden's British suits. 'Mundo had always mocked that jailhouse religion. It was for the curly hairs, the africanos. A children's cult of chicken blood. And he was a conquistador. But how did Holden get past Edmundo's guards unless he could depend on Changó's tricks? And as 'Mundo sought his captains at the table he heard a pop like thunder in some faraway store. Mansions disappeared and he wished he could have died at Pinar del Río as Comandante O . . .

It wasn't Rockaway, where the Frog had three brothers standing by themselves and could leave holes in their foreheads like red dimes. There were children flitting around the table. And Holden wasn't Buffalo Bill. He'd had his target practice on a firing range. So he went for the heart. Edmundo's captains wouldn't see any blood, and Holden had to count on confusion. The captains watched 'Mundo fall back into his chair. They couldn't take their eyes off the chief. An uncle pointed a bony finger at the Frog. But he said nothing. And Frog walked out with Lionel and Bern.

The two bodyguards were near the window with 9 mm guns. They'd heard Holden's thunder but they couldn't believe the Frog had gone past them like an invisible man. They looked at Lionel, looked at Bern, and before they could look into Holden's eyes he ran out from between the two morticians, socked the first bodyguard on the side of his head and walloped the second in the groin. As they tottered, Holden hit them again. "Come on," he said to Bern.

Holden got into the funeral truck. Bern started to mourn Don Edmundo. "That man was my biggest customer."

"You'll survive, Bern. I'm back in business."

"That's what I'm afraid of," the mortician said.

Lionel took Frog to the Algonquin. The boy was shaking a lot. "Kid," Holden said. "It had to be done."

"I understand," Lionel said. But he didn't stop shaking.

"Watch the truck," Frog said, and he walked into the hotel with Bern. Now he remembered why all the Brits stopped at the Algonquin. The lobby was made of wood, like the better, older English hotels where Holden had stopped when he was bumping British furriers and collecting patterns from greedy tailors on Saville Row. He liked Bond Street and Marble Arch and British taxi drivers, who were always polite in their polished cars and took Holden to whatever obscure rendezvous he had with the tailors.

"Ask for Schatz," Holden said to Bern, handing him the house telephone.

"I haven't seen Bruno in years. What should I say?"

"Say hello. Start the conversation. Tell him you're coming up. You have a couple of items from Don Edmundo to deliver. All I want is the room number. I'll do the rest."

"What if he decides to come down?"

"Then I'll whack him in the lobby," Holden said.

"This is the Algonquin, for God's sake."

"So what? You can always bump someone in a hotel lobby. I learned that from Red Mike. There are so many witnesses, no one remembers right. Some of the guys will swear I had a red hat or a blue nose. Bern, I promise. You won't even need an alibi. You can tell the district attorney to scratch himself."

"And keep my license?"

"Don't worry, Bern. Call the Swiss."

But he couldn't get Swiss on the telephone, and the clerk at the front desk wouldn't surrender Swiss' room to strangers, so the Frog went out to the truck with Bern and discovered Lionel at the wheel with a hole in his head. Billetdoux squatted behind him, clutching a gun with a long metal cuff. "Get in," he said.

Bern and the Frog climbed into the truck.

"Jesus, Billet, he was a kid," Holden said. "You didn't have to sock him so hard."

"He takes his responsibilities if he rides with you. You've been on a bloody rampage. You march into a man's hotel with the worst intentions. You ought to show respect . . . let's have your shooter, Holden."

Billet removed the PPK from Frog's shoulder cup and shoved it into his pocket.

"Billet, this is Bernhard Saxe, the mortician."

"We've met," said the bumper from Marseilles.

"Then you know he works for Don Edmundo."

"Worked, you mean. Edmundo's dead."

"He had nothing to do with it, Billet. Let him go."

"Don't dictate to me . . . Mr. Saxe, get behind the wheel."

Bern had to lay the dead boy down near his feet.

"Drive us to the fur district, Mr. Saxe."

He'll take us to that ghost town, Aladdin, Holden figured, and bump us in Nick Tiel's designing room. We'll rot for a month before anyone finds us. The Frog wasn't scared. It was a bumper's fate to sit in a funeral truck.

22 THEY ARRIVED AT THE FUR MARKET and Billet said, "I'm sorry about the boy, Mr. Saxe. But I couldn't take chances. Bury him somewhere and forget you ever saw Holden. Can you promise me that?"

Bern looked at Holden with a bit of shame. "I promise," he said, and he drove off as soon as Billet and the Frog climbed out of the truck.

"He's a top man," Holden said. "In the business all his life. His dad buried Dutch Schultz."

"I'll keep that in mind," Billet said, and he brought Frog up to Aladdin in the service elevator. He had his own key. They stepped onto the landing and Frog couldn't believe it. The cutters and nailers had their old roost. Frog could smell all the skins. The house was full of furriers.

"Did Swiss get himself a new designer?"

"You'll see."

They passed a bunch of nailers who kneeled to the Frog as if he were their homecoming prince and he entered Robert Infante's office with Billetdoux. Schatz was in his old chair. Andrushka sat on the desk. Holden felt remorse. He'd loved her and lost her. She'd grown into a woman in Swiss' arms.

"Hello, Frog," she said.

Swiss started to cluck. "You've done me more damage, Holden, than any man I ever knew."

"I'm glad," Holden said.

Billet slapped him on the cheek.

"I'm still glad," Holden said, with a mouth full of blood.

And when Billet went to slap him again, Swiss clucked a little louder. "No, no. He's much too valuable."

"How's that?" Holden asked, having to bite with blood.

"Edmundo's gone," Swiss said. "He wasn't very practical. He left no one in his place. Never organized. He ruled alone. And now his family is in complete chaos. Isn't that why you killed him?"

"I had a lot of reasons."

"Reasons?" Swiss said, waxing like some extraordinary owl in his chair. "That's what kept you alive . . . and the luck of that little girl. She was a great protector, Holden. Edmundo couldn't seem to part the two of you for very long. She was a goddess, I hear. Black magic and fainting fits. Your dad wouldn't have been clever enough to win her, Holden."

"I never won her, Swiss. She was short on fathers. And I found her under a table. My dad wouldn't have used a *santita*. He had Nicole."

The owlish eyes never arched, never betrayed Swiss' intentions. "Who's Nicole?"

"My mother," Holden said.

"You mean the bitch we hired for Holden Sr.? Was that her name?"

"Yes. And he wasn't Holden. He was Mickeljohn. Sidney Michael David Hartley Mickeljohn."

"I can see you've been talking to a certain tailor. He shouldn't have told you such things. It's dangerous to have a little information. It winds you up. And you get out of hand."

"You broke my father when you started stealing his name. Holden was a chauffeur. Mickeljohn was something else."

"He was a smalltime hood in the military police, Mickeljohn was. Utterly unreliable. Quite the ladies' man. He got us into more trouble than he was worth. But I was fond of him. That's my weakness, Holden. Once I take to a man, I commit for life."

"Save the violins, Swiss. My dad cracked skulls for you. You had your own bumper in arts and archives. You held on to him after the war, sent him to Avignon to find some paintings stashed under the streets. But it was a scam. Another one of your enterprises. The paintings were in Hamburg all along. No wonder my father hated Avignon. He saw that city from under the ground. He started killing people with his shovel. My mom wised up. She must have asked dad to get some money out of you. But he still believed in your bull. That's how he was. He was fond of military colors. He had a fight with her. She died. And you let my dad fall into purgatory. Like a snake without teeth."

"But that's my point, Holden. Your dad couldn't have come to the same conclusions. He was debilitated from the start. I'll be frank. If I'd had Billetdoux at the time, we might have put your dad out of his misery, once and for all."

"But you have Billet now. And I'm Mickeljohn's boy."

"Good God," Swiss said. "Do you think your dad could have walked into Mansions and shot Edmundo in front of his bodyguards? He didn't have your imagination. He was okay for France. He couldn't have survived out on the street. But you? This town likes boldness. There isn't a restaurant in the city that will ever let you pay for a meal again."

"But there are five district attorneys, Swiss, and at least one of them is after my blood. He could sell me to Manhattan or haul my ass to Queens."

"Not without implicating himself. He was in with Edmundo, all the way."

"But he's peculiar about his daughter-in-law. I love the woman. So does he."

"That's his aberration. It will pass."

"Meanwhile he has my shooter."

"Holden, I've chatted with Paul. He won't harm you. The mayor himself would kiss you if he could. You're a hero. You've taken out La Familia with one bullet."

"And I'm your military policeman in New York."

"We're furriers, Holden. New gangs will form and they'd love to steal from us, but they'll think twice with you around."

"I'm still not giving back Nick Tiel's paper."

"That's fine. We've rehabilitated Nick."

"Nicky's doing cuffs again? How? He had pink eyes the last time I saw him. He couldn't even speak his name."

"Ah, but we've had him in deep therapy while you were away. Anti-depressants, shrinks around the clock. He's started doodling. He'll catch up with himself. You ought to see his new paper."

"Nick recovered? There's no trusting science. A man can do anything. I'd like to see Nick."

Billet took him to the designing room. Nick answered after a dozen knocks. His cheeks were puffy. He'd gained twenty pounds. But he was scribbling furiously at his table. "Holden," Nick said. "Your mouth is bleeding."

"It's nothing."

Holden returned to that owl in the other room. "Better see a dentist," the owl said. "I think your jaw is broken."

"It's nothing."

"I insist."

Holden wondered what it would be like if Andrushka had never gone to Paris. She'd have ended up with Caravaggio in her bed, and Holden on the floor. She'd followed Swiss into her own art and archives division. And Holden had trouble learning a little Matisse. But she hadn't lost her beauty with a bit of fat.

"Frog," she said. And there was a teasing tenderness in her voice.

"What is it?"

"I'm in love with your suit. Bruno doesn't have anything to match it."

"It's a prototype."

"Explain to her what a prototype is," Bruno said. "It's pure theft. That suit came off the Duke of Windsor's back."

"Not quite. It came from his closets . . . and Swiss, I'll need a raise. Fifteen thousand a month isn't enough for New York."

"There's plenty a man who wouldn't complain about your salary. I've had a bad year."

"You stripped half my vaults. I want nineteen thousand a month."

"Sixteen," the Swiss said. "Not a penny more."

"Eighteen," Holden said.

"Seventeen and a half," said Andrushka, and Swiss wouldn't oppose his wife.

Holden would have kissed her, but Schatz was a jealous man.

He went down the elevator with Billetdoux. Billet returned the PPK. "I had to hit you, Holden. That's my job."

"It's nothing," Holden said. "A little blood." But his mouth ached. He spat into Windsor's handkerchief.

The two bumpers said goodbye and Holden marched up to Bryant Park. He searched the bushes, the walks, the open-air library lanes, the cafeteria tables, and couldn't find Gottlieb. He asked one of the chief pushers, who controlled the north side of the park. "I'm looking for a kid in dirty clothes. Seventeen. With gray eyes."

The pusher wore fingerless gloves. He had a band around his head. He looked like a narc. "You mean Holden's whore? He disappeared a week ago." The pusher might have been twenty, Lionel's age. "Are you the Frog?"

"Yes," Holden said. "I'm the Frog."

"What can I do for you? A little heroin, man. It's on the house."

"I need a cab," Holden said. And the pusher ran out to Sixth Avenue with his fingerless gloves. He whistled and danced and bumped into traffic until he lured a cab to the edges of the park. Holden got in. He didn't try his circular routes. He didn't change cabs. He rode down to Oliver Street and camped in Mrs. Howard's flat. The corpses were gone.

Holden slept for eighteen hours. Then he took a bath. He shaved with Mrs. Howard's old razor. He gobbled bran flakes out of her cupboard. He examined the *santita*'s dolls and realized how much he missed her.

He took a cab uptown to that cafeteria of kings. He felt like an infant, returning to the scene of the crime. But Holden didn't care. He wanted a bite to eat.

All the kings and queens and little countesses smiled at Holden. The waiters hovered around him. Count Josephus stood against the bar, with his back to Holden, and Holden took a seat near the window. The kings were quiet. Florinda left Fatso, her favorite king, to sit with Holden. Her mouth looked grim.

"Are you out of your mind? Detectives have been here most of the afternoon. They've been questioning everybody."

"It's like Rex's plays. A lot of barking. If the detectives wanted me, they know where I am. I'm safe among the kings. And I'm sorry. I didn't intend it to be a public execution. I had to nail 'Mundo."

"Oh, you," she said. "I'm not interested in that outlaw. He was Robert's partner. And he tried to get you killed. I went searching for you when you were shot. Went with Fay. She showed up at Mansions one afternoon, walked over to my table without a word, snubbed the count, and whispered in my ear, 'Help me find Holden.' My loving husband had told me you were dead or about to die. And I thought, I'm prettier than this blonde bitch, and Holden loves her, not me. But I couldn't refuse her, Holden. Besides, I was curious. And worried, worried about you. So I used Robert's connections, all the pimps around him. And a few cops. I didn't know there were that many Cuban villages in New York. I hired a chauffeur with a gun. And I talked to Andrushka."

"Andie helped you?"

"Yes. She drove with us in the car. Your three little wives . . . oh, I shouldn't include myself in that category. But sometimes I feel like a wife to you, Holden. It was Andrushka who found the name of that fat witch."

"Andie was in the car? She sabotaged the Swiss?"

"She's fond of you, Holden. You took her out of the filth at Aladdin. You're her first love. That's what she said."

"The three of you talked like that while you went for a drive?"

"Why not? I told Andrushka and Fay that you were the best lover I'd ever had."

"I'm speechless," Holden said. "It's like comparison shopping. I mean, women talk like that?"

"All the time."

"And what did Fay have to tell?"

"That you liked to make love in the toilet."

"It's worse than slander," Holden said. "I've been hit . . . and what happened next?"

"We couldn't find the witch. But she found us. And she said you were breathing, so we went home. But we got to be friends in that car. It was almost like a long ocean voyage."

"At my expense. I mean, you compared, you talked. At my expense."

"But we were all worried about you."

Holden ate his lunch. Ratatouille and London broil. He had two desserts. Florinda abandoned the Frog. She had an appointment with her hairdresser. "Holden, do me a favor," she said, "and stay alive."

He saw a rat in the window, a rat from Paul Abruzzi's detective squad. Holden decided to wait for Paul. He had a crème de menthe. The count kept avoiding Holden's table. But the little kings arrived with fountain pens and slips of paper. The fountain pens were sleek and silver, and could have been as old as the century, older perhaps, when the idea of a king carried its own special weight, and kings wouldn't have had enough time to collect in cafeterias and ask a bumper for his autograph.

"Hey, I'm not a movie star."

But he signed their slips of paper until he discovered Paul. The district attorney stood near him in a dark sack and Holden had to send the kings away.

"Congratulations," Paul said. "You walked into Mansions yesterday afternoon and settled all your business."

"Don't congratulate me, Paul. Just return my shooter."

"I already did."

"It was a dupe, Paul. Your gunsmiths must be great at preparing duplicate guns."

"Sidney, the boys were having their fun."

"Don't call me Sidney. I mean, you're not my father-in-law."

The district attorney put Holden's Beretta on the table, wrapped in a handkerchief. "It's a present from your Uncle Paul. I never liked you, Holden. But we have to get along. I can't afford another shooting."

"Edmundo died in Manhattan, Paul. You're off the hook."

"Don't be foolish. That man was tied to me. Or you wouldn't be out on the street."

"Good, but I want you to be the first to know. I expect to marry Fay."

The district attorney laughed into his fist. But his eyes were dull. "She already has a husband. She's married to my boy Rex."

"I still intend to propose."

"Holden, you've had a charmed life. Keep it that way. My daughter-in-law is not for you."

The kings had begun to gather again and Paul excused himself. He'd been recognized. And the Frog watched him pat a few men on the shoulder. Paul was agile in his black shoes. He swayed like a dancer, and Holden was miserable, thinking of Paul and Fay, Fay and Paul.

The Swisser was right. No one at Mansions would let him pay the bill. The cashier kept insisting, "It's on the house."

"I don't accept charity from strangers."

"Please, Mr. Holden. You're one of our oldest customers."

"Then tell the count to come over here."

The cashier shrugged until Josephus arrived from the bar.

"Holden, what's the problem?"

"I like to be greeted, count. I'm making Mansions my favorite restaurant."

"Is that smart?" the count asked.

"I don't have to be smart. When I come in, count, you say hello. Understand? Meanwhile, you can hold this." And Frog gave him the gun inside the handkerchief. "It's my shooter, count. Take good care of it."

The count went gray. "Holden, I can't. How will I explain your shooter to all the detectives?"

"Hide it from them, count. If there's a problem, go to Paul."

The air smelled sweet outside the restaurant. The bumper was in his element. He started walking uptown. He had that pewter animal in his pocket, with its head staring at its own tail. He fingered the animal's back. He was more comfortable with it than red and white *collares*. He couldn't fathom all the twists of a jailhouse religion. The bumper had never been to jail.

He went to Madison Avenue with the idea of visiting Fay. But somehow he couldn't approach the doorman and declare who he was. It was one thing to live with Fay in a mattress pad. But he turned reluctant near her territories. The Frog cursed his own shyness. Courtship had always been difficult to him. It would have been much less complicated to kidnap his darling.

He stood across the street from Fay's building, stood two hours, and when his darling didn't appear, he got into a taxi cab.

23 HE COULDN'T LIVE AT LORETTA'S. The rooms reminded him of the leopard girl. He couldn't live at his office. He didn't enjoy the company of furriers and Nick Tiel. He moved into his mattress pad. But the walls bothered him. They smelled of isolation, a bumper growing old.

He returned to Mansions, seized a table, and sat. But no amount of kings could soothe him. And it didn't matter how often Josephus said hello. Holden couldn't finish his London broil. He was about to leave when Fay walked into Mansions with Rex and their two daughters, girls who were older than the *santita* and had his

darling's blonde hair. Holden sank into his chair like a spy. His
darling sat with Count Josephus. The girls ordered lemonade. They
had beautiful complexions and they talked like the characters in
their father's plays. He never thought children could behave like
that, with all the bump and bother of adults. He watched his darling
move her mouth. He was as drawn to her as he'd ever been. But he
couldn't steal Fay from her own family. He might have sat there
with his London broil until the lights went out and the goddess Oyá
climbed on his lap to tease him and taunt him. Holden wouldn't
have minded Oyá's hostile attentions. But Fay looked up from her
avocado salad and saw the Frog. And that's when Holden fled. He
was a bumper fated to be alone.

He ran a few blocks, his heart shaking, and discovered Gottlieb
in a pair of two-hundred-dollar pants.

"Gottlieb, go away."

"I can't," the kid said.

"Who are you working for now? The Greek furriers? Did you
sell them Nicky's paper?"

"I'm not that dumb. I have the paper, Holden. I'm selling it
back to the Swiss . . . a cuff at a time."

"Then you're a dead person."

"No I'm not. I'm your whore. And we go half and half."

"You're a dead person, I said. You betrayed me twice."

"I didn't betray you, Holden. I acted for the firm."

"What firm?"

"Holden & Company. I'm your junior partner. I've been keeping strict accounts."

"You're a dead person. I'll whack you the first chance I get."

"Holden, it was good business. I had Swiss' ass to the wall."

"But you didn't refer to me."

"How could I? You were lying in pig heaven somewhere with
that Cuban mama. I had to take the initiative."

"I knew Swiss was full of shit. Nicky's eyes were heavy. He's
doped up. He can't create. Swiss is recycling Nicky's old cuffs."

"Does it really matter?" Gottlieb said. "We're rich."

"If we're so rich, how come you didn't find me?"

"Holden, I've been following you around for a day and a half. Longer than that. I visited your mattress in Queens. I played cards with the witch. I brought lollipops to the little girl."

"You're a dead person."

"Holden, I had to deal with the Swiss. Dolores couldn't protect you. She was running out of mattresses and men."

"So you decided to deal."

"No. It was Goldie's idea. He saw what was happening. He met me in Bryant Park."

"That man never goes midtown."

"He did for you. He told me how to treat the Swiss. 'Give him a nibble,' Goldie said. 'Nothing more.' He loves you, that old man."

And the Frog was depressed. You think you know the world, and then you fall on your ass, like Humpty Dumpty. "All the king's horses," he said.

"What?"

"I was thinking to myself. Take my share of the money, kid, and find Dolores. I want her to eat. And bring the little girl some dolls. Tell them, 'Holden is back on his horse.' "

"You never had a horse," Gottlieb said.

"They'll understand." And he removed Changó's beads from his neck. "Here," he said. "Give it to Dolores. Thank her for the god's hospitality."

"Where are you going?" Gottlieb asked.

"Home."

But he didn't have a home. He had a mattress pad. He went to a realtor, Di Robertis, who rolled money around for thieves in the fur market. Di Robertis was a short, clever man who'd given up most of his clients, but he happened to admire Holden. He found the bumper six rooms on Central Park West. It was in one of the great old towers. The price was a million two. "A lot of gold," Di Robertis said.

"I'll get it."

But Holden's vaults were in a reckless state. He couldn't gather more than a hundred thousand dollars. He presented himself to the building's co-op board. Holden was gloomy about his financial picture. He'd have to borrow from one of the mob banks. And the rates were prohibitive. He'd have carrying charges for the rest of his life. He wished now he hadn't given up Changó's beads. A god might be able to reason with a co-op board. And then, in the middle of the meeting, there was a knock on the door. Swiss had arrived from Paris. Di Robertis must have told him about the meeting. Swiss wore a fur coat. He was eighty-one, and he looked like a king. Not one of the royal hoboes who lived in a cafeteria, but a real king, with fury around him and a magnificent fur coat on his back. He wouldn't talk of Holden's current life. "I was with this man's father in the war," he said. And he entertained the co-op board for half an hour with stories of how he'd rescued Rembrandts from the German army. Even Holden was bewitched.

They walked out together. "Swiss, where will I get the gold?"

"Let me worry about that."

"Tell me the truth. Nicky will never design a cuff again."

The owl king glanced at Holden from the depths of his fur collar. "You know that. I know that. But he seems formidable to the rest of the world."

"You keep him there in the designing room like a prisoner."

"It's better than an asylum. He sits. He draws. He drinks coffee. His sketches make no sense. But he isn't harming anyone . . . Holden, I have to catch a plane. I'm due in Paris in six hours. Behave yourself."

And Holden lingered on that word. How should a bumper behave? He had a new apartment, thanks to the Swiss. He picked up his check at Aladdin. He avoided Nick Tiel. He threatened one or two furriers. But it was simple stuff. Suddenly everyone was paying their bills.

He bought furniture. Couches, carpets, a bed. His windows looked out onto the park. Fifth Avenue seemed across the world. The park itself was an impossible breach, a canvas of trees that could never be crossed. He'd once lived on the other side of the park, with

Andrushka, had looked at the very tower he was living in. And still he couldn't get that illusion out of his head. The park was uncrossable, an extraordinary veldt. He spied the vague, hidden roofs of the Metropolitan Museum of Art. A contraption, a pillbox where Andrushka had gone to study Caravaggio. The roofs of a dream.

And Holden began to feel that he was living in a city of walls. It was midnight, and for a moment, in the darkness, Holden thought New York was Avignon. The towers of Fifth Avenue were like the ramparts of that city, ramparts as Holden imagined them. And he himself could have been locked in the popes' palace with leopards springing from the wall.

He had a visitor in the morning. The kid. Gottlieb had arrived with his own cup of coffee.

"Didn't you trust me to fix you a cup?"

"I know you," Gottlieb said. "You never keep coffee in the house."

Holden remembered drinking coffee, but he searched his cabinets and couldn't find a coffee bean.

Gottlieb gawked at the rooms. "What a spread. It's like a cattle ranch."

"Gottlieb, get to the point."

"Dolores wants to say goodbye. She's going to Miami with the girl. It's not safe here for them."

"How's that? They can live with me."

"Holden, there's a crisis and the gods are going crazy. Come on. I'll take you to her."

It was Gottlieb who switched cabs, who took Holden into Brooklyn and out again until Holden thought the kid was copying his style. Then he discovered a map in Gottlieb's hand. The kid was following instructions.

"Dolores doesn't want a certain god on her tail."

"I don't understand. Dolores is a priest."

"Holden," the kid said. "I have enough trouble with human beings. What do I know about gods?"

They got out of the fifth cab near the Manhattan Bridge. And they walked along Market Street. There had once been a thriving market under the bridge. But now it was a city of old, abandoned stalls with an occasional shop that had survived, selling broken lamps and rubber tires, or a luncheonette that was so tiny, it couldn't hold two customers at a time. Dolores was lying on a couch in an ancient shop that looked like a chicken coop. The floor was a dark mass of feathers that had hardened into bricks. The *madrina* sweated a great deal. She must have lost fifty pounds in the weeks Holden had been away from her. She was a gaunt Carmen Miranda. When Dolores wheezed, the whole couch moved.

"What's wrong?"

"We must go to Miami," the *madrina* said.

"But La Familia has suffered and you have no more enemies in town."

"You must not say that. The other *madrinas* are jealous. They don't have a champion like you. They say I slept with Changó, tricked him into my bed, so that the lord would favor you in our fight with Don Edmundo. They have woken the spirits, and Oyá is mad. She is the lord's mistress, after all. And she will steal my daughter if I stay."

"Dolores, what can I do?"

"Do nothing. It is priests' business. We will pray to Santa Barbara when we get off the bus."

"But I can send you by plane."

"Please. Oyá will borrow the lord's thunder and strike all the planes you send. We will sit before Barbara's shrine. We will ask forgiveness. And if we are worthy, Changó will come to us in his red dress. Then we can return to the north."

"Will you give me your address?"

"I cannot write, señor. You have been lucky, and all the priests are jealous."

"Where's the girl?"

"With me, señor. But I am not certain she should look at your face. She could be harmed."

Dolores relented and called the little girl in Creole. Barbara arrived from under the couch. She wore a dirty smock and she didn't have her doll.

"*Querida,*" Holden said. He'd been a ghost until the *santita*, a bumper who lived in closets. He'd found a certain recreation in her eyes, a feel of himself. The girl had nourished him with those animal eyes.

"Froggy," she said, "will you miss me?"

And he started to cry, because he'd lived thirty-seven years as some kind of pilgrim. He'd loved Andrushka the twig. He'd loved Loretta Howard. And he'd loved his dad in a phantom way. But he'd spent his time dispatching people. The paradise man.

He wanted to hug the little girl, but Carmen Miranda scolded him from her couch. "You cannot touch the little one, señor. It is forbidden."

"Mother, I—"

"You must not call me that. Señor, you have to go. Oyá will curse our bus, and we shall never get to Miami."

Holden left that marketland under the bridge. He got into a cab with the kid. He was having murderous thoughts. The kid had helped destroy Mrs. Howard. But if Holden destroyed Gottlieb, he'd have one more person to mourn. "Adiós," he said, and dropped the kid off at one of the banks where the kid had a vault and then Holden continued uptown to Aladdin. He didn't have to collect any debts. There were mannequins in the showroom, but they couldn't excite him the way the twig had done. They were college girls trying to earn a dime for their tuition. They didn't have that frenzy of the twig. They flirted with Holden because he was rich and wore a king's suit. But the involvement in their eyes only saddened him. He was the Froggy who couldn't be brought to life by college girls.

He piddled around in his office and returned to Central Park West. He had an odd sensation outside his door. As if Oyá were still angry at him for interfering in Cuban politics. He shouldn't have been involved with African gods who sometimes wore a Christian face.

Oyá could swim in the Niger whenever she wants. He opened the door and gave a little scream.

Someone stood in Holden's rooms, wearing a red dress.

"Changó," he muttered. And then he noticed a head of curly blonde hair and a suitcase. He felt cheated. "Who let you in?"

Fay turned around and Holden had to fight an impulse to kiss his darling.

"I bribed the super," she said.

"I'm speechless. I mean, I pay a million two for this apartment and the security stinks."

"You're always speechless, Sidney. That's one of your nicest traits."

"But you could have been sent here to kill me. How would a super know the difference?"

"He wouldn't. But he trusted me. I told him it was a big surprise . . . that it was your birthday."

"It's not my birthday," Holden said.

"But you could pretend it was."

She'd worn him down and he'd only been home a minute. He wished he had some coffee in the house. Coffee would have bolted him awake. And he could have provided the necessary answers.

"Why did you run away from me at Mansions?"

"You were with your daughters and Rex. Your family. And I was frightened."

"You're never frightened . . . are you glad to see me?"

"I am glad," he had to admit. "Very glad. But you have a husband. You have daughters."

"My daughters can visit. All it takes is the crosstown bus . . . I'm not in love with Rex."

"And Paul, what about Paul?"

"He'll have to grow up."

"He's already grown up. He's the district attorney."

"Paul won't bother us."

"I know Paul. Paul's a brooder."

"So he's a brooder," she said. And Holden couldn't battle with his darling. He didn't care about the practicalities. Two daughters on a crosstown bus. He wanted Fay with him in his tower.

"I can't make coffee. I always forget to buy the beans."

"I won't drink coffee when I'm with you."

"You shouldn't have told Florinda that we made love in the toilet."

"Why not?"

"It's personal," he said.

His darling laughed. She started to unbutton his collar. "Yes. It's personal," she said. Fay was like that city outside his window, that mirage of walls. He couldn't say what love was about. A knock on the head. A naked woman in a bungalow. Curly blonde hair. The tremors in his darling's throat. That was more than enough for Sidney Holden.

She brought him into the toilet. She didn't examine the fixtures and the faucets. He held her from behind. He could taste her hair. She clutched the toilet seat. Holden's socks were on the floor, near the PPK. He entered his darling like that first little bump of a dream.

Something bothered him. A noise he heard. The movement of a key. Or a dark scratch, as if the leopards had come down from that wall in Avignon. Holden walked out of the toilet with the PPK in his hand. But the leopards had already pounced.

Paul stood above him with the PPK. Holden was on the floor. He had a headache. Paul was in his undertaker's suit. His voice was very sweet. "Holden, I'm not used to a blackjack. I had to borrow it from Dimitrios. Did I hit you too hard?"

"Not at all," the Frog said, with blood under his ear. "I don't have to ask you how you got in. You followed Fay."

"Holden, I'm the district attorney."

"In Queens you are. Not on Central Park West."

"It's all the same crib, Holden. Haven't you learned that?"

"What is it you want?"

"Fay. Only Fay."

"You can't have her. I told you. We're getting married."

"You're a ridiculous fellow. Sitting with your cock out. I could kill you, Holden, and swear it was self-defense."

"You'd have to convince a jury."

Paul looked at Holden with such contempt, the bumper began to feel lonely again. "Holden, you're a hardened criminal, a psychopath, with God knows how many murders behind you."

"But I had a stinking angel on my shoulder. The angel was you."

"No jury would ever believe that. And you won't be around to tell."

"But Fay will."

Paul started to laugh. "Fay has daughters to protect. She'll grieve for you. I don't doubt that. But she'd never put her family through the muck. Besides, she wouldn't make a very good witness. She's had a couple of breakdowns, Sidney."

"Don't call me that."

"All right, Frog. I won't. But you can't win no matter what."

"I'll decide that," Fay said, standing in one of Holden's robes. Her face had a deep burn, as if she'd come out of the most brutal sun, rather than Sidney's toilet. But Paul didn't seem perturbed.

"Are you comfy, dear, in your new nest? I didn't mind that rat's palace down in Chelsea. It was Holden's craphouse. But did you think I'd ever let you live with him out in the open? Among decent people? Dear, you don't know me very well."

"I know you, Paul," she said. "Get out of this apartment."

Paul kept laughing with his teeth. "I have Sidney's gun. And if you come near me with such a temper, I'll shoot his kneecaps off. He won't be much good to you, dear. So get dressed like a quiet little girl and come with me."

"I'm not coming with you, Paul. This is where I live. With Holden."

"That's preposterous," Paul said. "You have nothing in common with him."

"I had three semesters at Bernard Baruch," Holden said, getting off his ass and dancing in front of the PPK.

"Did you study Milton? Or Shaw?" the district attorney asked, with a sneer on his face.

"I'm married to Milton," Fay said. "And I don't need him. I need Holden."

And Paul's eyes turned mean. He could have been a little boy robbed of his candy. "Then I'll have to shoot your precious psychopath."

Fay stood in front of Holden. But the Frog couldn't let his own darling be his shield. He stepped outside the warm expanse of her body. "Go on, Paul. But make it good. Because if you don't finish me with the first bullet, I swear I'll shake you to death."

Paul never bothered to look at the Frog. He watched Fay; her eyes were like a mirror to his own black life. Fay didn't have the least regard or pity for him. He could neither woo her nor win her with Holden's gun. Bumping Holden wouldn't bring her back. There was a twitch in Paul's cheek, like an animal under the skin.

Holden retrieved his PPK and marched into the toilet to put on a robe; when he returned to Paul, the twitch was gone. Sidney was the pope of this tower. And Paul was the ruler of Queens.

"I wouldn't discuss this visit, old boy."

Holden didn't bite back. He let the district attorney have his little say.

Paul got onto the elevator and Holden went back to his darling. Fay swabbed Holden's head with a bit of wet cotton. "I'm starving," he told her.

"I'll make some ratatouille," his darling said. She was trembling, and Holden caressed her in the kitchen. "Ratatouille," she said.

"But there's no vegetables in the house . . . and no coffee beans."

"Then I'll improvise."

And Holden brought her suitcase into the bedroom while his darling searched the cupboards. The Frog had come home.